HOMESPUN

PINE RIDGE

BOOK FIVE

ASHLEY A. QUINN

TCA PUBLISHING

ONE

The warm late-May sunshine beat down on Alice Duvall's neck as she carried a box of pottery supplies to the trailer attached to her brother Knox's truck. She climbed inside and set it on the growing stack, then stepped out, lifting her face to the sun. The weather was nice today for her move, which made her happy. Rain and clay did not mix. Neither did rain and cardboard. Sighing, she went back inside to get another box.

"Ready?" Knox and their friends Brady and Thomas Archer stood around her kiln, preparing to move it.

Brady nodded and put a shoulder into the oven, tipping it enough for Knox and Thomas to slide a wide strap under it. They'd brought in an engine hoist to get it out of the building and onto the truck.

"Okay, you can let it down." Thomas stepped back and nodded to his brother.

"Christ, Alice. Did you buy the heaviest one on the market?" Brady huffed as he let the kiln settle on the floor. He walked around to the other side, prepared to tip it again.

She crossed her arms and leaned a shoulder against the wall. "Not even close." A smile crossed her pretty face. "And why are you complaining? You know you're having fun showing off your he-man side." The man was a brute. At six-foot-seven, he had several inches on either of the other men, as well as fifty pounds of muscle.

Knox and Thomas chuckled as Brady rolled his eyes. "Let's get this thing on the truck so we can focus on the other stuff." He put his shoulder into the kiln. "For a single woman, you have a lot of crap."

Alice shrugged. "Art isn't cheap."

Brady grunted. "You two ready?" He looked at his brother and Knox.

They nodded, and he pushed. Once the second strap was in place, Brady set the kiln down, then Knox gathered the straps on top of it and attached them to the hoist.

"Moment of truth. I hope this works." He grasped the lever on the back of the stand and pushed. The kiln lifted. Brady and Thomas slid a third, wider strap underneath, going the opposite direction of the other two. Knox set it down again, so they could hook the strap to the hoist. Once they were all secure, he pushed on the lever once more, raising it high enough to clear the threshold.

At the door, they turned it, setting it just inside the door. They would have to unhook it to get the stand over the threshold and outside. It was quite a process, but they finally got the kiln into the trailer.

Thomas stepped out and wiped his forehead on his shoulder. "I'm glad I don't have to do that again." He slapped Knox on the shoulder. "I hope you have some strong friends in Pine Ridge."

Knox pressed his lips together, amusement lighting his eyes. "I think we've got it covered."

Alice chuckled. They did indeed. Their friend Asa

Mitchell was nearly as big as Brady. Plus, he had some large ranch hands who would be more than willing to show off their strength. "I'm just glad I have friends on both ends willing to help." She smiled at Brady and Thomas.

"Hey, you offered to pay me in food." Thomas walked past her, glancing back. "I won't turn that down." His mouth twisted. "Especially since Rayna hates meat right now. I can't wait until she's past the stage where the smell of cooking meat makes her want to puke. It's been beans and tofu and lots of vegetables for the last two months." He waved a hand. "I'm not really complaining, though. I'll eat whatever keeps her stomach happy."

Alice wrinkled her nose. That sounded terrible. "Is she doing okay otherwise?"

He nodded. "She's doing great. The baby's growing well. Mason and Emma are excited to have a little brother or sister. Especially Emma. She can't wait to babysit."

Her heart warmed at the mention of his adopted children. Those kids, especially Mason, deserved every happiness in the world after what they'd been through. "Good. I'll have to come visit once he or she arrives." She hadn't seen much of Rayna lately. The other woman had been busy prepping her fields for the growing season and packing up their old house to move onto the ranch.

"We both will," Knox said. "Sofie and I can introduce our little one to yours. They'll be about the same age." Knox's wife was only a couple of months further along in her pregnancy than Rayna.

Alice smiled at her brother, happy for him. He'd been alone for a long time before Sofie came into his life. The change in him was drastic. He smiled more and didn't hide away like he used to. She was looking forward to living close to him again. She couldn't wait to spoil his new baby and his five-year-old stepdaughter, Olive.

They spent the next hour loading boxes from her pottery studio into the trailer. Once they were done, they left the trailer and the truck attached to it where it was, and piled into Alice's Subaru. She'd promised them all supper from Boone's for their trouble.

As she drove off the ranch, she couldn't help the melancholy that flooded her heart. This place had been her home since she was a kid until she bought her own house in town when she started teaching art at the elementary. After their mom died and their dad moved away, it was just Knox's home until a fire destroyed his horse barn and he decided to move his family to Pine Ridge to be closer to Sofie's mom. Alice had been a frequent visitor to the old ranch, though, thanks to the pottery studio they'd built on the grounds.

But now, the ranch belonged to Thomas and Rayna, and it was time for a new era for Alice. Sure, she'd miss her friends here, but Montana wasn't that far from Colorado. And she wanted to be near her brother and his growing family. She wanted to watch her niece and this new baby grow up. And maybe she'd meet someone to share her life with. Heaven knew her prospects around here weren't great. All the good men were taken, or she wasn't interested.

Not that she was in any rush. She was twenty-nine. But she was definitely ready for a family of her own.

"Alice, you need a bigger car," Thomas complained from the backseat.

She looked in the rearview mirror to see him glance at Knox.

"How come you get to sit behind her, and I'm stuck behind The Hulk?" He pointed at Brady, who sat in the front passenger seat.

Knox snorted. "Because I'm taller than you." She felt him shift behind her, his knees bumping her seat.

"By an inch."

He shrugged.

Alice chuckled. "I can turn around, and you can take your own truck to town."

Thomas waved a hand, a light smile on his handsome face. "Nah. I just like giving Brady a hard time." He pushed on the seat.

Brady barely moved, but a grin tilted one side of his mouth. "Watch it, or I'll sit on you."

"You wouldn't fit back here."

"Who says it has to be now?"

Alice glanced in the mirror again and caught Knox's eye. They shared a smile as they listened to the brothers' banter. These two and the rest of their family would be the people she missed the most. Especially their sister, Maggie. She was just glad she'd gotten all her goodbyes out of her system over the weekend. She didn't want to drive away tomorrow morning with tears in her eyes.

They reached town, and Alice steered the car through the quaint residential streets to the downtown area and parked. Thomas and Knox both let out groans as they unfolded themselves from the backseat. Alice led the way into the restaurant. A hostess led them to a booth by the window. They soon ordered, then sat back to wait for their food. Several people stopped to say hello to Knox and inquire about his family and how they were settling in up north.

When their food arrived, the three men inhaled their dinner. Alice refused to eat so fast she barely tasted her burger, especially since it was the last one she'd have from Boone's for a while. The others didn't seem to mind waiting on her, though. They sat there and talked while she finished.

Once they were done, they piled into the car again and drove back to the ranch so Thomas and Brady could get their trucks and head home. She tried to keep the tears at bay as she said goodbye to the men. She was going to miss them—all the Archers, really.

Sniffing, she hugged them, then waved as they drove away. Knox wrapped an arm around her shoulders, and she leaned into him.

"You know, as much as I'm sad you're leaving your friends behind, I'm glad you're moving up north with me and Sofie. It'll be great still having you close by."

Alice nodded. "Yeah. And it's not like we're saying goodbye to them forever." Between Knox's business dealings with them and their own personal history, she knew they'd be frequent visitors to each other's homes over the years to come.

Knox nodded. "Definitely not." He gave her a squeeze. "Come on. Let's head inside. Thomas left us a television. Want to watch something with me before we hit the sack? I bet we can find reruns of some sitcom to watch."

She smiled up at him and wiped her face. "Sure." Maybe a few episodes of *The Big Bang Theory* or even *Golden Girls* would cheer her up. Following him inside, she pressed a fist to her chest, holding back the melancholy.

They stopped in the kitchen and got themselves each a bottle of water, then sat down on the couch in the living room. Thomas and Rayna had moved a few things in, so Knox and Alice had a place to stay while they moved Alice out of her house. There were two beds upstairs as well.

Knox grabbed the remote off the coffee table and turned on the TV. He flipped through the channels until he found one playing a marathon of *The Big Bang Theory*. Alice sank deeper into the cushions, pulling her legs beneath her. As the show played, she felt herself relax, some of the sadness creeping away, thanks to the humor of the show. After the fourth episode, she stretched and yawned. Glancing at her brother, she saw him cover his own yawn.

"We should get to bed." She uncoiled herself.

He nodded. "Yeah." Turning off the TV, he stood.

Alice rose and picked up her empty water bottle. They tossed them in the recycling bin in the mudroom, then headed upstairs. She paused outside the room she was using. "I'll see you in the morning."

Knox glanced back, his hand on the doorknob to the master bedroom. "Bright and early." His mouth quirked.

She smiled back and went into her room. Gathering her nightclothes, she went down the hall to take a shower. Once she was clean and had brushed her teeth, she went back to her room and shut off the light, climbing between the sheets.

Fatigue pulled at her—it had been a busy day—but her mind refused to shut off. Huffing, she sat up and turned on the bedside lamp. She'd just read until she couldn't keep her eyes open anymore.

She got up and found her e-reader in her bag, then crawled back into bed. Turning it on, she immersed herself in her book.

When her head bobbed a couple of hours later, she put it down and turned off the light. Nerves still churned her belly, but exhaustion finally won, and she dropped off to sleep.

The blare of her alarm on her phone jolted her awake a few hours later. Groaning, she shut it off and sat up. She rubbed her gritty eyes and pushed her hair out of her face. With a yawn, she stretched and got out of bed and padded over to her suitcase to get some clothes. A quick trip to the bathroom to dress and do her morning routine, and she was ready to go.

Packing her suitcase, she double-checked she had everything, then zipped her bag and headed downstairs.

Knox stood at the counter, munching on a banana. He raised a brow at her and nodded in greeting.

"Mornin'." She walked straight to the coffeepot and poured some into her travel mug. She peeled the other banana, quickly eating it.

"You want one of these?" Knox held out a protein bar.

She took it. "Sure. I'll eat it in the car."

"We don't have to rush out, you know."

Alice shrugged. "No point in lingering."

He nodded. "Okay. I'm ready if you are. Let's load up."

She grabbed her bags and followed him out of the house. A wide yawn cracked her jaw as she stared out over the ranch in the early light. Gold lit the tops of the hills and the dew sparkled in the rising sun.

"None of that. We've got a long drive ahead of us and need to be alert."

Alice rolled her eyes at her brother. "That's why I have this." She held up her coffee cup, then narrowed her eyes. "Do *you* have coffee?"

He grinned. "It's already in the truck."

She smiled back. "Then let's go."

His chuckle faded as they went to their separate vehicles. Knox had driven down from Pine Ridge in his truck so he could haul the trailer back. Alice planned to follow him in her SUV.

Climbing into her car, she set her coffee in the cup holder and her purse on the passenger seat, then started the engine. Excitement zinged through her veins, battling with her nerves. This was a big move for her. She'd been praying for a way to move closer to Knox after he and Sofie announced they were moving to Pine Ridge. When the art teacher position came open at the school there, she'd jumped on it. She still couldn't believe the school board picked her.

But she was definitely more excited than nervous. This was the right move. And not just because she'd be closer to Knox. She couldn't wait to start teaching in the fall. As part of the interview process, she'd toured the school. It was a new building, and the art program had all the latest stuff. She'd have a kiln on-site. No more schlepping her students' art back and forth from school to the ranch to fire everything and praying nothing broke on the way.

Knox turned around in the wide drive in front of the ranch buildings and headed for the highway. Alice put her car in gear and followed. They turned onto the road and were off. She couldn't hold back the grin. Time for new beginnings.

Two

The scent of coffee pulled Alice out of her slumber. She stretched and opened her eyes, smiling as her brain registered her surroundings. It was her first morning in Pine Ridge.

Throwing the covers back, she got dressed and took care of her morning routine, then headed downstairs. She rounded the newel post and wandered down the hallway to the kitchen. Daisy Mitchell looked up and smiled.

"Hi. Sleep well?"

Alice nodded. "Yeah. The bed in the guest room is like a cloud. I slept great. Thanks again for putting me up until I find a place of my own." Knox's friend Asa and his wife Daisy offered Alice a place to stay until she found a house. She'd have stayed with her brother, but they were currently living in one of the little bungalows on Asa's ranch while their own house was being built on the property they bought. There wasn't room for her in the small two-bedroom place they currently called home.

Daisy waved a hand and poured her a cup of coffee. "No problem. The house is too quiet since Aunt Nori and Silas moved into their own place last month."

She took the mug. "I doubt I'll make it any louder."

"Maybe not, but I'll have someone to talk to during the day for a bit, anyway. It gets lonely in here."

Alice smiled, sitting down at the island. "You need a houseful of kids. Have you and Asa talked about starting a family?" The couple had been married about six months now.

"Sort of. We wanted to wait until all my injuries healed but haven't really discussed it any further. I'm healed, but I'm in no hurry. A baby would be nice, but I'm kind of enjoying being a newlywed. I might feel differently once Sofie starts to show more." She shrugged as she sat down. "We'll see. I've got time. I'm only twenty-nine, and Asa just turned thirty-four."

Alice nodded and took a sip of her coffee. That's how she felt about her lack of a significant other as well.

"So, do you have any plans for today?" Daisy asked.

Her head bobbed, and she set the coffee mug on the counter after taking a drink. "I made an appointment with a realtor to look at houses in town."

"I hope you can find something. There isn't a lot on the market. Knox and Sofie found that out. Though they were looking for land. I still don't think there are too many houses available."

Alice wrinkled her nose. "I don't want to settle, but I also don't want to stay here forever."

"You take as long as you need. If nothing else, you can move into Knox and Sofie's place once their house is finished. Or maybe our ranch hand Jasper's house. He's been spending most of his time at his girlfriend's house and driving out here for work. I imagine he'll probably move in with her soon. Her place is nicer than his, and she needs to be in town for work."

"What does she do?"

"She's the sheriff."

Alice's eyes widened. "Oh. Yeah, I guess I can see how she'd need to be close to the police station."

Daisy nodded. "So, yeah, there are plenty of options for you."

"Sounds like it." Alice tipped her head and studied her hostess. "Would you like to come with me today?"

The other woman straightened in her seat. "Me?"

Alice nodded.

"Oh. Well, sure. That would be great." A bright smile lit Daisy's face.

"Good. I thought about asking Sofie, but she's got her hands full with Olive, and Knox needed to get back to work. I really didn't want to go alone."

"Well, I'm glad you asked. What time do we need to leave?"

"The appointment is at ten."

Daisy glanced at her watch. "We've got a couple hours yet. That works. I have a few things I need to do around here still."

"Are you sure you aren't too busy?"

"Pfft, no. It's just laundry and stocking the bunkhouse cookie jars. The only thing that can't wait is feeding the chickens, which I'm going to do now." She stood up and pushed her stool in.

"Want some help?"

"If you want to, I won't turn it away."

Alice followed her to the mudroom.

"You can wear my extra boots." Daisy pointed at a pair of black boots tucked into a corner. "They might be a little big on you, but it's better than you getting chicken poop all over your tennis shoes."

"For sure." Alice chuckled and stepped into the boots. "I have a pair, but they're buried in a box in the trailer still." At least she knew where the box was, though. She'd marked the more important ones with hot pink duct tape, then they'd stacked all those near the door so she could get to them quickly.

"Well, hopefully today you'll find a house and won't have to live out of boxes for long."

Alice hoped that was the case. She was eager to settle in.

Daisy picked up a basket from on top of the washer, then the two women walked across the yard to the chicken coop. Inside the pen, she opened a storage closet on the back side and removed a pail.

"Do you want to collect eggs or feed them?"

"I'll do the eggs."

"Sounds good." She handed Alice the basket.

They split up, and Alice wandered inside the coop. Most of the hens ran outside when they came in the pen, so she was able to get through each roost with little effort. There were a few hens, though, that didn't want to move. She nudged them aside and collected the eggs nestled in the straw.

Daisy appeared in the doorway as she moved toward the last roost.

"Be careful of that one. She doesn't like us taking her eggs."

Alice's mouth twisted. "Wonderful." So far, she'd managed to avoid being pecked. "Any tips?"

"Just be quick."

Blowing out a breath, Alice held the basket up next to the hen, pushing on her side. The chicken let out a loud squawk and pecked at the basket. Alice slid her hand under it and beneath the hen, snatching the egg hiding in the straw and backing away.

Daisy chuckled. "Nice technique. Did you get them all?"

"I think so." She moved toward the door. "Have you finished filling the feeders?"

"Yep." Daisy backed up, and they headed for the gate to go back to the house.

Alice lifted her face to the sun. "I'm glad spring has arrived. I'm not a fan of winter."

"Same here. I was happy to finally ditch the cane."

"You're walking well."

"Yeah, my balance is back to normal. I still get headaches on occasion, and my legs ache and get tired sometimes, especially if I've been really busy." She shrugged. "With time, most of the leg stuff should go away. I might always get headaches now, though. Migraine medicine helps. I'm just glad the seizures have gone away."

Alice couldn't imagine how much Daisy's life had changed in the last year. "Well, I'm glad you're doing well. Knox was pretty upset when Asa called to tell him what happened. I was too, for that matter. Asa's a good friend, so we all hurt for him."

Daisy smiled. "I'm glad he has friends like you and Knox. And the Archers. It kept him from completely self-isolating over the years."

"He did the same thing for Knox. I still can't believe he married Sofie. I never thought I'd see the day my brother would get hitched."

"Well, I'm glad things worked out the way they did." Daisy climbed the back-porch steps and opened the door. "He's so wonderful with Olive. And he makes Sofie happy."

Alice followed her inside and put the eggs on the counter. "It's mutual. He loves them both very much." She glanced around. "Do you have egg cartons to put these in?"

"In the pantry."

She glanced to where Daisy pointed and walked over to get several from the shelf. Together, the two women checked and cleaned the eggs.

"Thanks for your help. I'll run those over to the bunkhouse later when I take the cookies." Daisy smiled.

"You're welcome. I'm going to wander around a bit outside, if that's okay?"

"It's fine with me. If you saddle a horse and ride over the ridge behind the buildings, you'll find the river."

"Oh, that sounds nice. I'll probably save that for another day when I have more time, but thanks for the tip."

"Yep." Daisy waved a hand and pulled some canisters forward. "Have fun exploring."

"I will." Alice smiled and headed back outside into the warm sunshine. She took a deep breath of the clean Montana air, letting the peace of the ranch wash over her. She missed living in the boonies. Town was fine, and it was close to school, but there was something about waking up in the morning to nothing but the birds and cattle that fed her soul. She was really hoping the realtor had a few properties just outside of town to show her. A bit of a drive to school was okay. She just didn't want to be thirty minutes away like her family's ranch in Colorado was. It was too much of a hassle in the winter.

Alice wandered through the yard, visiting the various barns and familiarizing herself with the Stone Creek. It was a large cattle operation, but they also had sizeable goat and horse herds. The horses she could understand—running cattle required them—but not the goats. Knox kept goats because their mom liked them, and he and their dad could never get rid of them after she died. She wondered what the story was here. Perhaps Asa and Silas just liked them.

She stopped outside the goat pen and watched them play. There were quite a few babies running around. Their tiny bodies zipped around the pen between the larger adults, butting their heads against hay bales and their mothers' rumps.

Shaking her head and giggling, she walked away, heading for one of the horse barns. She knew from the last time she was here for Daisy and Asa's wedding that the Stone Creek had three. Two for their everyday stock—which also consisted of most of Knox's horses until his ranch was ready—and a smaller one for foaling mares and their newborns.

And she was all about the baby animals, so she wandered into the foaling barn first, hoping one of the hundred horses on the ranch gave birth recently. Foals were almost as much fun to watch as baby goats.

Alice blinked as she entered, helping her eyes adjust to the lower light level inside the barn. A soft whicker met her ears, and she followed it down the aisle to a stall near the end.

"Oh! Aren't you just beautiful?" She peered over the bottom of the split door into the stall at the shiny gold foal with bright blue eyes. Its mother—her own coat a slightly darker shade of gold than her baby's—walked up, blowing air in Alice's face as she sniffed the newcomer.

She laughed softly. "Hi, Mama." She lifted a hand, scratching the side of the horse's face. The mare stepped closer and leaned into her touch. The baby trotted over, its tiny tail bobbing. Both horses' ears twitched a moment before Alice heard the murmur of male voices. She straightened and glanced toward the door as it opened. Asa's massive frame filled the doorway. Another man, who was a few inches shorter, entered behind him. They paused when they saw her.

"Alice, hi." Asa smiled.

"Good morning." She gave them a small wave. "I was out for a walk and decided to see if you had any foals." Her eyes traveled to the stall next to her. "These two are beautiful. Where did you get the mare? She isn't one of Knox's."

Asa and the other man came closer. "No. I found her through one of his friends. Her colt is from one of his stallions, though."

"That explains his lighter coloring. They're both beautiful." Speaking of beautiful, her eyes strayed to the stranger with Asa. The man looked to be about Asa's age, but that was where the similarities stopped. Where Asa's coloring was dark, this man's was lighter. His rich, amber-colored hair was cut short, almost military in style. Sharp hazel eyes studied her. Alice studied him right back. He was mighty fine to look at. The seams of his gray polo shirt strained against the muscles bulging in his shoulders and biceps. She imagined there were some rock-hard six-pack abs under that shirt too. Dark jeans hugged his powerful thighs and black boots added to his over six-foot height.

"They are. And Rosalind is a sweetheart. I'm hoping Horatio inherited her disposition. Right now, he's got too much spunk to tell."

She chuckled. "Of course he does. He's a baby." She looked at the man. "Are you here thinking about buying him?"

A frown drew down the man's eyebrows, and his gaze sharpened. "Me? No. I'm inspecting the new fire suppression system in the barn."

"Oh."

"Alice, this is Wade Kaczmarek. He's one of the county fire inspectors." He glanced at the man. "Wade, this is Knox's sister, Alice. She just moved here."

She held out a hand. "It's nice to meet you."

He took it, giving it a firm shake. Alice tried to keep her eyeballs inside her head at the touch. A fierce jolt raced through her body, like she'd touched an electrified fence. Wade cleared his throat as he let go of her hand, the frown on his face turning contemplative. She tried not to stare at him as she wondered what the hell that was all about. Rolling her shoulders, she tried to shrug off the sudden ants-in-her-pants feeling his touch provoked.

"You too." Wade straightened and put both hands on the clipboard he held, then glanced at Asa. "You know, for a man who likes his solitude, you seem to have opened a guest ranch lately."

Asa grinned. "It's just family." He shrugged, thumbs hooked in his pockets. "And we're just a stopover. Knox and Sofie's place will be ready in a few months, and you want to look for a house in town, right?" He glanced at Alice.

She nodded, suppressing the lingering shivers rippling through her. That was something she needed to examine later when she had a chance to think. "I'm actually going this morning to meet with a realtor. Daisy's coming with me."

"There are a couple nice houses for sale on the north side of town," Wade said. "I don't know what your budget is, but they're reasonable in price."

"Good to know, thank you."

His head bobbed once, then he looked at Asa. "You ready to get this show on the road? I have to be back in town by ten for a meeting."

"Right." He looked at Alice. "I'll see you later. Don't let my wife talk you into a fixer-upper. She got into all those home design shows while she recuperated from her accident. Thankfully, the wedding took up most of her attention, but she's been talking about paint colors and curtains."

Alice grinned. "I'm not afraid of a little hard work. But I also would like something move-in ready."

"Good deal." He glanced at Wade and gave a quick tip of his head. "Come on. We can start with the control panel."

"Sounds good. Ma'am, it was nice meeting you."

"You too." Even if he did set her nerves all aflutter.

The men walked away, and Alice couldn't stop herself from turning to watch. Wade Kaczmarek had a nice ass.

THREE

"Oh, I like this one." Daisy peered through the windshield.

Alice put the car in park and stared at the two-story, turn-of-the-century craftsman. She did too. The pale-yellow siding and white trim were clean and cheerful. Manicured flower beds boasted neatly trimmed shrubs and spring perennials, adding pops of purple, pink, and red to the front of the house.

"Let's go see if the inside matches the outside." She turned off the engine and got out of the car, glancing at the realtor, Lorraine Newman, as she walked over from her vehicle.

"What do you think?" The woman raised her sunglasses and smiled.

"It's cute. Is the inside just as nice?"

"Mostly. It could use some updating in a few rooms, but it's livable."

Alice's mouth twisted. Now she was a little nervous. "Okay. Let's take a look."

Lorraine led the way up the sidewalk and took the key from the lockbox on the door, letting them inside. Alice stepped over the threshold and winced.

"Wow." Daisy stepped in behind her. "Someone really likes yellow."

"That's for sure," Alice muttered. The door opened into the living room and the walls were a bright, almost neon yellow. The stark white sheers hanging over the windows did little to soften the color. Nor did the honey oak casings. Paint would be the first thing on her list if she bought this place. Thankfully, that was an easy fix.

"I agree. The color is a little off-putting, but the bones of the house are great." Lorraine stepped further inside. "It has all its natural woodwork still. The floors are newer, but still hardwood. Let's go into the kitchen." She pointed down a short hallway at the back of the room behind the stairs.

Alice followed, praying the kitchen wasn't stuck in a time warp or painted an equally shocking color. Holding her breath, she stepped out of the hallway. Bright white cabinets greeted her, but the walls were a softer yellow, more like the exterior of the house. She still wasn't a fan, but she could live with it while she tackled the living room. The appliances were new, and the tile on the floor complimented the cabinets and walls.

"This is much better," Daisy said.

"Yeah." Alice glanced around. "I'm still not a fan of the yellow, but it's not as bad."

"Good." Lorraine pointed toward a door on the left side of the room. "The dining room is through there."

Alice headed that way. "More yellow." It was the same color as the kitchen, but it also had white wainscoting and hardwood floors.

"Is the whole house yellow?" Daisy asked as they followed the realtor back to the living room.

"Yes. I think it's their idea of neutral. The only room that isn't is the kid's room. It's pink." She paused in the hall.

"There's a half bath here for guests." She leaned in and flipped on the light.

Alice poked her head in. It was a basic guest bath—and also the bright yellow of the living room.

"Let's go upstairs." Lorraine led them up the staircase to the three bedrooms and full bath occupying the second story.

More shades of yellow greeted them, none as loud as the living room, though. The little girl's room was a pale bubblegum pink. Alice thought it was great for a kid's room, but for her, it, too, would need to be painted.

"I'll let you walk around a bit. Definitely check out the yard and the garage. Both are very nice." Lorraine started for the stairs. "If you need me, I'll be out front." She walked away, leaving Alice and Daisy alone.

"So, what do you think?" Daisy looked at her once the other woman was out of earshot.

"I think it needs a lot of paint. But the bones are nice. I like all the original wood moldings."

"Me too."

"Let's go look at the yard." Alice led the way downstairs and out the back door in the kitchen to a decent-sized lot. A six-foot wooden fence encircled the property, which Alice appreciated. She planned to have Knox's kids be frequent visitors, and it would be nice not to have to fence the yard first.

They poked their heads inside the garage on their way back out front. Alice liked the place, but painting that much house would require a lot of work. She wasn't sure she wanted to spend her summer painting her house. Not when she and Sofie had a storefront to get ready as well. The little artisan gift shop they wanted to open was going to take up a lot of her time.

Rounding the corner of the house, she spotted the realtor on the porch, phone to her ear. The woman smiled at them and held up a finger. She ended her call and pocketed the phone.

"So? What do you think?"

"It definitely needs some work. Mainly paint. Do any of the other homes have the charm of this one, but a more neutral color palette?"

Lorraine tipped her head back and forth. "Sort of. Pretty much everything on the market right now in your price range needs something done to it. Let's go look at the one two streets over. It's more dated than this one and not as happy on the outside, but the paint colors are easier on the eyes. And it's vacant, so you'd be able to move in sooner."

Alice sighed. Maybe she should just save her money and move into an apartment for now. Or rent a house. Then she could buy some land and build a place. But did she really want to do that? She wanted to say she would never move again, but if she met someone and got married, she might. It would depend on where he lived and then where they wanted to live together.

Why couldn't this process be easier?

Getting in the car, she followed Lorraine's vehicle through the neighborhood to the next house. It looked similar to the other one, but the exterior needed some love. Overgrown hedges lined the front under the windows, and the sidewalk was cracked and crumbling. The white paint wasn't peeling, but it was a little dingy.

"She's right. It's not as nice on the outside."

"Yeah." Alice turned off the engine. "But if it doesn't require me to paint every single room, it might be worth it."

Daisy chuckled and got out. "You could hire someone to paint the rooms for you."

Alice shut her door and walked up the sidewalk. "True. Maybe Asa would let me hire away some of his ranch hands for a day."

"It wouldn't hurt to ask."

That was definitely something to think about.

"Okay." Lorraine paused outside the house. "This place is laid out pretty much like the other one. A lot of homes in this neighborhood were built around the same time. It still has the original woodwork, but it's carpeted. I think there's hardwood under it, though, if you wanted to tear it up." She wrinkled her nose. "Which you probably will, anyway." She removed the key from the lockbox and inserted it into the lock.

Alice's stomach dropped. That did not bode well. Taking a deep breath, she walked inside. The smell hit her first. Cat pee—from what smelled like fifty cats—and stale smoke.

"Oh, my." Daisy covered her nose.

"This is better than the last one?" Alice arched an eyebrow at Lorraine.

The woman shrugged. "It's not yellow. And most of the odor is in the carpet. The upstairs smells better."

"Let's go up there, then." Alice didn't wait. She made a beeline for the staircase and headed up, taking note of the worn carpet on the treads. At the top of the landing, she glanced around. It did smell better up here—less cat pee. But the stale smoke smell remained, and the carpet was as dingy as the exterior. It would definitely need replaced.

"What's the asking price for this house?" She looked at Lorraine, who rattled off a number. Alice nodded. "Good. I'd need the extra to redo the floors. You're sure there's hardwood underneath?"

"Pretty sure. All these homes had hardwood floors when they were built. I can't imagine anyone tearing them up unless they were severely damaged. It wouldn't be cost effective to rip up the boards, then put down plywood sub-flooring for the carpet."

Alice nodded and wandered into the master bedroom. She

wondered if the homeowner would object to her lifting a corner of the carpet in the rooms to check.

Leaving the room, she did a quick turn through the other bedrooms, which were a lot like the ones in the other house. The bathroom needed some updates—namely a new vanity—but she liked the tile on the walls and floor.

Lorraine motioned for them to follow her back down to the main level, then turned into the short hallway to the kitchen. The walls were white, the cabinets red oak. Tired and dirty linoleum stuck to her shoes as she walked inside.

"I think this place is a hard no." Alice wrinkled her nose. "You said it was dated, but you didn't mention dirty." Even in here, she could still smell the faint whiff of ammonia. "I met one of the fire inspectors this morning at the ranch when he was checking out a new fire suppression system in the foal barn. He mentioned some nice properties for sale on the north side. What can you tell me about those?"

"Oh." Lorraine frowned slightly. "They're a little pricier. And some of them need some work. But not like this one." She named an amount that was at the tippy-top of Alice's budget.

"I'd still like to see them. I don't plan to go anywhere anytime soon, so I don't mind going that high. I want to be comfortable in my home."

"Okay, then. Follow me." Lorraine turned on her heel and led them back through the house. After locking up, they climbed into their cars and drove across town.

Alice eyed the houses on the street with surprise when they turned into the neighborhood. They were not what she was expecting. "Pine Ridge has a Victorian side?"

Daisy grinned. "Gorgeous, aren't they?"

A smile lit Alice's face as she parked. She hurried from the car. "Yes! The inspector didn't mention the style. Just that they were nice." She stared up at the tan and cream Victorian

Lorraine stopped in front of. Its gabled roof and wide porch called to her. She didn't care that the paint peeled in a few places or that the landscaping needed some work. A place like this, she would paint the exterior anyway. Bright, vibrant colors.

"There are two houses for sale in the neighborhood. This one is the least expensive, and it's vacant." Lorraine told her the price. It was thirty thousand dollars under her cap.

"That's not bad." It was still forty thousand more than the other two houses, but for a Victorian, she didn't care. She headed up the walkway. *Please don't have nasty carpet or smell like cat pee.*

Lorraine opened the door, and Alice walked inside, her heart in her throat at the thought of what she might find. Gleaming hardwood floors and dark wood moldings greeted her. The walls were all a cream color. "Oh, thank God." Alice moved deeper into the interior. Because it was vacant, the fourteen-foot ceilings and expanse of blank floor made it feel much larger than it was, but the rooms still weren't small. And the light was fantastic. Sunlight streamed through the stained-glass upper windows, casting rainbows of color around the empty room.

"This place is amazing." Daisy spun in a circle, then paused to look at Lorraine. "Why didn't you bring us here first?"

"I always start at the bottom of the price range and work my way up unless the client asks to start somewhere specific."

Alice didn't care how the realtor did things; she was just glad she was here now. And she wasn't waiting for a guided tour. Taking off down the hallway that ran beside the staircase in front of her, she found the kitchen. Her mouth dropped open as she looked up at the ceiling. Every bit as high as the rest of the downstairs, it was covered in tin tiles.

Daisy gasped behind her. "Oh! That ceiling is incredible!"

"It is." Alice tore her eyes away from it to look at the rest of the room. Deep green cabinets with burnished brass handles lined most of the wall space. A white subway tile back splash ran the perimeter of the room above quartz counters, and in the few places where the walls were visible, the white paint faded seamlessly into the tile. Wide-plank hardwood floors and stainless-steel appliances rounded out the space. She wandered over to gawk at the six-burner, double oven, stainless-steel stove. It rivaled Daisy's range. Oh, she could have fun in here.

Turning, she glanced out the French doors. They let in an abundance of natural light. So did the large windows over the copper sink.

"As you can see, this space was recently renovated. So were the bathrooms," Lorraine said.

"I'd like to see those." But not before she checked out the pantry and the mudroom. She walked over to the pantry door and opened it, gawking again at the floor-to-ceiling shelves.

"Oh my goodness. I think Asa and I need to have a talk about our kitchen." Daisy peered over her shoulder.

Alice snickered and glanced at her. "And he told me not to let *you* talk *me* into a fixer-upper."

Daisy laughed. "Little did he know this trip would backfire on him." Her eyes roved the empty shelves again. "But I need this pantry. Mine's busting at the seams."

They backed away, and Alice shut the door, turning to Lorraine. "What's wrong with this place?"

The woman frowned. "What do you mean?"

"It's vacant and recently renovated. Why is the price so low?" A house this size in this condition, Alice would expect it to be well out of her price range.

"There's really nothing wrong with it. It's only real problem is the heating system. It's older." She held up her hands. "It still works, but not well. It really needs to be replaced. And it doesn't have central air."

Alice frowned. "That's it? No hidden bug or mold problem?"

Lorraine shook her head.

"No ancient wiring? Or corroded plumbing?"

Again, the woman shook her head. "Trust me. Around here, a bad heating system will make for a hard sell."

"So why didn't they upgrade it when they upgraded the kitchen and bathrooms?" Daisy asked.

"They ran out of money. This place is a flip, and the owners are new to that sort of thing. They didn't do things in the right order or budget for surprises and had to leave the heating system as is so they could complete the other renovations. Like I said, it still works, but it's on its last legs, and it's not very efficient."

"Well, I guess that makes sense." And she could definitely have a new heating system installed. She glanced around, looking for vents, but saw radiators instead. A frown marred her face. That wasn't good. That meant putting in central air would be more complicated than merely replacing the unit. "Okay. Let's look at the rest of the house."

"Certainly." Lorraine motioned to the hallway.

They toured the rest of the house, but Alice didn't see any surprises. Unless she counted the gigantic soaker claw-foot tub in the master bathroom. It was a thing of beauty.

When they went into the cellar, she understood better why the house was priced to sell. The boiler unit really was ancient. She wasn't sure she felt safe using it. If she bought this place, she'd definitely have it replaced before winter. The hot water heater too. It had a twenty-year-old date written on it. The only other thing that bothered her was the age of the electrical panel. Lorraine said the house didn't have any electrical issues, but she would be interested to see what an inspector said.

"Okay. I think I've seen enough. Can we look at the other property in this neighborhood?" Alice turned to the realtor.

"We sure can. And we can walk if you'd like. It's around the corner."

"Sure." Alice looked at Daisy, sending her a curious frown and glancing at her legs. "Is that okay with you?"

Daisy waved a hand. "I'm fine. Let's go."

"Okay, then." Alice spun on her heel and went upstairs.

Outside, Lorraine led them down the sidewalk and around the corner, stopping in front of another Victorian. This one was a little smaller, but much more stately. Bright white, it had intricate gingerbread trim lining the entire roofline. A porch swing hung from the rafters, swaying slightly in the breeze. More gingerbread trim on the screen door beckoned them inside.

"This is really cute, Alice. I like the exterior of this one more than the other house." Daisy glanced around the porch as they mounted the steps.

"The trim is great, yeah. How much is this one?"

Lorraine glanced back as she inserted the key in the lock and quoted the price. It was five thousand over her budget.

Alice's face pulled. This one would have to be perfect if she were to pick it at that price.

The realtor pushed the door open, and Alice and Daisy followed her in. Like the other house, it, too, had high ceilings and an abundance of natural light. It didn't have the stained-glass windows of the other house and all the trim had been painted white. It was furnished nicely, though. The house felt lived in and she had no problem seeing how her own furniture would fit in the space.

"The kitchen and dining room are through there, and there's a half bath and an office down that hallway." Lorraine pointed to a door to the left, then to a hallway on the right.

"Let's check out the kitchen first." Alice wasn't sure anything could top the one at the other house.

In the dining room, she paused to take it all in. The room was two-toned, painted a dusky lavender on top with white square panels on the bottom. A walnut table and chairs took up the center of the room under a brass and crystal chandelier. A matching china cabinet sat against one wall and a buffet on the other under the window.

"Nice," Daisy said.

It was. But Alice still wanted to see the kitchen, so she kept going, pausing just over the threshold. It was smaller than the other house, but that didn't surprise her. The entire house was smaller. Like the other kitchen, it had high ceilings, but no tin tiles. The cabinets were white and the walls a soft blue. White tile with a gray leaf pattern covered the floor, complimenting the quartz counters. It also boasted new stainless-steel appliances and French doors leading to the backyard. The stove wasn't as fancy as the other house, though.

"You like the other one, don't you?" Lorraine asked, a knowing smile on her face.

Alice gave her a sheepish smile. "Yeah. Even with its problems, that house had a lot of character. This one does too, but it's lost some of its old-world feel with all the white." She gestured to the trim around the windows and doors.

"Do you want to see the rest of it?"

"Yes. I think I want to put an offer in on the other house, but just in case there are more issues with that place than what we know about right now, I'd like to have another option."

"All right, then, let's head upstairs." The woman whirled and led them back through the dining room to the stairs.

The second story was more of the same. White trim, modern. It just didn't have the character of the other house.

"So, you like the other Victorian, then?" Lorraine shielded her face from the sun as they stood out front.

Alice nodded. "Yes."

"Okay. Let's walk back to the cars and go to my office to talk about the offer details."

"Sounds great." They wandered down the sidewalk and around the corner, heading to their cars.

"This is a great neighborhood," Daisy said, getting in the car.

"Yeah." Alice buckled her seatbelt and started the car. "I see a lot of swing sets in the yards and bikes in the driveways. It looks quiet and safe." She just wondered if maybe it was too much house for her, though. As a single woman, Alice didn't really need all that space. But it would be nice for when Knox's kids stayed with her. She planned to spoil them rotten while she could. And maybe one day she'd fill all those rooms with children of her own.

Downtown at Lorraine's office, she parked, and they went inside. It didn't take long to hammer out the offer details. Alice decided to offer ten thousand below the asking price and see what they said. Lorraine promised to send it this afternoon.

"So, lunch?" Alice stepped out into the sunshine and looked at Daisy.

"Sure. We can go visit Sara."

"Sounds good to me."

"It's just down the street a couple of blocks, so we can walk."

That worked for Alice. It was a nice day.

In just a few minutes, they were inside Sarafina's Diner. Alice's mouth watered at the delicious smells. Burgers and fried chicken with a dash of pie.

"Hey."

Alice looked over at the window in the wall behind the counter to see Sara's smiling face.

Daisy waved. "Hi. Alice put an offer on a house, and now we're hungry."

"That's exciting! Go find a seat and I'll come out to hear about it in just a couple of minutes."

"Okay." Daisy gave her a thumbs up, then turned to find them a seat in the diner. "Do you have a preference for where we sit?"

"No. Anywhere but the counter." The booths or the dining chairs were more comfortable than a bar stool.

"Over there?" Daisy pointed to a table by the window.

"Sure."

They wove through the tables and sat down. A server appeared, smiling as she handed them menus.

"Hi, Daisy."

"Hi, Rachel. This is my friend, Alice." She cocked her head. "Though I guess I could call you my sister-in-law. Or the sister of my brother-in-law. Sofie is now technically my sister-in-law since her mom married Asa's dad." She waved a hand and opened her menu. "Whatever. You're family." She grinned at Alice, then up at Rachel.

"It's nice to meet you," the other woman commented with a smile.

"You too," Alice said.

"So, do you guys know what you want to order?"

"I do, yes. Alice?" Daisy looked across the table at her.

"Oh. I guess I should look at the menu." She opened the folder and quickly scanned it. "I'll take the turkey bacon avocado panini."

Rachel wrote it down. "Daisy?"

"The same."

"Do you want a chocolate milkshake?"

"Yep."

"Oh, that sounds good. I'll have one too." Alice handed Sara her menu.

"Okay. I'll be back soon with your orders." She took the menus and left.

"So, how much trouble am I going to get into with Asa?" Alice tossed Daisy a mischievous grin.

Daisy chuckled. "None. As much as I want the pantry that house has, there's no way to put it in our kitchen without some major renovations. I don't want it that much."

The bell over the door sounded, and Alice glanced over. Her brain froze when she recognized the man who walked in. It kick-started, sending her heart rate into overdrive. She turned away and prayed he either didn't see them or wouldn't come over. Wade Kaczmarek made her insides feel all gooey, like gelatin. And while she appreciated his physique and handsome face, she didn't much care for the flock of butterflies rampaging through her emotions. It was unsettling.

"Oh, it's Wade." Daisy raised an arm and waved.

Alice bit back a groan. So much for ignoring him. She glanced up as he stopped in front of their table.

"Hi, Wade." Daisy gave him a bright smile. "Did the fire suppression system check out?"

"Hello. Yes, it did. That pretty mare and her baby are safe tucked into that barn."

"Good. We just ordered. Would you like to join us?"

Alice's stomach flip-flopped at the thought of sharing such a confined space with the man. Would the same tingles she got from his handshake come back if she accidentally brushed against him while he sat across from her? Or beside her?

"Thanks for the invitation, but I can't stay. I just came to grab the sandwich I ordered. I need to get back to my office. How did the house-hunting go?"

There was a pause, and Alice realized he was talking to her.

"Oh, um, it went fine. I put an offer in on one of the places you suggested I look at."

"Really? Which one?"

"The tan and cream Victorian."

He gave a short nod. "That's a great place. It belonged to an older couple for decades. Before they both passed away and it sold to a couple who are first time home flippers. They filled a couple of dumpsters, then marched a bunch of new stuff in. I haven't seen the interior, though."

That brought Alice's head up. She gave him a curious frown. "Do you drive by it often?"

"You could say that. I live next door. Blue Victorian with the white trim."

Her eyebrows shot up. He didn't strike her as a Victorian house kind of person. "You live in an old Victorian?"

His smile was amused. "My daughter thought it looked like a fairy tale house and fell in love with it. I couldn't say no to her."

"Oh." He had a daughter? Did that mean he was married too? She didn't see a ring, but that didn't mean much. Asa hardly ever wore his. Neither did Knox. They both said it was safer. Especially if they needed to work with machinery.

Rachel walked past, interrupting Alice's thoughts, and greeted Wade. "Your sandwich is at the counter. Give me just a minute and I'll check you out."

"Okay, thank you." He nodded and smiled at her.

She moved on with a tray of food balanced on her hand.

Wade turned back to them. "I better go get in line. Daisy, it was good to see you. Alice, I guess I'll be seeing more of you if we become neighbors."

Alice nodded. "I guess so." She forced a smile onto her face and hoped it reached her eyes. She wasn't sure how she felt about living so near this man. Then she gave a hard, mental eye roll. What did it matter? He was probably married. That fact would make it easy for her to forget about the shivers he sent through her body.

He waved and walked away. Alice did her best not to stare, reminding herself he was off-limits. But no matter. It was damn hard not to look. He looked as good going as he did coming. Those cargo pants hugged his tush just enough for her to see the muscles flex as he moved.

Daisy's soft chuckle drew Alice's attention.

"What?" She frowned at her friend.

"Don't 'what' me. He makes your lady parts wake up and take notice." Daisy grinned across the table.

Alice's cheeks flushed bright red, and she shifted in her seat. "What makes you say that?"

"Oh, please. You're talking to a woman who was very recently in your shoes."

"My shoes?"

Daisy nodded. "Asa made me hot and bothered from the get-go. I denied it, of course, but it didn't change the fact that he set my undies on fire just by walking into the room. He still does, only now I don't mind." She gave a saucy grin. "And you could do a lot worse, you know. Wade's a good guy. He and Asa have been friends since they were kids."

"I remember seeing him at the wedding, but he didn't have the same effect on me then that he does now. I don't quite understand why."

"He was still married then. Separated, but married."

Alice glanced over to see him walk out the door. Well, at least she wouldn't be lusting after another woman's husband. "Do you know what happened?"

"His ex-wife is a dumbass, selfish bitch."

Eyes wide, Alice turned back to her friend. "Whoa. Don't hold back."

Daisy rolled her eyes. "It's true. She left him with three young kids. Decided she didn't want to be a mom or a wife anymore. I don't know the entire story, just what Asa told me after Wade told him. But I do know he's doing what he can for his kids."

Alice frowned. "So, she doesn't have any contact with them?"

"Nope."

She shook her head. "I can't imagine walking out on my kids, if I had any. It'd tear my heart out."

"Same here. But, like I said, I don't know the whole story."

Glancing out the window again, Alice watched a fire department SUV pull out of the lot. She was still wildly attracted to the handsome inspector. But now curiosity gripped her about the kind of man—the kind of dad—he was.

She frowned and looked away. The attraction she felt made her uncomfortable. Not because he creeped her out, but because her feelings were stronger than any she'd ever experienced for a man she just met. She didn't know what to make of them or how to handle them. The instant sizzle wasn't something she'd ever dealt with. And knowing now that he was a single dad of three didn't help her any. If anything, it just confused her more. Yes, she was ready to have a family, but did she want one that was ready made? Would he want more kids? Because she wanted a baby of her own.

Alice bit back a snort. Why was she even contemplating that? She'd had two short conversations with the man, and she was already envisioning their future? She rolled her eyes at herself and sighed. *Get a grip, Alice.*

But as she smiled up at Rachel, who appeared with their orders, she couldn't help but wonder what would happen if they went on a date. Where would that lead? Would his kids approve?

She didn't have any answers and wasn't sure she ever would. One thing was certain, though. Her move to Pine Ridge was already shaking up her boring life.

Four

"Daddy!"

Wade grinned as his five-year-old daughter, Bronwyn, spotted him as she came through the back door at his parents' house. She ran to him, arms outstretched.

"Hey, munchkin." He gave her a smacking kiss on her cheek as he scooped her up. "Did you have a good day with Grandma and Grandpa?"

She nodded. "Yep. Grandma and me baked cookies after school. Oatmeal raisin." A frown drew her rich brown eyes together. "I didn't think I'd like them, because they have fruit in them, but they're yummy." She wiggled in his arms to be put down. "Do you want one?"

He set her on her feet. "Not right now, sweetie. But we can take some home with us. I'll eat one after dinner."

"Okay."

"So, how was school?" Bronwyn was in her last year of preschool. He couldn't believe she'd start kindergarten in the fall.

She shrugged, the frown returning, though pensive this

time. "We painted. Our family. I didn't know whether to put Mommy in the picture. I did, but she's off to the side."

Wade's heart lurched at the pain in his daughter's voice. Then his anger surged. He tamped it down. It didn't do any good for him to get upset with Emily. She'd made her choice and left him with the fallout. He was determined to manage it as best he could and make sure his kids led happy, fulfilling lives without her.

"That sounds fine, sweetie. You can add her in however you want. Are you ready to go? Where are your brother and sister?" He glanced around, but the living room and kitchen were empty.

"They're out back with Grandma and Grandpa." She hooked a thumb toward the sliding door. "I came in for a juice box."

"Oh, okay. Well, go get your juice box while I collect your siblings, all right?"

"Okay." She scampered off, and he walked through the door to the yard.

"Hi, honey."

He glanced over to his mom, Peg, who sat in a patio chair arranged around a table. She had eighteen-month-old Elise on her lap. The toddler held a plastic phone and was busy pushing buttons to make different sounds.

"Hi, Mom." He glanced out at the yard. His three-year-old son, Henry, kicked a soccer ball around with his grandpa.

"How was work?"

He sat down next to her. Elise gave him a toothy smile and crawled across Peg's lap toward him. He gave his daughter a big smile and picked her up, pressing a series of smacking kisses to her jawline. "Hi, baby girl."

"Dada!" She held up her toy and babbled at him.

Smiling, he nodded along, then answered his mom's question. "It was fine. Busy as usual." His thoughts strayed to his stop at the Stone Creek and the beautiful, blonde bombshell he met there, Alice Duvall. If ever there was a woman who looked like she belonged in a beauty pageant, it was her. She could pass for a Barbie look-a-like with her blonde hair, blue eyes, and tall, curvy frame. He remembered her from Asa and Daisy's wedding, but not this intense attraction. That was new. And unsettling.

"What happened?"

"Huh?" He blinked and focused on his mom. "What do you mean? Nothing happened."

"Uh-huh. Then what's with the sudden frown?"

"Oh. I was just thinking about someone I met." He cursed, mentally. Why did he say that? It would just encourage her to ask questions.

Peg studied him for a moment, then a smile broke out on her face. "A woman?"

"Who said it was a woman?" He cleared his throat and focused on Elise, bouncing her on his knee. Dammit, when would he learn? Better yet, when would he ever be able to conceal his expression from her?

"The twinkle in your eye told me."

He rolled his eyes, a smile breaking free. "Okay, yes. It was a woman. Alice Duvall. Knox Duvall's sister. She just moved here, and she was in the barn I inspected this morning at the Stone Creek." He glanced over the yard, not really seeing much of it as he thought about what else he'd learned today. "We apparently might end up as neighbors."

"Oh, really? How so?"

"She mentioned she was house-hunting, and I told her there were some nice places on the north side of town." Why he did that, he still didn't know. The words had been out of his mouth before he could stop them. "She liked the Coulson's old house and put in an offer on it."

A wide smile spread over Peg's face. "Really? That sounds lovely. What's she like? Anything like her brother?"

He bounced Elise again as he thought about Alice's pretty face and quiet demeanor. "Yeah, I guess. Their coloring is similar. She's on the tall side. Quiet." Though, there was a liveliness in her eyes that said once he got to know her, she wouldn't be so demure. "I didn't really talk to her for long, so that's about all I can tell you."

Bronwyn walked out, saving him from any further inquisition.

"What's for dinner, Daddy?"

"Pancakes."

Her eyes lit up. "Shaped like Mickey Mouse?"

"Are there any other kind?"

She giggled.

"Come on." He stood up, holding Elise. "We should get home so I can get them started." Plus, if he stayed any longer, his mother would be sure to ask more subtle questions about Alice. It didn't matter to her that he really didn't have any interest in getting involved with a woman. She thought he needed one—that his kids needed a mother. To him, they were doing fine on their own for now. He had no desire to open himself up for that kind of heartache again, and he'd be damned if he'd expose his children to it.

So, no matter how much his mom wanted to set him up with the beautiful Alice Duvall—or how much his body sat up and took notice of her—he wasn't interested in anything more than friendship. Full stop.

"Henry. Time to go, bud."

The boy turned at the sound of his dad's voice and ran over. "Hi, Daddy."

"Hey, bub. Go make sure you have all your stuff. It's time to go home."

"We're having pancakes for dinner!" Bronwyn announced.

Henry cheered. "Oh, boy!" He ran inside to find his backpack.

"I do believe you just made their day." Wade's dad, Bill, walked up, smiling.

Wade returned his smile. "Pancakes make any day a win."

"That they do." Bill looked at his wife, waggling his eyebrows.

Peg huffed. "We're having pancakes, too, aren't we?"

He laughed. "You're the cook. I'll eat whatever you make."

She rolled her eyes. "I swear, you're taking lessons from Henry with those puppy eyes." She huffed again. "Fine. We can have pancakes."

Bill's smile widened.

Wade chuckled and leaned forward to kiss his mom's cheek. "Thanks for watching the kids. I'm still looking for someone to fill in for Shelby, but I'm not having much luck. Maybe once school lets out for the year, I'll have more options." His regular sitter, Shelby Nicholas, fell off a horse just over a week ago and broke her leg and sprained her wrist, leaving him without steady childcare until she healed. Thankfully, his parents stepped in.

Peg waved a hand. "I don't mind. It's been fun having them around. Makes your dad leave closing up the store to someone else and he comes home earlier." She nudged Bill in the stomach.

Bill feigned a grunt and rubbed the spot. "Someone's got to play soccer with Henry. And I think that when you do find a replacement for Shelby—and even once she comes back—we should continue to shoulder some of the childcare duties." He glanced at Peg, lifting an eyebrow.

She beamed and nodded. "Yes, I agree. We'd love to have them more. I think this has been one of the good things to come from Emily leaving. It brought you home. As far as I'm concerned, they're welcome whenever they want to come over."

"I know, but I don't want to put a damper on your retirement years by asking you to babysit all the time."

"Nonsense. That's what grandparents are for. And it's not like we'll be full-time babysitters forever. Shelby will be back."

"If you're sure?" Wade would forever be grateful to his parents for their support over the last year. He hadn't been the best son the couple of years before that. It took Emily leaving for him to see it, but she'd subtly shifted him away from his family over the course of their marriage in an attempt to keep them in Nashville. But Pine Ridge was home, and he'd missed it. All of his family was here. Hers was too—what was left of it, anyway—but she didn't seem to care. All she wanted was glitz and glamour. All the things being a wife and mother wasn't.

"We're sure," Bill answered for his wife.

Wade gave a quick nod. "I'd still like to find someone to fill in. I know you have other responsibilities and things going on you can't just shove to the back burner for weeks on end. Once I do, we can discuss how often you want the kids and what days work best."

"That sounds great." Peg stretched up to peck a kiss on his cheek, then put one on Elise's. The toddler giggled and leaned over to smack a sloppy kiss on Peg's cheek. Smiling at the little girl, Peg looked up at Wade. "We'll see you Sunday at church?"

He nodded. "We'll be there." That was another thing he'd changed since Emily left and they moved home. She'd gradually stopped going to church, even going so far as keeping Henry and Elise home. Bronwyn pitched a holy fit, though, and demanded to go with Wade. He was sure it was just another thing that drove a wedge between them.

Wade looked at Elise. "Say bye-bye to Grandma and Grandpa."

Elise waved a chubby fist and grinned. "Bye-bye."

Peg grabbed her hand and kissed it. "See you later, sweetie. Be good for Daddy."

"We'll walk you out," Bill said, ushering them all inside. "We want to say goodbye to Wyn and Henry."

They walked inside, where his older two children finished packing up. Henry had his backpack and jacket, while Bronwyn stood on a stool, putting cookies in a zippered bag. She grinned sheepishly at her grandma when they walked in.

"Daddy said we could take some home." She shrugged.

Wade chuckled and looked at his mom. "I did. She said she helped make them."

Peg smiled. "She's fine. I was going to send some with you, anyway." She walked over and lifted the girl off the stool to set her on the floor. "Did you leave some for me and Grandpa?"

Bronwyn giggled. "Yes."

"Good." She kissed the top of the girl's head.

Wade smiled and herded the kids toward the door. Peg handed him Elise's diaper bag and Bronwyn's art project from school.

"Thanks, Mom."

"Yep. Have a good night. We'll see you Sunday."

"We will." He waved and headed for the car. Bronwyn buckled herself into her seat while he secured Elise and Henry. Climbing into the driver's seat, he fastened his seat belt and put the car in reverse. "Okay. Let's go make some pancakes."

Bronwyn and Henry cheered. Elise clapped because of her siblings' excitement, making Wade smile. He rolled out of his parents' driveway, tooting the horn, and headed for home.

FIVE

The hum of voices filled the church rec room after Sunday's services. Alice sipped a glass of punch as she stood near the wall and people-watched. She only knew her brother and his family, but everyone they'd introduced her to seemed friendly.

Her eyes strayed to the far side of the room, where Wade stood, holding the most adorable little blonde girl she'd ever seen. Well, except for maybe her older sister, who played in the kids' corner with her brother and a couple other kids, including Alice's niece, Olive. She'd seen him with all three children when he entered the rec room before the two older ones made a beeline for the toys. Now, he talked with an older couple, whom she figured for his parents. The man bore a striking resemblance to Wade.

"Alice."

She tore her gaze away from Wade and his family at the sound of Sofie calling her name. Glancing over, she saw the other woman motioning to her. Alice headed her way.

"I want you to meet someone. This is Cynthia Hughes. Our minister is single, so she sort of runs all the women's functions in the church." She gestured to a woman in her sixties standing beside her.

"Hello." Alice held out a hand.

Cynthia smiled and shook it. "Nice to meet you."

"You too."

"I was telling Cynthia about your background and how you'll be the new art teacher at the elementary this fall. She said you should do something with the Sunday schoolers."

"Oh. Sure. I can do that. It sounds like fun." Her mind immediately cycled through the Bible school crafts she'd done in the past. "What are they learning about right now?"

"We usually follow with whatever Pastor Rick is doing, so the kids get the same lesson as the adults. Then the parents can discuss it with their kids at home and reinforce what the kids learned in Sunday school with what they gleaned from the sermon."

"Okay. That sounds great. So long as you give me a couple of days so I can come up with an idea and materials, an art project shouldn't be a problem."

"Wonderful." Cynthia smiled. She opened the small purse slung over her shoulder and took out her cellphone. "Why don't you give me your phone number, and I'll call you later this week."

Alice rattled off her number, and Cynthia input it into her phone.

"I'm excited to see what you come up with. We try, but none of us are the best artists in the world. And the teacher you're replacing doesn't go to this church." She glanced away, waving at someone. "Alice, it was lovely to meet you. If you ladies will excuse me?"

"Of course." She smiled, watching the older woman hurry away to talk to someone else. "She seems busy." She looked at Sofie.

"Oh, yes. Cynthia Hughes is a force to be reckoned with.

But she's super nice. So, how are you enjoying our little church?"

"It's nice. Everyone's been very welcoming." She cast a look over the parishioners, then back at her sister-in-law. "How do you like it? Knox said you grew up Catholic, but this is a Protestant church."

"It's different, but I stopped going to Mass a long time ago. Back when I was still married to Lance. He didn't want to get married in the Catholic church, and he didn't want me going to church without him, so I eventually just quit going. If I did go, it was to his church. When Knox suggested we find a church and start going, we looked around, even going to the Catholic church in town. But this is the one that felt like home."

Sofie pressed a hand to her stomach and grimaced.

"Are you okay?"

"Yeah. Just getting hungry. If I wait too long to eat, I get nauseous. I'm at that point."

"Well, let's find Knox and make him take you to lunch." She knew her brother would take one look at the green cast to his pregnant wife's face and whisk her out the door.

"I know where he is. But I need to get Olive first." She nodded toward her daughter.

"Why don't you go get him? I'll get Olive."

"Are you sure?"

"Of course."

"Okay. We'll meet you at the car, if that works?"

"That's fine." Alice shooed her away. Sofie walked off with a nod.

Spinning on her heel, Alice threaded through the crowd to the children's corner. "Olive."

The dark-haired girl looked up.

"Hey, it's time to go, sweetie."

"Already? We just started playing." She looked at Wade's daughter. "This is Bronwyn. She's in my class at preschool."

Alice smiled and waggled her fingers. "Hi. I'm Olive's aunt, Alice."

The girl smiled. "Hi."

"It's nice to meet you. I'm afraid Olive will have to play again another time, though." She turned her attention to Olive. "Your mom is ready for lunch, so we need to go."

Olive sighed, but didn't protest. "Okay." She glanced at her friend. "I'll see you at school."

Alice held out a hand to Olive. The girl took it, and Alice turned, but stopped short at the wall of man behind her. "Oh!" She glanced up into Wade Kaczmarek's face. He still held the blonde toddler.

Wade's free hand shot out to cup her elbow, steadying her as she rocked back on her heels. "Sorry. I didn't mean to startle you."

"That's okay. I didn't realize you were back there."

He glanced down at Olive. "Hey, Olive."

"Hi, Mr. Catch-rack."

Alice bit back a grin as Olive butchered his last name. Wade tried to as well, but failed. A corner of his mouth lifted, and he shot her an amused smile.

"Heading to lunch?"

"Yes. Not sure where, but I know there will be food soon."

"Same here. Mom made a feast, like always on Sundays." He glanced past her. "Wyn, Henry, it's time to go."

There was a clatter of tin pans and plastic food as the kids put the toys away.

Alice tugged on Olive's hand, looking down at the girl. "We better get going before your mom gets hangry."

Olive giggled. "Yeah. The baby does that to her a lot."

Smiling, Alice glanced at Wade. "It was nice seeing you again." She looked at his kids. "And it was nice meeting you.

I'm sure I'll see you around." She just hoped it was in a class-room and not so much with their handsome-as-the-devil dad. He set her hormones into overdrive. With that baby in his arms, she could fly to the moon without a rocket booster.

"Come on, Ol." She pulled in a deep breath. "Your parents are waiting on us." With a nod, she led Olive away. At the door, she couldn't help but glance back. Wade still held the little girl, but now he also held the little boy's hand as they stood with his parents. Bronwyn hovered around them, bouncing on the balls of her feet as she played peek-a-boo with her sister.

She stepped through the doorway, cursing herself for taking another look. Now, the image of him being a doting dad was burned into her brain.

Six

Alice parked her SUV outside the storefront she and Sofie rented for their new boutique. Excitement zinged through her. It would be her first time inside. Over the last couple of days, she'd unpacked some essentials and just settled in, relaxing after the stress of moving. But now she was ready to see the building Sofie picked out.

She walked up to the door and pulled, stepping into the dim interior.

"Hi." Sofie popped up from behind the counter.

"What are you doing back there?" She meandered further into the room, glancing around. The space was nice. All the walls were a light gray except the back, which was brick. The counter needed some sprucing up. The cream laminate was beyond drab. She hoped they could wrap it in wood and stain it.

"The internet guy was here earlier today. My pregnancy brain forgot to bring the computer, so he used his tablet to make sure it was running. I was just plugging in all the cords so the computer has internet access."

"Oh. That's great."

"Yeah. Now we can start inputting inventory and sync it to our other devices. And get real-time reports on sales once we open. So, do you want a tour?"

"Of course."

Sofie smiled and came out from behind the desk. "Main room, obviously. Knox is going to build shelves on this entire wall." She motioned to the wall to Alice's right. "On this wall," she turned around, "will be the art prints. We might add more shelves. I think it'll just depend on how much interest we get from local painters."

"Okay. That sounds good."

"Knox is also building a display case for your pottery. It's going to look like a two-sided hutch. I figure we can store extra inventory in the cabinets." She turned and pointed to the checkout counter. "That abhorrent thing is going away."

"Oh, thank God. It's hideous."

Sofie chuckled. "Right? I found a jewelry display case I want to put in its place, then we'll build out the end into an L-shape with shelves beneath to house the computer tower and any miscellaneous stuff we need to keep at the register."

"That works. Where are we with inventory?"

"I think we're looking great. We have your pottery and my jewelry. I talked to a couple of local painters who said they'd love to put some pieces on display. Also, Billy Jeffries is going to contribute some woodworking pieces. He makes some gorgeous jewelry boxes and toolboxes. He might make some larger pieces too, like picture frames and even hope chests. We still need a metal worker, but Jasper knows someone. And the craft store lady, Ellen, she's actually a great seamstress and makes clothes, so she's putting together a line for us to carry here. She also knows of a local woman who makes her own paper, then uses it to make greeting cards. I have a meeting scheduled with her tomorrow to talk about having her put together a small display of cards—blank and stamped. We can be a one-stop shop for gifts, then."

"Wow. Sofie, you've really done a lot of work in the last few months."

She shrugged. "We've been in a holding pattern with the house, so this has helped keep my mind off of what's going on there and bugging the contractor for updates."

"Still. We're a lot closer to opening than I thought we'd be at this stage."

"Yeah. It's come together pretty quickly. I'm hoping we can get it up and running before the baby comes."

"We've got what? Five months?"

Sofie nodded.

"I think that's doable. We might be able to open by the end of summer at this rate."

A wide smile brightened Sofie's face. "That's what I think too." She spun on her heel. "Come on. I'll show you the back room and the basement."

"There's a basement?"

"Yep. We'll have plenty of room for extra inventory."

They went through the doorway to the back. Alice glanced around. It was a pretty standard back room. Fairly open, the twenty-by-twenty-foot space had plenty of room for some tables. At the back of the building, there were two doors.

Sofie pointed to one. "That's the bathroom. The one beside it is an office."

"Oh, that's nice. We'll be able to lock things up."

"Yeah. That's what sold me on this place, actually. The other storefront I looked at was just a little bigger, but it didn't have an office. I think we need that space."

Alice agreed. There were some things—like personnel files and petty cash—that she didn't want accessible to just anyone.

"This is great, Sof. I can't wait to start moving stuff in and get it all setup for opening. What about staff? I'll only be able to work evenings and weekends once school starts."

"I'll work as much as I can until the baby comes. My friend Marci has already offered to babysit during store hours, which is great. I won't have to go far to drop the baby off. It's just going to be my maternity leave we'll need to cover. We might be able to find a retiree through the church."

"Oh, that would be ideal. Someone who doesn't have a lot of outside responsibilities, who's just looking for a little extra spending money. It would give you a break too."

Sofie nodded as Alice talked. "That's what I thought too. I'll talk to Cynthia and see if she can think of anyone who might want the hours."

"Awesome." Alice clasped her hands in front of her chest and bounced on her feet. "I'm excited!"

"Me too. There's nothing like this in town. I think it'll do well."

"I hope so." She gave the room another once over. "You feel like walking around town? I'd like to see some of the other shops. See what the other shopkeepers are doing."

"Sure." She motioned toward the door. "My purse is under the counter."

Alice followed her out front, then outside. "Which way?"

Sofie pointed to her left. "There's more down this way."

The two women strolled down the sidewalk, ducking into shops as they went. Alice found several things she knew she needed for her house after she settled in. Once she closed on a place, she'd have to come back downtown and go on a bit of a spree.

In an eclectic little boutique called Secret Garden, two blocks down from their storefront and across from the sheriff's department, Alice thought she'd died and gone to heaven. The place was a hotbed of Bohemian and Victorian décor. She saw several vases that, if she ended up with that Victorian house, would need to go on the fireplace mantle.

The murmur of a child's voice and a lone male drew her attention as she neared the back of the store. Hiding behind all the vintage wares was a thoroughly modern toy section. She rounded the corner and saw Wade standing in the aisle with his son. His youngest was strapped into a carrier on his chest.

"Oh, hi." She smiled at him and the kids.

"Alice. Hello." He returned her polite smile. "This is my son, Henry. And my youngest, Elise." He pointed to the boy, then ran a hand over the toddler's blonde head.

She gave them a small wave. "Hello." Awkwardness hit Alice as they all continued to stand there, not saying much. She shifted her weight and glanced at Henry. The boy studied a wooden food set. "That looks fun."

He looked up at her. "It's pizza. I like pizza." A frown wrinkled his forehead. "Daddy, do you think Stevie likes pizza?"

"I'm sure she does, bud. Is that what you want to get?"

The boy bit his lip. "Maybe."

Wade's chest rose and fell as he stifled a sigh and glanced at Alice. "He was invited to a birthday party on Saturday."

"Ah. And his friend is a girl? Did I hear that right?"

Wade nodded.

Alice held up a finger and crouched next to the boy. "Henry. Can I make a suggestion?"

"Okay."

"Is this a friend from school?"

He nodded.

"Think about what she likes to play at school or the things she talks about."

His brow wrinkled again. "She likes to color. And kitties."

"Okay, good. So, how about we look for coloring books or something with cats?"

His eyes lit up, and he put the wooden pizza back on the shelf before dashing away. Alice straightened and looked at Wade, who cast an amused half smile at her. "I think you hit on something."

She chuckled. "Seems like."

Henry returned, carrying a white stuffed cat with sparkly pink eyes and a coloring book with cats on the cover. He handed both items to his dad.

"This is what you want?" Wade held up the stuffed cat, staring at its wide-eyed face.

"Yes. She'll love it!"

"Okay. Why don't you go grab a pack of crayons or markers to go with the book?"

The boy scampered off again. Alice smiled as she watched him go.

"Thanks."

She turned her attention to Wade, steeling herself for the punch of attraction that always hit her when she looked at him. Especially now, wearing his daughter. A man holding a baby—even one that was more toddler than baby—was sexy. When the man was already sexy? And single? Well, she was a goner.

She cleared her throat. "For what?"

"Helping him find the right gift. I can shop for my own kids, but other people's always trip me up."

"Oh, you're welcome. I'm glad I could help."

Sofie wandered over, smiling at Wade. "Hi. You're Bronwyn's dad, right?"

He nodded. "Olive's mom?"

"That's me."

"What are you two out shopping for? The new baby?" He nodded to Sofie's middle.

"Not really. Alice wanted to browse. See what all Pine Ridge has to offer."

"Oh. And are you finding it to your liking?"

Alice nodded. "Yes. There are some nice shops."

Henry came back, holding a pack of scented markers. "Can we get these, Daddy? They're the smelly kind." He scratched at the sticker on the front, then raised it to his face and sniffed it.

"Sure." He glanced at Alice and Sofie. "We need to get going. It was good seeing you both."

"You too," Sofie said.

Alice smiled and waved as they walked away. She did not turn around and watch. Melting into a puddle at the sight of his denim clad backside was not on her agenda today.

Sofie chuckled.

"What?" Alice glanced at her.

"Don't think I didn't notice the way you looked at him."

"And how was that?" She picked up a package of toy food and turned it over to see what all it contained. She should get some toys for her new house, so Olive didn't have to bring a bunch of hers when she came over.

"Like you wanted to lick him like an ice cream cone from head to toe."

Alice felt her cheeks heat. "You're imagining things."

"No, I'm not. What I want to know is why you're denying it. He's single. You're single." She narrowed her eyes. "Do you not like that he has kids?"

"What? No. I think they're adorable."

"Thinking they're adorable and wanting to date a single dad are two different things."

"I know."

Sofie arched an eyebrow.

Alice huffed. "I don't have anything against dating a single dad."

"But?"

"No but. He just unsettles me, is all." Her eyes widened, and she waved her arms as she realized how that sounded. "Not in a bad way. I just feel—electrified around him. I've never felt that way before. It's strange. Thrilling, yet strange."

Sofie patted her shoulder and smiled. "Don't ignore that. Trust me. It's worth it."

Alice wrinkled her nose. "Ew. I don't want to think about how you know that."

Sofie laughed. "I won't go into detail, I promise."

"Good." Alice chuckled, then sobered. "It's not just those feelings that are holding me back, though. I get the impression he's not interested."

"What? Girl, his eyes clocked all your curves when you weren't looking. More than once."

"They did?" She frowned.

"Yes. But I get why you'd say that. He seems a little distant."

Alice nodded. "Daisy told me his wife left them. All of them."

Sofie's eyes widened. "Olive mentioned her friend Bronwyn didn't have a mom, but I thought she meant she died."

"Nope."

"That's terrible. Any parent—man or woman—who can just walk away from their kids is a special kind of selfish. I should know. I was married to one just like that."

Alice agreed. "Now do you see why I'm not keen on having the hots for Wade Kaczmarek?"

Sofie nodded. "Yes. I won't say anymore, except I think if your feelings are strong enough, don't sit on them forever. You might be what he and those kids need."

That was a concept Alice hadn't considered. She set the toy back on the shelf and sighed. It bore some thinking. But she was getting ahead of herself. Whether Sofie thought he was attracted to her or not, she hadn't seen it. If Wade wasn't interested, it wouldn't matter what Alice wanted.

SEVEN

W ade cursed as he exited his truck, noting the empty parking lot. He was so late. Slamming the door, he ran into the church. He'd been called away to a fire scene just as church started. In addition to being the fire inspector, he was also an investigator. It was unusual, but their department was small, so he wore a lot of hats.

Typically, when it was his weekend to be on call, there was no rush for him to get to a scene, but his boss thought this one looked suspicious. And since someone was injured in the fire, time was more crucial. He was just thankful Cynthia Hughes said she'd watch his kids until church ended so he could at least go quickly assess the scene. Normally, it wouldn't be a problem—he'd just tell his parents what was going on and they'd take the kids, but his dad was sick, so he and his mom had stayed home.

He ran through the rec room doors and stopped, letting his eyes adjust as he glanced around. He didn't see Cynthia, but he saw Alice Duvall. She sat in a chair, holding a sleeping Elise while Bronwyn and Henry played nearby.

"Hey." He started across the room.

"Hi, Daddy." Henry got up to run over and give him a hug. Bronwyn waved from her spot, giving him a big smile.

He waved back and hefted Henry into his arms as he crossed the room, glancing around again. "Where's Cynthia?" He looked at Alice.

"She had to leave. I guess she tried calling, but couldn't get a hold of you, so I offered to stay with the kids."

"What?" He set Henry down, then reached into his pocket and took out his phone, groaning when it failed to turn on. "Dammit. My battery died."

"Did you forget to charge it?"

"No. I need a new phone. I just haven't had a chance to get to the store to get one. Guess that's the first thing on my list tomorrow. Thank you for staying. I appreciate it. I tried to hurry, but that scene—it was a mess." His boss had been right. It was definitely arson. Wade found multiple points of ignition —all from gasoline. "I'm still not done with it."

"Do you have anyone to watch the kids?"

"No. I was going to ask one of the firefighters to sit with them while I finish my assessment. I cleared part of the scene for the crime scene techs to come in and start processing, but there's still more to do. I only left because I had to be back here and I didn't have anyone else to come get the kids." He ran a hand through his short hair and sighed.

"I can stay with them."

"What? No. I can't ask you to do that. They'll be fine in the car with one of my colleagues."

The droll look she gave him normally would have made him smile, but he was too frazzled to find humor in much of anything right now.

"You didn't ask. I offered. And I don't mind. So long as you don't mind me in your house."

"I don't mind. Are you sure?"

"Yes. I was just going to work on some pottery this afternoon, but I can do it later."

"If you're sure you don't mind, that would be great. I'm really in a bind." He hated asking for help, but he knew the kids would be much more comfortable at home than in the car while he worked. Plus, they needed lunch.

"I'm sure. Now, how do you want to do this? It would probably be easier if I followed you home. Then you don't have to transfer car seats." She continued to rock, rubbing Elise's back as she talked.

"That works." He turned to his two older children. "Bronwyn, Henry, it's time to go."

The kids quickly picked up the toys they got out. Alice stood, still holding a sleeping Elise.

"Do you want me to take her?" Wade pointed at his youngest.

"No. She's good. I'll follow you out. Could you grab my purse?" She nodded toward her handbag on the small bookcase beside the toys.

He picked up the leather bag and ushered Bronwyn and Henry outside to his SUV. Bronwyn climbed into the rear seat while he buckled Henry into his and Alice put Elise in hers. The toddler stirred as she changed positions, rubbing her eyes.

"Dada?"

"I'm here, sweetie." Wade reached over the seats to give Elise's leg a pat. The girl strained against the straps.

"Dada!" Her face turned red and crocodile tears formed in her eyes.

Wade bit back a groan. He'd waited too long to pick them up. Elise tended to get—irritated when she didn't eat on-time. He feared she would shriek the whole way home now.

He double-checked Henry's buckle, then shut the door and rounded the car. Elise shrieked from inside.

Alice met him with an amused smile. "Have fun on the ride home."

"Yeah. She just needs some lunch and she'll be fine."

"Well, then let's get her home so I can feed her."

He nodded and opened the driver's door. Alice retreated to her Subaru and got in. Wade did his best to tune out his daughter's cries as he drove home. Henry's whimpers added to the cacophony, upset that his sister was so loud. Bronwyn covered her ears and yelled over the noise for Elise to stop.

The car was barely in park in his driveway before he climbed out. Opening Elise's door, he unhooked her from her seat. "Wyn, can you unbuckle your brother, please?"

"Sure." The girl unfastened the buckles on Henry's seat and let him out. Wade knew he should be concerned that she was so good at it—she was only five—but today he was grateful.

Scampering out of the car and up the front steps, Bronwyn and Henry left him in their dust. Alice emerged from her car and gave him a sympathetic look.

"Let's get inside and find her a snack. I don't think she's going to wait for lunch to be ready."

Wade agreed. He unlocked the door and let them in, making a beeline for the kitchen.

"Where are her snacks?" Alice set her purse on the counter and looked at him.

"In the pantry." He pointed to a door on the far side of the room, settling Elise into her highchair. The toddler arched her back and screamed.

Alice hurried across the kitchen and threw open the door.

"Grab the Cheerios. She likes those."

She emerged with the box. "Where are your bowls?"

"Just scatter some on the tray. I'll get her some milk." He moved toward the cabinet where he kept the sippy cups while

Alice opened the cereal box and dumped some on the high-chair tray.

Elise's screams calmed to hiccups as she scooped up a handful of Cheerios. Wade let out a breath and filled a sippy cup with milk. He screwed the lid on, then set it on the tray with the cereal before turning to the other children. "You two want some milk?"

They both nodded.

"You can each have a pack of fruit snacks too. Or an applesauce."

The kids hurried into the pantry. Wade poured them each a drink and set the cups on the table as they climbed into chairs.

"What do you want me to feed them for lunch?"

He turned to Alice. She stood by the counter, looking prettier than usual in her lavender sundress and white sweater. White sandals adorned her feet. Her blonde hair hung loose around her shoulders, making her look more like a co-ed than a woman only a few years his junior. His groin tightened, and he clenched his teeth, willing his body under control. He wasn't interested in having a woman in his life in any other capacity than as a friend. No matter how beautiful and kind she was.

"Um, sandwiches are fine. Or mac and cheese. There are some boxes in the pantry."

"Mac and cheese!" Bronwyn said, popping up to her knees on her chair.

"Yeah," Henry echoed. "Mac and cheese!"

Alice smiled. "The masses have spoken. We'll have mac and cheese."

Both kids cheered. Elise banged on her highchair tray, responding to her siblings' enthusiasm.

Wade smiled and leaned over, kissing the top of the

toddler's head before straightening to look at Alice. "Thank you again for watching them. I really appreciate it."

"It's no problem. We'll have fun. After lunch, I think I'll have Bronwyn show me where you keep all your art supplies and we'll do a project of some kind."

"That sounds great. I can't wait to see what they do." He glanced at the older kids. "You two be good for Ms. Duvall, okay?"

"Okay, Daddy." Bronwyn nodded as she took another drink of her milk.

Henry parroted his sister.

Wade turned to Alice. "If you need anything or something happens, call the fire station. They'll get me on the radio. The number is in the drawer by the fridge."

"Okay. I'm sure we'll be fine." She made a shooing motion. "Go. Investigate."

He smiled, backing toward the door. "Thanks again."

"Sure."

With a wave, he spun and left the kitchen, heading for the front door. Some of his stress eased as his body caught up with his mind. The kids were in good hands. Elise didn't fall asleep for just anyone.

Blowing out a breath, he exited the house and climbed into his car. Time to go to work and catch an arsonist.

EIGHT

"Dis!" Elise held up a dandelion to Alice.

"I see that. Do you want to glue it to your butter-fly?" Alice took the flower, smiling at the girl.

Elise nodded. "Yeah. Butt-fly." She climbed into the patio chair in front of her paper with the outline of the butterfly Alice drew. All three kids had wanted to play outside after lunch, so she let them out into the fenced yard to play while she washed the lunch dishes. She liked Wade's kitchen. It had a large picture window above the sink that looked out over the backyard. She'd been able to keep an eye on the kids while they played on the swing set and in the sandbox.

When their energy started to flag a bit, she'd found three sheets of paper and drawn a butterfly on each, then told the kids to find items from the yard to glue to it to fill in the outline.

"Where should we put this?" She handed Elise the dandelion.

The girl put it on the butterfly's head.

"That's perfect." Alice opened the glue bottle and put a dollop on the head. "Press the flower on there."

With her tiny fingers, Elise placed the flower on the glue, then smashed it down with the flat of her hand. Alice rolled her lips in, amused. The girl looked so proud of her smashed flower head.

"Okay. Hop down and find more stuff for your butterfly."

Elise dropped to her butt, then turned, sliding off the chair to run back out into the yard. Henry and Bronwyn ran up with items to affix to their butterflies. She helped glue them on, then they headed out to find more things to fill up their papers.

"That's really creative."

Alice shrieked and spun around, a hand on her chest over her pounding heart. Wade stood just outside the house. "Oh my goodness, you scared me!"

He smiled. "Sorry. I wasn't trying to."

She blew out a breath and waved a hand. "I know. I just didn't hear you."

"These are neat." He walked forward to look at the butterflies. "I never would have thought to do something like this."

Alice shrugged, her heart rate kicking up for a different reason now. His nearness turned her body into a live wire. "Creativity is sort of my thing."

"So I've heard. Asa told me you're the new art teacher at the elementary starting this fall. He also mentioned you're opening a store downtown with your sister-in-law."

"I am, yes."

"Busy lady."

"I don't like to be idle." Her face pulled. "Which is kind of where I'm at now. Other than making pottery inventory for the store, I don't have much to do until I close on a house. The store won't open until late summer at the earliest. And I can't get in to work on my classroom until a few weeks before school starts. I'm kind of twiddling my thumbs for the foreseeable future." And it was driving her crazy. She thought she'd enjoy the forced break, but she was just restless.

He glanced up and studied her, a contemplative look on his face. "This might not be anything you'd even want to consider, but would you be willing to be my babysitter? My regular one fell off a horse and broke her leg. She's out at least another month."

Alice's spine straightened. Babysitter? She wasn't sure being around him, being in his space, would be any better for her than the restlessness plaguing her now.

"Daddy!" Bronwyn ran up. "Did you see what we made with Alice?"

Wade smiled at his daughter. "I did. Your butterflies are very pretty."

Alice melted at the sight of the big, strong fireman smiling at his little girl. Nope. It definitely wouldn't be better for her. But she couldn't say no. This family needed help, and she was in a position to give it.

Besides, his kids were great.

Bronwyn held up the two small sticks she found, showing them to her dad. "Can you help me glue these on?"

"Sure. Where are we putting them?" Wade picked up the glue bottle.

"Up here." She pointed to the antennae.

"Okay." He laid down two lines of glue, and she pressed the sticks on.

"I need a head." Bronwyn tapped her chin, then her eyes lit up, and she ran away.

Alice chuckled. "She has a lot of energy."

"You don't know the half of it."

"But I will." She turned to him. "I'd be happy to fill in until your sitter can come back."

"Seriously?" His shoulders sagged. "Thank you. You have no idea how much pressure that takes off of me. With Dad sick and Mom not wanting to leave him alone—or risk getting the kids sick—I've been scrambling, trying to rearrange my schedule this week and find people to watch them. I really appreciate this, Alice."

"I get it. I've had parents who've told me how hard it is to find sitters when school's canceled or something unexpected comes up. I'm happy to help."

"I hope you still say that after you spend all day with them. There is one thing I should mention, though."

She frowned. "What's that?"

"Our department is very small, and we do things a little unconventionally, so I wear multiple hats. We have two fire inspectors and two fire investigators. I happen to be both. I work as the inspector two days a week, then I'm an investigator the other three days. One of those is an overnight shift, because I go out on runs. I come home Tuesday evening, eat dinner with the kids and put them to bed, then go back around eight and don't come home again until after five the next night. Thursday and Friday are my inspector days."

Her eyes widened. "Oh."

"Yeah." His mouth twisted. "Are you okay sleeping here? The kids have been going to my mom and dad's, but they're more comfortable at home."

"Um, yeah, that should be fine." It would be weird at first, but she'd get used to it. It's not like Wade would be home while she slept.

He smiled, sending her heart aflutter again. She willed it to beat normally. It wouldn't help either of them if she passed out from an arrhythmia.

"Thank you. I'll definitely make it worth your while."

Her mind went to all the places it shouldn't, and she blushed. She knew he meant monetary compensation, but her body wanted something else.

Alice fanned her face, pretending she was just hot from the

warm sun. "Whatever you want to pay me is fine. I don't need the extra cash." Truthfully, she'd probably end up spending a good portion of it on art supplies to do projects with his kids. And on field trips. She didn't plan to keep them at home while he was at work. They were going to have fun. "Just write me a list of when you need me."

He scratched his temple. "Um, that would be all week. And overnight Tuesday. My parents might take them later in the week if you need a break, but it'll depend on how my dad's feeling and if Mom gets sick."

"That's fine. What time do you need me here tomorrow?"

"I leave for work at seven-thirty. Are you okay dropping Bronwyn off at preschool? She's still got two weeks left. They don't normally get out until the first week of June, plus there were a lot of snow days this year."

"Sure. Just make sure the school knows I'll be doing drop-off and pickup."

"I'll call them in the morning." He took out his phone, then frowned. "I'll call them from work in the morning. I forgot about my broken phone." He sighed. "We still need to exchange numbers, though. Hang on." He ran inside and came back a moment later with a pad of sticky notes and a pen. After scrawling his number on the paper, he pulled it off and handed it to her. "Now, tell me your number."

Alice gave it to him, then he slipped the notepad and pen into his pocket.

"Thank you again, Alice. You've taken away a big worry. I didn't know what I was going to do this week other than take time off until my parents could help out again."

"I'm glad I'm able to help. Your kids are great, by the way. We've had fun this afternoon."

He smiled. "You mean Elise didn't scream the house down?"

She laughed. "Not once she had a full belly, no. Henry got

a little cranky after they played for a bit, but I think it was just because he was tired. That's when I got out the paper and sent them on a scavenger hunt for butterfly parts."

"I need to remember this. They could do just about anything with it. I could even draw a different thing for each child."

"Yep. It's a great, quick activity when you need something, but don't have a lot of extra supplies on hand for an art project. And they're pretty."

"They are. I'm going to hang all these up." He turned Bronwyn's paper so he could see it better, then smiled at Alice again.

"Twine strung between two hooks—you can use those removable hooks—with some clothes pins, makes for a great art gallery."

"I'm going to learn all kinds of things while you're around."

Alice smiled. "About art, definitely." She glanced at the kids. They still wandered through the yard, looking for things for their butterflies. Elise seemed more interested in plucking every dandelion she could find, though. Her tiny hand was full of the bright yellow weeds.

"Well, I better get going." She really did need to work on some pottery. She'd set a quota per week, so she'd have enough pieces to open the store by the beginning of August.

Wade let out a sharp whistle and all three kids stopped what they were doing and ran toward them.

"Man." Alice glanced at him. "You need to teach me that trick."

He grinned, then turned his attention to the kids. "Alice has to go, but she'll be back tomorrow. She's going to be your babysitter until Shelby can come back, okay?"

Bronwyn and Henry cheered. Elise toddled up and held out her flowers to Alice.

"Dis!"

Smiling, Alice scooped the girl up and took the bundle of dandelions she offered. "Thank you, sweetie. They're lovely."

Elise clapped, then patted Alice's cheek before wiggling to get down. Alice set her on her feet, and she ran into the yard to get more dandelions.

"I better go before I take home any more," she said with a chuckle.

"There will be a vase full of them for you when you get here in the morning."

"Oh, I'm sure." She looked at Bronwyn and Henry. "I'll see you guys in the morning, okay?"

"Okay!" Bronwyn said, then looked up at Wade. "Can we go play?"

He nodded, and they took off.

Alice watched them go, then turned, dandelions in hand. "I'll see you in the morning. About seven-fifteen? You can give me a quick tour before you go to work. I found what I needed for lunch, but I'm sure there are other things you like the sitters to know."

"Yeah. That sounds good."

She gave a short nod. "See you then."

"Okay. Thanks again."

With another nod, Alice slipped inside. As the door closed behind her, she glanced back. Her heart did a hard thump as she caught sight of Wade walking out into the yard to pick up his youngest. He swung her into the air, making her squeal in delight.

Her heart flip-flopped, and she paused, almost turning back. She didn't want to leave, which surprised her. Blowing out a breath, she forced her feet to move, and couldn't help but wonder if she'd made a grave mistake by agreeing to babysit. It didn't take those kids—or their handsome father—

long to find the door to her heart. If she wasn't careful, the four of them were going to own it.

NINE

Wade glanced at his watch as he heard the knock on the door. Seven-fourteen. Alice was prompt. He liked that. Grasping the doorknob, he steeled himself for what awaited him on the other side. Just because he didn't want a relationship with a woman didn't mean he found Alice Duvall unattractive. Quite the opposite. Her bright, golden hair and silvery blue eyes matched her sunny disposition. And her curves put his body on notice.

Enough stalling! He blew out a breath, then twisted the knob and opened the door. She smiled at him, stealing his breath. The woman was the definition of beautiful. She reminded him of some homespun beauty queen.

"Good morning." She offered him a cheery smile.

He cleared his throat and stepped back so she could enter. "Good morning."

She walked past him. He averted his gaze as it landed on her backside, which was encased in tight denim that stopped mid-calf. Canvas shoes adorned her feet. He shut the door. "You ready for the tour?"

"Yep. Are the kids up yet?"

He shook his head. "They usually get up around eight. Bronwyn doesn't have to be to school until nine, and it's only five minutes away."

Her head bobbed.

"You can put your purse on the table, there." He pointed at the walnut entryway table.

She set it down, then shrugged out of her lightweight white zip-up hoodie, exposing her sunny yellow t-shirt, and laid it over top of her bag.

"Let's go through the downstairs first, then I'll take you upstairs and show you their rooms."

"Sounds good."

He led her into the living room off to the right.

She looked around in wonder. "I love this room. We didn't spend much time in it yesterday. They wanted to play outside."

Wade knew what she saw. High ceilings made the living room—which was already large—appear larger. A giant brown leather sectional took up a good portion of the room. A television was mounted over the fireplace, which was bracketed by built-in bookshelves. Stained-glass topped the windows facing the street and cast pops of color on the hardwood floors and light blue walls.

Her eyes traveled over the dark wood moldings and rosettes on the corners of the door frames. "This is amazing." She looked at him. "Did it look like this when you bought it?"

He shrugged. "Sort of. We painted the walls and refinished the trim. The room was a deep red, which I didn't like. It was too dark. I changed the rug too. It came with a Persian-style tapestry, but I figured this was more kid-friendly."

Alice looked down at her feet, and he followed her gaze. The gray and blue carpet under them had some give, and the pattern hid stains well.

She looked up with a smile. "I like it."

"Me too. Come on. I'll show you their playroom." He motioned her to follow him through the doorway at the back of the room. He stepped inside and paused while she took it in. This room looked more formal, with its dark wood paneling going halfway up the walls, but the plethora of toys told another story. It was a fun space for his children. One where they could make a mess and be kids. It, too, had hardwood floors covered by a rug, but this rug was a gray-on-gray floral. Their feet sank into the nap. It was soft and plush. Perfect for kids.

"They spend most of their time in here or outside. We do TV in the evenings for a little while. And they can watch a bit in the afternoons after lunch if they want. Usually, when Elise is sleeping, I let Wyn and Henry watch some cartoons."

"Perfect. That will give me a chance to clean up from lunch."

He nodded, then pointed to the left. "That leads to the hallway." Walking over, he opened the door and motioned her through to the hallway that ran beside the stairs.

"Kitchen is back there." He pointed down the hall to the left. "Bathroom is there, and my office is through there." He pointed to the two other doors set into the wall. "Don't let them in the office unless you're in there, too, for some reason."

"Other than to get drawing paper from your printer, we shouldn't need to be in there."

"They have an art cabinet in the playroom."

Alice's head bobbed. "Okay. The kids were already outside yesterday when I went looking for paper. I found it in your office first. I'll check the cabinet next time."

"That's fine. Take whatever office supplies you need for whatever you want to do with them. I just don't want them messing with the piles of papers on the desk. Some of it's bills, other stuff is for work."

She nodded again.

"Let's go upstairs now."

Alice turned and headed for the staircase, tiptoeing to the second floor. Wade followed just as quietly, not wanting to wake the kids just yet. Once on the landing, he paused and pointed.

"My room is at the end of the hall." He kept his voice low as he pointed to the left. "Elise is directly across from me. That's the bathroom the kids share." He gestured to the door in front of them. "Down there are Bronwyn and Henry's rooms. There's a spare bedroom between them where you can sleep on the night's I need you to stay over. There's also a twin bed in Elise's room. Sometimes, she can be hard to put to sleep, so I put that bed in there rather than lying down on the floor while she drifted off. Too many nights I found myself falling asleep on her floor and waking up the next morning with a crick in my neck."

Alice wrinkled her nose. "Good plan."

"It gets used, that's for sure." Smiling, he pointed toward his room and Elise's. "That doorway leads to the third floor. I keep it locked. Right now, it's just a catch-all. Eventually, I'd like to make it into something, but I'm not sure what. The key is in my desk drawer, if you need up there for some reason."

"Okay." She nodded. "Let's go down to the kitchen and you can show me what they normally eat for breakfast." She turned and started down the stairs on light feet. Wade followed.

Rounding the banister, they went through the dining room to the kitchen, and he led her into the pantry. When he turned, he realized going inside was a mistake. She was far too close for comfort.

He swallowed hard and tried to ignore the scent of her almond and honey shampoo. "So, they like a variety of things in the morning. Anything from oatmeal to cereal to pancakes. It just depends on the day and how much time we have. Mom usually feeds them oatmeal or toast and eggs. Shelby does the same. Sometimes, she gets adventurous and makes pancakes. I usually make waffles or French toast on the weekends. There are some days, though, where one of them only wants cereal. I don't fight it unless that's all they've had for a couple days in a row."

A smile tugged at her lips. "Picking your battles is a good strategy."

"Agreed. Starting the day with a temper tantrum because I made Henry eat oatmeal instead of the Cheerios he wanted is never fun. Though there are far worse things he could eat for breakfast. I just like them to have more protein in the mornings."

She nodded. "So, they can have whatever this morning?"

He nodded. "I always ask before I start cooking, so I don't put anything to waste. Anyway, they have snacks here and here." He touched a couple of shelves. "For lunch, just sandwiches or mac and cheese. We have peanut butter and lunch meat. There are also some chicken nuggets in the freezer. Hot dogs too. There might even be some mini pizzas. We have lots of fruit and vegetables in the fridge too. Elise can't have strawberries, but anything else is fine."

A small frown marred Alice's forehead. "How allergic is she to them?"

"She gets a rash and they upset her stomach. Never anaphylaxis, though."

"Okay. Is that all strawberry stuff—even things that are just flavored with it?"

"Popsicles are okay, so long as they aren't the real fruit ones. She's been fine with strawberry gelatin too. Just read the labels before you give it to her. If it mentions the fruit anywhere, don't do it."

She gave him a thumbs up and backed out of the pantry. "What do you do for dinner?"

"I should be home in time to make it every night except Wednesday, unless I'm at a scene and running late. In that case, I'll call."

"All right. Did you contact Bronwyn's school yet?"

He shook his head. "I couldn't get the phone to hold any kind of charge, even if I left it plugged in. And I don't have a landline. I'll call from my office at the fire station. I'm going to replace my cell once the store opens at nine."

"Okay. Where's Bronwyn's school? You mentioned it's only a few minutes away. I haven't been here long, so I don't know where anything is yet except for Sarafina's and the grocery store."

"Come into the office. I'll draw you a map."

They wandered out of the kitchen into the hall. He opened the office door and walked to the desk, sitting down. Taking a piece of paper from the printer, he grabbed a black marker from the cup and drew a rudimentary map, adding street names and a couple of landmarks.

Alice took it and studied it. "This should work great. Some of the street names even look familiar."

"Yeah." He stood. "You have to cross one and go down another to get here." He glanced at his watch. "I need to get going. I think we covered everything. You know where the emergency numbers are." He snapped his fingers and pointed. "Car seats. I'll take them out of my SUV and leave them in the garage, if that's okay?"

"That's fine. It won't take me long to install them."

"You know how?"

She nodded. "I watch Olive every once in a while, so I've had practice with her seat."

"Okay, good." He rounded the desk, motioning her to the door, ready to get going. "You can wake the kids up around eight. Don't let Bronwyn lounge in bed any later than eight-fifteen. She likes to drag her feet in the mornings, and if she sleeps any later than that, you'll be scrambling to finish getting her ready."

Alice chuckled. "Sounds like my kind of kid."

"Not a morning person?"

"No. This"—she circled a finger around her face—"takes two cups of coffee if I'm up before eight. Any less and I'm a zombie, no matter how much sleep I get."

"You'd be a pretty zombie, though." Wade's eyes widened as he realized what he said. *What the hell? Where did that come from?* He bit back a groan, watching a pretty blush steal over her cheeks. "Sorry."

"No, it's okay. I know what you meant."

She did? That was good, because what was going through his head probably wasn't the same thing she was thinking. And he shouldn't be thinking it. He didn't care how gorgeous she was—and she was plenty gorgeous. He didn't want a relationship. He had enough to focus on with work and his kids.

Clearing his throat again, he headed down the hall to the coat rack, where he grabbed his department windbreaker. "Call if you need anything. Try the station first. Just in case my phone's not set up yet."

"Okay. Be safe and have a good day."

He shrugged into his jacket. "I will. I'll see you around five."

She nodded. Wade beat a hasty retreat down the hallway and out the back door to the detached garage. He cursed under his breath as he left the house. This next month was going to be torture. He wasn't sure how long he could be around Alice Duvall without his body overriding his brain.

Yanking open the door, he entered the garage. She wasn't even his type. His ex-wife and all his past girlfriends were on the smaller side, with light brown to brown hair. Alice looked like a blonde beauty queen from Nebraska.

But there was something about her that his body refused

to ignore, no matter how much he told himself all he wanted from her was friendship.

Wade slammed his car door and pushed the button to raise the garage door. He needed to put the woman out of his mind. She was his babysitter. He'd be damned if he'd become the cliché and be the dad who screwed the nanny.

TEN

"Morning, Wade."

Coffee in hand from his quick stop at Sarafina's, Wade smiled at Joy Cardano, the administrative assistant he shared with his partner, Jed Braun.

"Hi, Joy."

"Sheriff Lattimer called. She wants an update on the arson investigation."

He nodded. "Set up a meeting for later this morning. I need an hour or so to go over my notes and check on the status of what the crime scene unit gathered. Then I need to run an errand. My cell phone died, so I need to replace it."

She reached for the phone. "Will do."

Wade continued past her into his office and sat down at his desk. Turning on his computer, he took a sip of his coffee, waiting for it to boot up. Once the login screen appeared, he input his password, then opened his email. No new messages had come through from the crime scene investigators. He hadn't really expected any. They were probably just beginning their assessment of the evidence today. Any fingerprint evidence—which was fast-tracked yesterday—would go directly to the police department. The rest of it would be slower to process.

Still, he picked up the phone to call the lab and see what all they gathered from the scene and where they were in processing it. Once he had their report, he typed it up and gathered the notes he took at the scene. Glancing over them as he put them in a folder for his meeting later with the sheriff, something niggled in the back of his mind, and he paused. A frown lit his face as he leafed back through his notes. Something about the owner of the property bugged him.

Wade shoved the papers aside and pulled up the property database on his computer, typing in the name Tim Willard. Several properties popped up under that name. He wrote down the addresses, then cross-referenced them with their fire calls. His eyes widened as he discovered two other properties destroyed by fire on the list.

Pulling up the incident reports, he read through them. He hadn't been the fire investigator for either fire. That was his partner, Jed Braun. He'd ruled both as accidental.

Suspicion deepened Wade's frown. It seemed like too much of a coincidence for there to be fires at three properties owned by the same person. Especially when this most recent one wasn't an accident.

He hit print, then opened his calendar to see when his meeting was with Sheriff Lattimer. He still had a couple of hours. Rising, he scooped the reports out of the tray and added them to the folder. Picking up the phone, he dialed Jed's cell number. He had a few questions.

"It's my day off, Kaczmarek." Jed's tone was droll as he answered, but a hint of amusement ran through it. "Though I guess I should thank you. You just gave me a break from Lisa's honey-do list."

Wade chuckled. "Glad I could be of service. I have a question for you."

"Shoot."

"I have a meeting with Sheriff Lattimer in a little while to go over the details of that fire on Spruce Street yesterday. When I was gathering up my notes, a detail about the property bugged me, and I realized it was the name of the property owner, Tim Willard. I looked him up. He's had fires at two other properties in the last six months. You investigated them both and ruled them accidental. Yesterday's was an obvious arson. Can you give me some details about the other fires? Or better yet, can I take a peek at your case files?"

"Um..." Jed blew out a breath. "One was an old house, right? And the other a large garage in the business district?"

"Yes."

"The house came down to wiring. A contractor turned on the electrical in preparation for some renovations and it sparked a fire. The garage came from a trash fire lit by some squatters. The files are in my filing cabinet. You're welcome to look at them."

Wade scratched at his temple, leaning his elbow on the desk as he held the phone to his ear. "I'll do that. Something just doesn't feel right."

"I don't know what to tell you. The wiring at the electrical box was fried at the house. And at the garage, it was obvious the fire started in a thirty-gallon trash can. It was full of grease rags and left uncovered."

"Okay. Thanks."

"No problem. Hey, you want me to come in and go over the files with you?"

Wade grinned. "Nah. You better get back to Lisa's list."

Jed sighed. "Yeah." He grumbled under his breath. "She's got me sanding and painting the kitchen cabinets. We're going gray."

"Sounds exciting." Wade chuckled.

"Very much so." His voice was dry. "Okay. I'll talk to you later. Call if you have any more questions."

"I will, thanks." Wade bade him goodbye and hung up.

Standing, he left his office and went to Jed's, using his keys to open the door and get into the filing cabinet. It didn't take him long to locate the two files. He took them back to his office and glanced through them. Nothing struck him as out of the ordinary. They stated the same thing Jed just told him.

With a sigh, Wade made copies of everything—his notes included—and added them to his pile to take to his meeting with the sheriff later, then put the case out of his mind. He needed to go replace his phone, then get to all the other work he had to do today. Without more information, the Willard fire wasn't going anywhere.

Leaving his office, he went to the shopping center on the outskirts of town to his cellphone carrier and replaced his phone. Thirty minutes later, he came out with an upgrade and went back to his office. There, he worked his way through both investigator and inspector reports. Fifteen minutes before his meeting with the sheriff, he grabbed the folders on the Willard case and left again, driving the short distance to the sheriff's department. Once he signed in, he wove his way through the halls to her office and knocked on the door.

"Come in." Her voice came through the closed door.

Wade twisted the knob and stepped inside. "Good morning."

"Hi, Wade. Have a seat."

He sank into one of the chairs in front of her desk.

"I take it from the stack of folders in your hands, you have something?"

"Maybe. Yesterday's fire was definitely arson. I found several points where gasoline was poured and lit. What caught my attention this morning was the name of the property owner." He handed her the top two folders. "There have been two other fires at his properties in the last six months. My colleague investigated them and ruled them both accidental."

A frown creased her brow as she took the folders. "Do you agree with his assessment?"

"On paper, yes."

"On paper?"

He nodded. "I'd need to see the scenes to one hundred percent agree. But I doubt that's possible. Both buildings have likely been razed by this point."

She looked at the addresses, then nodded. "They have. So, you suspect the other two fires were actually arson, but clever cover-ups?"

"Maybe. I can't see Jed missing something like that, though. It could be that the first two were coincidental. Willard owns about a dozen properties in the area. Maybe he liked the insurance checks he got for the other two buildings and decided to try for a third one. Or someone decided to do it for him."

"Hmm. There haven't been any other suspicious fires lately?"

He shook his head. "No, ma'am."

"Okay. I'll look into him and see if there's anything to dig up. Keep me posted if you turn up anything? I'll do the same."

"Sounds good."

She raised the folders. "Can I keep these?"

"Yes. Those are copies. This too." He handed her his file of notes.

"Okay, thanks."

He stood, hesitating before he walked out. "I hope I'm wrong. If Willard is setting these fires, he could be dangerous. Someone already got hurt, and he may not hesitate to hurt others if he thinks he's in danger of getting caught."

She nodded. "I agree. I'll dig deep. I promise."

With a short nod, he left her office. He knew she'd do her due-diligence, but he couldn't stop the roil of unease in the pit of his stomach. He had a bad feeling about this case.

ELEVEN

The bell tinkled over the door at Ellen's Craft Shop as Alice held it open. Henry and Bronwyn passed through, and she followed them in, carrying Elise. She'd waited to shop for art supplies until Bronwyn got out of school for the day. She wanted all the kids to have an input on what they did.

"Hello."

Alice smiled at the older woman sitting behind the counter who greeted them. "Hi." Elise bounced in her arms, so she set her down. The little girl toddled over to a display of fake flowers and buried her face in them.

The woman laughed. "Oh, she's adorable. All of your children are."

"They are, but they're not mine. I'm just the babysitter. We're looking for some crafts they can do."

"Oh, well, I have several kits. Though they're probably too advanced for the little one." She came out from behind the counter.

Alice picked Elise up to follow the woman down the aisle to a rotating rack. The girl whined and pushed against Alice's hold. "Sorry, baby. You have to stay with us." She looked at the woman. "What about finger paint? She could do that while the other two do something else."

The woman nodded. "That's over here." She pointed and walked to her left.

"Okay. I think we'll take one of those kits." She nodded to a box of finger paint that contained the primary colors, plus green, white, and black.

"Do you want the leak-proof, tear-resistant paper too?"

"Yes." It was more expensive than regular watercolor paper, but it was worth it if she didn't have to clean paint off the table because it soaked through or they ripped the paper because it became saturated.

"You sound like you know what happens without it." The woman looked up as she straightened with both items in her arms and smiled.

"Oh, I do. I'm the new art teacher for the elementary, starting this fall."

"I heard Betsy was retiring. I'm Ellen Wendell." She held out a hand.

Alice shifted Elise to her other hip and took it. "Alice Duvall."

"Duvall? Is Sofie Duvall your sister-in-law?"

Alice nodded, her brows dipping as she remembered something Sofie said. "She mentioned you. You're creating some custom clothing for our store."

Ellen nodded, smiling. "I am, yes. I also order in a lot of the items she needs to make her jewelry. She brings Olive in on occasion, too, looking for art projects."

"Olive's my friend," Bronwyn interjected.

Ellen turned her eyes on the little girl and smiled. "She is? That's great. What's your name?"

"Bronwyn Kaczmarek."

"Oh, you're Bill and Peg's granddaughter. I thought the

three of you looked familiar." She glanced at Alice. "They own the feed store. How did you end up being their babysitter?"

"Their dad was in a bind, so I volunteered. It's my first day. Well, I guess officially it is. I watched them for a little while yesterday because he had an emergency at work."

"That boy works too much." She sighed. "But I guess it's necessary now." She quickly schooled her features and offered the children a bright smile. "So, what kind of craft do you guys want to do with Miss Alice?"

"Paint!" Henry said.

Bronwyn nodded. "But I want to paint something besides paper."

Alice's face lit up as a thought hit her. "I have an idea. Why don't we make some birdhouses? Ellen, do you have balloons and white tissue paper? And Modge Podge?"

Ellen helped her find everything—plus a few other items Alice had to have, just because—then rang her up at the register.

"You guys have fun now. Try to keep the paint on what you're painting, okay?" She smiled at the kids as she handed the bags and receipt to Alice.

"That would be nice, yes. I'm still papering the tabletop with newspaper, though. And they're wearing trash bags as smocks."

Ellen laughed. "Good idea."

Grinning, Alice ushered the kids to the door. "Come on. Let's go home and make a mess."

Bronwyn's eyes widened. "You mean it?"

"Of course I mean it."

"Oh, boy! Henry, did you hear that? We get to make a mess! On purpose!"

"Within reason, Wyn," Alice amended. She could see the kids deciding they needed to paint their arms or something if she gave them carte blanche.

Ellen laughed. "Have fun."

Alice tossed her a grin and held the door open for the kids. "Thanks."

They walked outside to the car, where she buckled them all in before heading back to their house. The drive was short and did little to dampen the kids' enthusiasm for the coming project. Bronwyn and Henry ran inside, eager to get started. Elise toddled in after them, squealing as she headed for the playroom.

Alice set the bags on the island. "Wyn, Hen, can you find some newspaper to spread over the counter?"

"It's in the recycling. Come on, Henry." Bronwyn scampered out the back door to the covered trash bins.

Shaking her head and smiling at them, Alice found the package of balloons she bought and opened it. She had one white balloon partially blown up when the kids came back inside.

"How's that gonna turn into a birdhouse?" Bronwyn climbed onto a bar stool and set the papers down.

Alice finished blowing up the balloon and tied it off. "We're going to papier-mâché the balloon. Once it hardens, we'll cut a hole for the birds and pop the balloon, leaving just the hard outer shell." She'd also bought some waterproofing spray, so it didn't turn into a soggy mess the first time it rained.

"Cool."

"It's very cool." She picked up the second balloon and blew it up. "Okay, let's get a couple of trash bags so you don't get glue all over your clothes. I need to get you two some smocks. Maybe your dad has some old shirts he doesn't want that you can use. I'll have to ask him." She dug under the sink and came out with two trash bags.

"While I cut holes in these, I want you two to tear up this tissue paper. Like this." She picked up a piece of tissue paper and ripped it. "Make sense?"

Both kids nodded.

"Good. I'm going to check on your sister, then make your smocks. Don't touch the glue yet."

They nodded again, and she walked into the hall and poked her head in the playroom. Elise banged a small metal pot on the kitchen set. She glanced back at Alice with a toothy smile.

"You silly goose. That's not how we play with the kitchen." She walked into the room and scooped the girl into her arms, blowing a raspberry on her belly and making her giggle. "Come on. Let's go paint."

Elise clapped. "Leese paint!"

"Yep." Alice went back to the kitchen and set the girl on the floor while she slipped a trash bag over the highchair seat. The tray would wash, but the seat would be harder to clean. After cutting holes in two kitchen trash bags for Bronwyn and Henry to wear as smocks, she helped the kids slip into them. With Elise, she stripped the girl down to her diaper and put her in the highchair with some of the special paper and dollops of finger paint. Elise stuck her fingers in the red paint, then immediately put them in her mouth.

Alice sighed. "And this is why I bought the edible kind."

Henry laughed at his sister's now painted face. "You're not s'posed to eat it, Elise!"

"She's okay, Henry. It won't hurt her." She would definitely need a bath, though. They all would, she had a feeling.

"What do we do now, Alice?" Bronwyn asked.

"Now, you get to play with glue."

"Is this the mess part?" The girl's eyes sparkled.

"Yep." Alice picked up the Modge Podge and poured some onto two disposable plates. Then she opened the package of foam brushes and took one out, picking up Henry's balloon. "Dip your brush in the glue and paint it on the balloon like this." She smeared some of the glue over the surface. "Then take some of the tissue paper and lay it over the glue." She put several pieces of tissue paper onto the glue she smeared. "After you do that, you put a little more glue over the top." Alice dipped the brush in the glue again and smeared it over the tissue paper. "Easy enough?"

Both kids nodded. She handed the balloon and brush to Henry. "Have at it."

"When do we get to paint them?" Bronwyn smeared glue on her balloon.

"It'll be a couple of days, probably. You have to put several coats of the tissue paper on to make them sturdy enough for the birds."

"Oh." Disappointment colored her voice.

"I know you're eager to make them look pretty, but we need to make sure they won't fall apart when birds build nests inside."

"Yeah, that makes sense." She dipped her brush in the glue again.

"Good. While you guys do that, I'm going to make you a snack."

"Can we have apples?" Henry asked.

"Sure. Do you want some peanut butter with them?"

He nodded. So did Bronwyn.

"What should your sister have? Applesauce?"

"She likes that," Henry said.

"Okay. Applesauce it is. And maybe a yogurt tube."

While the kids worked, Alice busied herself slicing apples and adding peanut butter to them. She retrieved an applesauce pouch from the pantry and a yogurt tube from the fridge. When she turned around and glanced at Elise, she couldn't help but laugh. The toddler had paint all over her chin and cheeks and in her hair. "Oh, dear. I think your snack will have to wait, Elise."

The girl just grinned and banged her paint-covered hands

on the paper. Paint splattered and drops splatted onto the floor. Alice would have to mop once they were done.

Bronwyn and Henry laughed when they looked at their sister.

"She's a mess!" Henry said.

"Mommy wouldn't like this." Bronwyn shook her head.

Henry's smile died, and he looked down, spinning his brush in the glue.

Alice's heart stuttered. This was the first time either of them had mentioned their absent mother. It was a testament to Wade's parenting that they were as happy and well-adjusted as they were after such an event. She knew what it was like to lose a parent—Alice's mom died when she was in high school. But she couldn't imagine what it would feel like to have your mom leave just because she didn't want to be a mom anymore.

She cleared her throat. "It all washes off, so she's fine. There's nothing wrong with making a mess that washes. Finish your first layer of papier-mâché so you can have your snack."

More subdued now, he nodded.

Alice's heart ached for the boy. She glanced around, searching for something to cheer him up, and her eyes landed on the iPhone speaker dock on the counter. Music always helped her feel better, so she took out her phone and pulled up a playlist she used at school for her students and put her phone in the dock. The first song on the list filled the kitchen. She sang along, dancing around the kitchen to it. Giggles followed her as she put on a show. A smile wreathed her face, glad she'd put the smile back on Henry's.

The kids finished their first layer of papier-mâché, and she helped the older two wash their hands so they could eat their snacks. Elise needed a bath.

Alice chuckled as she lifted the toddler from her chair. "You're such a mess. Your daddy will be happy, though. He'll have a nice, clean, bathed baby and won't have to do it later." She glanced at the other kids on her way out of the kitchen. "You two finish your snack, then you can go watch some TV for a bit until it's time for the next layer of papier-mâché. Okay?"

Both kids nodded, their mouths full of apple. Alice left the room, heading down the hall and upstairs to the kids' bathroom. She closed the door and set Elise on the floor to turn on the bathtub faucet. When she turned around to put the girl in the tub, her eyes widened. Colorful hand prints decorated the vanity.

"Oh, baby girl. Guess I should have washed you up with some wipes a bit first." Her face twisted. "I hope that comes off." She caught sight of herself in the mirror. "Crap." She blew her bangs out of her face. She should have known better than to pick up a paint-covered child. "Some art teacher I am."

Elise banged on the vanity doors, leaving behind more prints, and squealed. "Live it up, kid. You get a little older and you'll get more than a bath if you paint the vanity." Bending over, she unfastened the tabs on the toddler's diaper, letting it fall to the floor, and lifted her into the tub.

The water immediately turned a murky brown as the paint dissolved from her skin. Alice wrinkled her nose. "You're going to need a bath after your bath."

Elise splashed, sending droplets of the dirty water all over the tile walls. Alice resigned herself to cleaning the entire bathroom once the girl was done.

She found a rag and the baby bath wash and set about washing the finger paint off of Elise. Once she had her clean, she drained the tub and soaped her again to get rid of any residue left by the dirty water.

"Let's get you dressed, yeah?" Alice lifted the girl from the tub and wrapped her in a towel, then carried her down the hall to her room. She found a clean t-shirt and shorts and quickly dressed her before heading back downstairs.

In the living room, she found Henry and Bronwyn curled up on the couch watching a cartoon on TV. The credits rolled as she entered.

"Perfect timing."

The kids looked back.

"Can we watch more?" Bronwyn asked.

"Not at the moment. I need the three of you to go in the playroom while I go up and clean the bathroom. Your sister left hand prints all over the vanity. And I need to clean the paint residue out of the tub." The playroom was the safest place she could think of to leave Elise alone for a few minutes. It had a door to the hallway, and she saw a baby gate near the door to the living room.

Bronwyn giggled and hopped off the couch. "Bet you don't let her paint again anytime soon. You've got paint all over your shirt."

"I know. But next time I know to wear a paint shirt too. Come on." She hustled them toward the playroom. "Wyn, close the hallway door, please."

The girl walked over and shut the door. Alice put Elise down, then set the baby gate in the doorway. "You guys stay in here. If you need something, yell. I'll only be a few minutes, okay?"

They nodded. Elise found the pots and pans she had earlier and started banging them again as Alice walked over the gate. She shook her head, hoping the other two didn't go deaf before she got back.

Upstairs, she found the cleaning supplies under the sink and sprayed the front of the vanity and the bathtub. Rummaging in the linen closet, she found some old rags and used one to scrub off the hand prints and wipe out the tub. Standing back, she surveyed the front of the vanity. Satisfied it was clean, she rinsed the rag and laid it over the edge of the hamper to dry, then went back downstairs. Instead of going directly into the playroom, she took the opportunity to use the restroom, then checked on the kids' projects. They were dry enough for another layer.

Leaving the kitchen, she went down the hall and opened the playroom door, poking her head in. "You two ready for another layer of papier-mâché?"

Bronwyn and Henry got up and ran out of the room. Elise waved the baby doll in her hand at Alice. "You can bring your baby." She picked her up and headed for the kitchen. This time, she gave the girl some fat crayons and paper.

It took them a couple more rounds of papier-mâché to make the bird houses sturdy enough to paint. They were finishing the last layer when she heard the front door open.

"Daddy's home!" Henry laid his brush down and pushed away from the table, running from the room in a swish of plastic from the trash bag smock he wore. Bronwyn quickly followed once she finished gluing on the strip in her hands.

Alice heard Wade's deep voice greet the kids. Their chatter got louder as they got closer, then the three of them appeared in the doorway to the kitchen. She fought to keep her heart from racing out of control. He had Henry in his arms and a smile on his handsome face. His forearms flexed as he set the boy down.

"Dada!" Elise banged on her highchair, breaking Alice from her spell.

He nodded a greeting at Alice as he passed, walking over to press some smacking kisses to his daughter's cheeks. "You smell good." He glanced at Alice with a soft frown. "Did she already have a bath?"

Alice nodded. "Yeah. I let her finger paint. She had it everywhere."

"Brave woman. I haven't worked up the courage to let her do that yet."

A chuckle escaped her. "After today, I can understand why."

He grinned, then looked down at Henry, who tugged on his pants' pocket.

"Did you see what we did?" Henry pointed at the table.

Wade looked over. "What's this?"

Henry led him closer. "Bird houses."

"Bird houses?" He glanced at Alice with another soft frown.

"We blew up balloons, then they layered tissue paper over them with Modge Podge," Alice explained. "They got enough layers on, I think, that tomorrow, we're going to paint them and cut holes in them. I bought some shellac, so they can actually hang them outside."

He leaned a little closer to get a better look, then straightened. "That's pretty neat. So, did you guys have fun today?"

"Yep!" Bronwyn said.

"Uh-huh," Henry added.

"Were you good?"

Both heads bobbed. Wade looked at Alice, a question in his eyes, and she smiled.

"They were very good. Henry and Elise played most of the day after I dropped Bronwyn off at school. Later, after we picked her up, we went to the craft store in town and found stuff to make these and the finger paints. They were just finishing their last layer."

"Oh, well, you better do that then. We don't want to accidentally mix glue with our dinner, do we?"

Henry and Bronwyn giggled.

"You're silly, Daddy." Henry climbed into his chair and picked up his brush.

Wade grinned. "I'm just saying. That would be kind of yucky."

"Very," Alice agreed. She moved to the table and started cleaning up what she could while the kids finished up. Wade picked up the pack of tissue paper, and she glanced at him. "You don't need to help. Why don't you go do whatever it is you normally do when you get home from work? I'll finish cleaning this up. I can start dinner, too, if you tell me what you were planning to make."

"Oh. Honestly, I usually just jump right into meal prep." He straightened, still holding the tissue paper.

"Go ahead and do that, then. I'll help them finish and get them cleaned up."

"You're sure?"

"Yes." She shooed him away. "Go. Cook."

He held out the tissue paper. "Okay. Thanks."

"Of course. I authorized the mess. It's not fair that I'd leave it to you to clean up just because you came home before we were done." She'd be livid if her babysitter did that. Part of caring for kids was teaching them to clean up after themselves. What kind of an example would she be if she left it for Wade to deal with?

"I appreciate it." He headed for the pantry.

It took Henry and Bronwyn another fifteen minutes to finish their final layer of papier-mâché. When they were done, Alice moved their projects to the back of the island, out of the way, then helped them wash their hands. She rinsed their brushes at the sink, then gathered the newspaper and plates with glue from the table, as well as their trash bag smocks and dumped everything in the trash can.

"Before I forget, do you have some old shirts the kids can use as paint smocks? The trash bags were a quick solution today, but I don't want to keep using them. It's just a waste."

Wade glanced up from the stove where he sautéed some

smoked sausage links in a frying pan. "I think so. I'll try to remember to look tonight. If I forget, feel free to rummage in the back of my closet. There are several old flannels in there that already have paint stains. I have some t-shirts at the bottom of my dresser drawer, too, they can use. They're just plain white." His gaze traveled over her paint-stained shirt. "You might want to get one for yourself."

Alice laughed softly and glanced down. "Yeah. I didn't think when I picked Elise up to take her for a bath. She pressed those paint-covered hands all over me. She decorated the vanity in the bathroom too. But that cleaned up easily." She pulled her shirt away from her stomach. "I hope this washes out, but if not, it's my new paint shirt."

"I think you should wear it whenever. Start a new trend." One corner of his mouth kicked up.

Alice laughed. "I could probably get away with it. People would just shake their heads and say, 'She's an artist.'"

His laughter joined hers. "Do you want to stay for dinner? There's plenty here."

"Oh." Her smile faded with her surprise at his invitation.

"Stay, Miss Alice!"

She glanced back at Bronwyn.

"Pweez?" Henry added.

Alice's heart squeezed. Oh, she was in trouble. She couldn't deny those two much. "Okay."

They cheered.

"Help me set the table." She motioned for the kids to come help, and they ran for the silverware drawer. Alice opened the plate cupboard and removed two adult plates and three kid plates, setting them on the counter beside Wade.

He nodded his thanks, then went back to the pantry and came back with two cans of green beans. "There are two bags of roasted potatoes in the freezer. The steamer kind. Can you get them out and pop them in the microwave?"

"Sure." She found the bags and set the timer on the microwave, adding an extra ninety seconds since there were two bags.

He finished the sausage and split it among the five plates, then did the same with the green beans he heated in a saucepan. The microwave chimed, and Alice split the potatoes onto the plates. She helped him carry them to the table, taking Elise's to cut up her food into tiny bites before giving it to the toddler.

"Thank you for dinner." Alice speared a bite of sausage.

"Yeah, thanks, Daddy." Bronwyn ate some green beans.

"You're welcome."

"So, how was your day?" Alice slid the bite of sausage into her mouth as she glanced at him.

His head bobbed. "Fine. Routine." A slight frown dipped his brow. "Well, mostly routine. I'm still dealing with that arson investigation."

"How's it going?"

He shrugged and speared some green beans. "We have some leads. I handed everything over to the sheriff. She's investigating alongside me. I just hope we find who did it before there's another fire."

Alice's eyes widened. "You think there will be more?"

"Unfortunately, yes. I found a pattern in several fires. It might not have been the first this person set." He ate the food on his fork.

Alice frowned as she thought about that. She'd heard someone got hurt in the last fire. She hoped no one else did and that he and Sheriff Lattimer could figure it out soon.

Their discussion turned to more mundane things as they finished eating. Once the kids were done, Alice helped Wade clean up.

"I should be going." She folded the rag she used to wipe Elise's hands and face and laid it over the edge of the sink. "It's getting late." She wanted to throw a few pottery pieces before she headed to bed. She needed to pack for tomorrow night as well. It would be her first sleepover at the Kaczmarek residence.

Wade nodded. "Yeah. I need to get Wyn and Henry in the bath and ready for bed. Thanks again for filling in until my sitter can come back to work."

"It's no problem. We had fun." She motioned to the door. "I'm going to say goodbye to the kids, then head out. I'll see you in the morning."

"Okay. Don't forget tomorrow's my overnight. I'll be back for dinner, then leave again for the night."

She nodded. "Already planning what to pack."

He smiled. Alice's heart skipped. Dammit. Why did he have such an effect on her? She stifled a sigh and blamed it on fatigue. It had been a long day. Fun, but long.

Waving her fingers at him, she said goodnight and walked into the hall to go to the playroom, where the kids went after they finished eating. She poked her head around the door. "I'm leaving. You guys be good for your dad. I'll see you in the morning." Elise ignored her, but the older two got up and came over to give her a hug. She squeezed them tight and gave them each a kiss on the cheek before saying goodnight. Gathering her purse and jacket from the entryway table, she let herself out. Birds chirped their end-of-day song, and a light breeze blew.

Alice took a deep breath of the warm evening air and headed for her car, a little sad to leave. Today had been fun. The Kaczmarek kids were great. And they'd already stolen a piece of her heart. That bothered her a bit. She didn't want to lose it permanently once their other sitter came back to work. Somehow, she vowed, she would stay a part of their lives. She climbed into her car and started the engine. Maybe through all this, she and Wade would become friends.

Her body heated, wanting more than that. She clenched her teeth and put the car in reverse, tamping down that silly thought. The man gave no indication he wanted anything more from her than babysitting. Friendship could be a natural extension of that. Hoping for anything more was just lunacy and setting herself up for heartbreak. She refused to even entertain the thought.

But as she drove back to the Stone Creek, her body still hummed at the memory of Wade's bright smile and tender looks when he interacted with his children. A man who loved his kids—and was single—was hard to resist. It said a lot about his character. He was someone she wanted to get to know better.

She blew her bangs out of her face and shook her head. "Friends, Alice." The man didn't seem like he was in the market for a relationship. And she couldn't blame him after the way his wife left. She wouldn't be either if her husband picked up and ran off, leaving her to care for three kids with no warning. Friendship was all she was going to get. No matter how much he made her body sing. And she wouldn't push for more. She had too much respect for herself—and for what he was trying to do, raising those kids alone—to throw herself at him.

TWELVE

The door banged shut just as Alice opened the oven door to remove the lasagna she made for dinner. Choruses of "Daddy!" echoed through the house as the kids ran to greet their father. Moments later, she heard his boots on the hardwood floor of the hallway, alongside the quieter patter of small feet, as he neared the kitchen.

"It smells good in here. You made dinner?"

Alice smiled as he walked in. "Yep. I figured since you have to go back to work in a few hours, your time home would be better spent relaxing and hanging out with the kids than cooking. This is ready if you want to wash up and have a seat."

"You're going to spoil us all." He headed for the sink. "But I'm not complaining. Tuesdays and Wednesdays are always rough because of my schedule."

"What does your other sitter do on those days?" She looked at the kids. "Go wash your hands in the bathroom, please." They took off.

"Not cook, unless I ask her to. Which I don't very often." His mouth pulled. "She's not the greatest chef."

Alice chuckled at the look on his face. "I'll have to come

over and make you some freezer meals after she comes back. She can just pop them in the oven, then, on Tuesday and Wednesday nights."

He shut off the water and tore off some paper towels to dry his hands. "You don't have to do that. Wednesdays are usually pizza nights since I'm generally exhausted. Tuesdays, we just wing it."

She picked up a knife to cut the lasagna and shook it at him before spearing the casserole. "Well, there will be no winging it while I'm here. Go sit."

"Can I do anything?" He ignored her and walked closer.

"You can take the salad over to the table and put some on the kids' plates." She wanted to argue but also didn't want him to feel like she was taking over, so she caved and gave him a task. "It's on the island."

He turned and picked up the bowl, taking it over to the table the kids set a few minutes ago. They scampered back in as he put salad on Henry's plate.

"Yuck. I don't like salad." The boy wrinkled his nose as he climbed into his chair.

Alice grabbed her hot pads and lifted the casserole dish, carrying it to the table. "We all have to eat things we don't necessarily like, Henry. Salad's good for you, so you can eat some."

He grumbled but didn't say anything else.

Bronwyn hopped into her chair. "I like salad. It's yummy."

"I'm glad." Alice put the casserole dish down on the trivet in the center of the table, then sat down.

Wade lifted Henry's plate and dished lasagna onto it. Alice handed him Elise's, then cut it up while he filled Bronwyn's and his own.

"Do you want me to fill yours?"

"Sure." Alice handed Elise her spork, then set the plate in front of her.

Wade took Alice's plate and filled it, handing it back.

"Thanks."

"You're welcome. This looks really good. Remind me to give you money for groceries."

She waved a hand and picked up her fork. "Deduct whatever from what you insist on paying me."

He huffed. "You're doing a job, Alice. You deserve to be paid."

She shrugged and cut off a chunk of lasagna. "To me, this is fun. And I don't mind helping. But I understand where you're coming from. Pay me whatever you want, Wade."

Dinner passed quickly as the kids talked, regaling their dad with tales of their day. Alice glanced at Elise and wrinkled her nose in dismay.

"Two days in a row, kid? Really?" The girl had pasta sauce all over her face and hands. The ends of her blonde hair around her face were tinged orange.

Wade laughed. "You have a thing about letting her make a mess, don't you?"

With a sheepish smile, Alice shrugged. "Honestly, I wasn't thinking about the mess she'd make when I made dinner today. Just that it would be easy and filling. I'll give her a bath. Again."

His grin widened. "You do that. Wyn, Henry, and I are going to go out back and kick the soccer ball around."

The kids cheered.

"Oh, boy!" Henry pushed back from the table. "I like soccer. Lots more than salad."

Alice laughed and grabbed his shirtsleeve, halting his getaway. "You still have to finish it, young man."

Henry's shoulders sagged, and he looked at his dad. "Do I really?"

Wade nodded. "Yes. Alice is right. Salad is good for you. You can finish your dinner before we play."

The boy heaved a sigh as big as he was and climbed back into his chair. Glaring at his plate, he forked a piece of lettuce and stuffed it in his mouth. Alice bit back a grin. He was cute.

To his credit, he finished the rest of his food without complaint. Once the last bite was gone, he picked up his plate and took it to the sink. "I'm ready, Daddy."

"Me too." Wade deposited his plate in the sink. "Bronwyn, are you done?"

The girl nodded, eating the last bite of her food. "Yep." She carried her plate to the sink.

Wade glanced at Alice. "You okay in here with the orange sauce-monster?" He pointed at Elise, smirking.

Alice sighed. The toddler was even more of a mess than before. Now she had melted cheese smushed in her hair. "Yeah. Send help if you don't see me in about twenty minutes."

Laughing, he herded the kids toward the door. "Got it. Come on, guys. Let's make our escape before she makes us help."

Giggling, Bronwyn and Henry ran outside. Wade grinned at Alice and followed them.

Heaving another sigh, Alice looked at Elise. "Are you finished eating?" Her eyes roved over the highchair tray. There really wasn't much left. It was all in her belly or on her body. Finding a rag and wetting it, she ran it over Elise's hands and face. "I'm not making the same mistake again. You're not ruining another one of my shirts." Once she had most of the gunk off the girl, she took her out of the seat and carried her upstairs to give her a bath.

The water wasn't quite as dirty this time, but Alice still had to rinse the residue out of the tub. She put clean clothes on her, then headed back downstairs to join the others outside.

THIRTEEN

Wade glanced over as the back door opened. Alice walked out carrying a freshly washed Elise. His stomach turned over as he took in his babysitter's flushed face and the sweaty tendrils of hair clinging to her forehead. She looked a little frazzled, but still gorgeous. He turned away, focusing on the ball coming toward him.

"Do you want to play, Alice?" Bronwyn stopped the ball, putting her foot on top of it.

"No. You go ahead. I'm going to sit down for a minute." She put Elise in the grass. The girl ran for the sandbox.

Wade noticed Henry's attention stray to his little sister. The boy wanted to play in the sand too. "Why don't we take a break?"

"Okay." Henry ran to the sandbox and sat down with Elise. Bronwyn went to the swings.

"Did they wear you out?" He sat down next to Alice at the patio table.

She smiled and nodded. "A little bit. You'd think I'd be used to it, teaching all day. It's different, though, when you're at home with them. They aren't corralled into groups at tables. They run everywhere, constantly needing to keep busy, but also always changing their minds. And they hardly ever all want to do the same thing."

"Tell me about it. Elise has become much more independent in the last few months, and it's just increased the amount of discord. She's very vocal about what she does and doesn't want."

"I've noticed. She is pretty good about staying content, though, once you find something she likes." She smiled as she watched them play. "They're really great kids, Wade."

"Yeah. For all that's happened in their short lives, they're happy. I've tried hard to keep them to a routine and not let their mother's actions affect them too much." He shrugged. "It's nice to know it's working."

"What happened? If you don't mind me asking? I'd like to know the basics in case one of the kids asks, or someone says something to one of them about her."

Wade frowned, his buoyant mood souring as thoughts of his ex-wife filtered in. She was right, though. She needed to know at least some of what happened. He ran a hand over his short hair and stared out over the yard, not really seeing anything. "Emily and I were college sweethearts. She was a music major I met at a party. I was a forestry major there with my roommate. I didn't even want to go, but he talked me into it. After that night, she and I were inseparable. I asked her to marry me right after our graduation ceremony, and she said yes."

"You were happy."

It wasn't a question. He could tell she'd picked up on how things were good for a while.

"Yeah. For several years, actually. We went to college in Missoula, but afterward, she wanted to try to make a career out of music, so we moved to Nashville. Emily really can sing, but she has a voice like so many other women. It was pretty, but nothing about it makes her stand out, you know? I still loved to listen to her sing, though."

Bronwyn jumped off the swing and ran over to the deck box that held their backyard toys. He pointed at her. "Then that one happened."

"She wasn't ready to be a mom?"

"It wasn't like that. She was ready. Bronwyn wasn't an oops. Neither was Henry. Elise was the oops. Emily's plan was to have a couple of kids, then try to get on a touring band."

"What was she going to do with the kids? What were you doing for work?"

"I was a forest ranger in the Appalachians. And part of their fire service. We put the kids in daycare, which revolved around my schedule, usually. When she was home, her rehearsal schedule could be erratic. And she'd play gigs in the evenings."

"So, what changed?"

"She got offered a place on a big-name artist's band as a backup singer, then had to bow out a couple weeks before they left on tour because she was pregnant with Elise and having problems. She had that hyperemesis gravidarum. Do you know what that is?"

Alice nodded. "Extreme morning sickness, right?"

"Basically, yes. She was hospitalized for a couple of days so they could get some fluids in her and try to get it under control so she could at least keep water down. But it kept her from going on tour. She changed after that. Started resenting being a mom. Being tied down. All she wanted was to play her music. It's like it became an obsession. Nothing was going to get in her way."

Bronwyn hopped by on a pogo stick, making them both smile. He still marveled at how good she was on it. He wished they had a place that offered gymnastics lessons closer than Billings. She'd be good at it.

"After Elise was born, she withdrew more and more. Started taking more gigs, finding new tours to be part of. Sometimes, she didn't come home for several days straight, even though she never left Nashville. She said it was easier to stay downtown, since she'd go from gig to rehearsal to gig again. Elise was six months old when she told me she was going on tour with the same artist whose tour she had to bow out of. The woman offered her another chance. I was excited for her until she told me she didn't plan to come back."

He swallowed hard as the memory hit him. That was one of the hardest days of his life. His voice was gruff when he spoke again. "She told me she wasn't cut out to be a mom. That I was doing a great job at being mom and dad, so she thought it best if that's what we did." He inhaled a shaky breath. "She'd packed up her things while I was at work and had them all loaded into her car already. After she laid that bombshell on me, she kissed the kids goodbye and left. I got divorce papers in the mail two weeks later."

Alice gasped. "I'm so sorry, Wade."

"Me too. But not for me. For them." He nodded at the kids. "They didn't do anything to deserve that kind of treatment. She hasn't called, sent a card, or anything since she left. It pisses me off. I knew she was career-driven when I married her, but I never thought she'd abandon her kids."

"Have you tried to contact her?"

He nodded. "When she missed Bronwyn's birthday, I called her cell. It was disconnected, so I tried her attorney. He said he'd get a message to her. I never heard back. I tried again when Elise turned one. Even sent some pictures for him to forward. Crickets." He glanced at Alice. Her blue eyes looked like hardened steel, and her mouth was set. She shook her head.

"That's terrible."

He shrugged. "It is what it is. I do what I can to make life good for them. Moving back here was the first step to that. I knew I'd need help, so I called my parents and told them what happened. Dad immediately offered me a job at the feed store. We stayed with them for a few months until I could sell our house in Nashville and find a place here. In that time, a spot with the fire department opened up. A couple months later, so did the fire investigator's position. It meant less time away at night and a raise, so I applied and got hired. The chief asked me to apply for the fire inspector spot when it came open, and we worked out a plan that kept me home every night but one. And I get most weekends off. Jed and I rotate who's on call on the weekends. I just have to be available for those."

"That's great."

"Yeah." A soft smile formed on his face. "I feel like we're finally settled, you know? All the upheaval of the last year—it's done, and we can just live now."

She glanced away, watching the kids play. Wade smiled at Henry. He'd dug a trench in the sandbox and Elise ran a toy car through it.

"Bronwyn mentioned her yesterday." Alice broke the silence and looked at him. "She said her mom wouldn't like the mess Elise made of herself. Henry got really quiet at that. He seemed both sad and unsure if he should do what she would have wanted or continue to be a little messy."

Wade frowned and stared at his son. Henry didn't talk about Emily much, and he wasn't sure how much he remembered about her. "Emily didn't like it when the kids made a mess. She's a very tidy person, so all the kid stuff bugged her some. Especially all the toys strewn everywhere. Bronwyn still tends to be tidier than a lot of kids her age."

"Does it bother you? The messes, I mean?"

"Not really. I don't want to leave the house in a perpetual state of disarray, where it always looks like a tornado just blew through, but if they want to dump out a bucket of blocks or play food, then not pick it up right away, I don't care. We clean up at the end of the day. That's good enough for me. I just want them to be kids, you know?"

Alice gave him a soft smile. "You're a good dad, Wade Kaczmarek. I'm amazed at how well-adjusted Bronwyn and Henry are. They know you love them. And it's helped them cope with the fact their mother left."

He shrugged. "They're easy to love. I think that's the hardest thing to understand about not just why she left, but why she never calls or sends cards. It's been radio silence for over a year."

Alice rolled her lips in, watching the kids a moment before turning those pretty light blue eyes on him. "Maybe it's too hard for her." She held up a hand. "I'm not defending her actions. Just playing a bit of devil's advocate. Maybe the reason she cut all ties was because it was easier to start her new life if she pretended you all didn't exist."

Wade's mouth flattened and his eyebrows drew down. "I thought about that. And it might play a part. But I also think she really did just want to move on. We're her past, and she's not interested in dwelling on it." His mood took a nose-dive as he thought about his ex-wife. About her betrayal. Not just of him, but of their kids. Whatever her reasons for ghosting their family, they were selfish. Their children didn't deserve it. He waved a hand. "Whatever her reasons, I try not to spend too much brain power on it. I just want to keep moving forward."

"I think that's probably what I would do too." She bent her arm at the elbow where it rested on the arm of her chair and leaned a finger against her face as she stared out at the kids. "If one of them says something about her—asks a question or my opinion—what do you want me to say?"

Surprise made Wade turn to look at her. None of the other caregivers in his kids' lives had ever asked him that. He gave Shelby and Bronwyn's teacher a cursory explanation about their mom being out of the picture and left it at that. He liked that Alice wanted to be sure she followed his wishes. Which was to be honest with them.

"You can answer however you feel is appropriate. I've always been honest with them. I try not to speculate. When they ask if I think she loves them, I tell them I believe she does—because I do. She just does it in a different way. Mostly, I just make sure they feel worthy, and that it wasn't anything they did that caused her to leave."

She nodded. "I'll reiterate that, then, and tell them they can talk to you more about it when you get home if they want."

"That sounds good. Thank you for asking. I appreciate it."

She nodded, but before she could say more, Henry ran up with the soccer ball.

"Daddy, can you come kick the ball again?"

"Sure." Wade stood up, then glanced at Alice. "Do you want to join us now?"

"Um, sure. I think I'm rested enough." She got up, smiling at Henry. "Show me what you've got, kiddo." She jogged out into the yard.

Wade smiled as he watched her. She was great with the kids, and they seemed to love her. He thanked his lucky stars she'd dropped into their lap. It made Shelby's absence bearable. And it made his attraction to her—which he didn't want—something he could endure. His children were happy. Nothing else mattered.

Fourteen

"Just a few more minutes, sweetie." Alice glanced over her shoulder into the backseat at Elise, who strained against her buckles and banged her toy against her seat. The toddler had not been happy when Alice plucked her out of the sandbox to go pick up Bronwyn from school. Not even when she gave her a snack cup full of Cheerios after she buckled her into her car seat. The cup went flying, narrowly missing Alice's head. Henry just shook his head at her and remarked that she wasn't happy.

Alice glanced at the clock, then at the school doors, willing them to open. She tapped her fingers on the steering wheel and did her best to tune out Elise's tantrum. At least she wasn't in full-on meltdown mode.

Finally, the teachers who ran the pickup line came outside, walkie talkies in hand. Alice willed the line to go quickly. Creeping forward, she lifted the placard with Bronwyn's name on it so the teacher could see. The woman called her name into the walkie talkie. A moment later, Bronwyn ran out of the school and got in the car.

"Hi, kiddo."

"Hi, Alice. Guess what?" The girl twisted in her booster seat, putting on her seat belt.

"What?" Alice made sure she was buckled, then drove away.

"We're having a music play this Thursday. I get to sing a solo, and we rehearsed today. Can you come?"

"That's exciting. Of course I can come. What time is it?"

"I dunno. Daddy knows, though. He put it on his calendar, so he wouldn't forget."

"Okay. I'll ask him."

"Yay!" Bronwyn clapped her hands. "What's wrong with Elise?"

Alice glanced in the rearview mirror to see Bronwyn leaning as far away from her sister on the other side of the car as she could. Henry sat in the middle with his hands over his ears. Elise's tantrum had grown worse. She was crying now.

"She's mad because I made her leave the sandbox." And she had only a short nap today. The girl hadn't wanted to go to sleep, then only slept for about thirty minutes. Normally, she was out for an hour or two. Alice had a feeling she was teething, because she also wanted to chew on everything.

That thought gave Alice an idea. At the next intersection, she pulled a U-turn.

"Where are we going?" Bronwyn sat straighter in her seat and looked out the window.

"The grocery store. I think popsicles are in order today."

"Popsicles?" Henry lowered his hands. Alice could see the interested look on his face in the mirror.

"Yep. What kind do you think we should get?"

"Lime!" Bronwyn shouted.

"I like raspberry."

"What kind does Elise like?"

"She'll eat any kind," Bronwyn said.

"Well, we'll get both." Alice turned onto the main thoroughfare and turned toward the grocery store. It only took a few minutes before she turned into the parking lot.

Elise calmed a bit as Alice opened her door to take her out of the car and she saw where they were.

"You want a popsicle?"

The girl hiccupped and gave a small nod.

"Let's go get some. But you have to calm down, okay?"

She hiccupped again. Alice glanced back. Henry and Bronwyn stood behind her.

"You two ready?"

"Yep." Bronwyn bounced on her toes.

Henry nodded.

"Okay. Henry, hold my hand. Wyn, stay close." She led the children across the lot to the front doors. They swished open, letting them inside, and Alice made a beeline for the freezer section. "Pick the ones you want. The real fruit kind, not the sugary ones." She let go of Henry's hand to point at a particular brand.

Bronwyn opened the door and grabbed a box of lime popsicles. Henry pointed to a shelf he couldn't reach.

"Raspberry, right?" Alice reached for the box when he nodded. She grabbed it and let the door close. "Let's go pay for these and go home."

The store wasn't busy, so checkout was quick, and they were soon back in the car. Elise was much calmer for the ride home.

Once inside the house, Alice had them sit at the table—Elise in her highchair—and gave them each a popsicle. When they were done, she cleaned the toddler up while the other two washed their hands.

"I'm going to take advantage of your numb mouth, Leese. Let me feel those gums." She washed her hands, then slid a finger into the girl's mouth. A large lump met her finger on the left side of the toddler's mouth. "Oh, baby girl. No wonder you're cranky. I wonder if I can give you some pain meds."

"Can we play outside?" Henry asked.

"Sure." She opened the door and let them out. He and Bronwyn dashed to the swing set. Alice put Elise in the sand-box, then took out her phone to call Wade. She wasn't sure how he normally handled teething.

The phone rang three times before he picked up, sounding a bit breathless.

"Hey, Alice. Is everything okay?"

"Things are fine. Are you all right? You sound out of breath."

"I was in the gym, lifting weights."

"Oh." Alice tried not to think about how he'd look, muscles bulging and sweaty. But it was no use. The image popped into her head and refused to leave.

"So, what's up?"

She cleared her throat. "Um, Elise is teething. A molar. Can I give her some pain medicine?"

"Oh, man. Poor kid. Yeah. It's in the medicine cabinet in my bathroom. The dosage is on the bottle. You might want to alternate them. Ibuprofen first, then acetaminophen three hours later. It'll keep her comfortable and save all our sanity. There are some teethers hiding in the freezer somewhere too."

"Okay. I stopped at the store on the way home from picking up Bronwyn and bought popsicles. That seemed to help."

"Good. If they're the sugar-free kind, you can give her another one later."

"They are."

"That works."

"Great. I'll let you get back to your workout. Thanks."

"Of course. I hope she's not being too much of a bear for you."

"Only a little. She's fine."

"Okay. I hope she sleeps for you tonight. Teething turns her into an insomniac."

Great. Alice blew out a breath. "I might sleep in her room, then." It was her second overnight in the Kaczmarek house. The first one went fine, but she didn't have a teething toddler. She hoped the pain medicine helped Elise sleep. "Should I wake her up during the night to give her the pain medicine?"

"I wouldn't. If she's sleeping, let her sleep. But have it ready for when she does. Just use your best judgment."

"All right." She glanced over at Elise, who seemed happy for the moment. "Thanks, Wade."

"Anytime. Other than teething, is everything going okay?"

"Oh, yeah. They're fine. We're hanging out outside right now."

"Good. Okay. Give them my love. I'll see you tomorrow."

"Yep, I will." They said goodbye, and Alice hung up, pocketing the phone. She blew out another breath, hoping to expel thoughts of Wade in workout gear.

It didn't work.

Rolling her eyes at herself, she glanced over to the swing set. "Wyn, I'm going to run inside and get some pain medicine for your sister. Will you keep an eye on her? Make sure she doesn't eat sand?"

The girl hopped off her swing. "Yep!" She ran over to the sandbox.

Alice smiled and went inside. She ran upstairs and went into Wade's bedroom. Pretending she had blinders on, she hurried past the king-size oak bed with its dark gray comforter and went into the bathroom. Men's toiletries littered the countertop of the double vanity. She opened the medicine cabinet and scanned the bottles, quickly finding both liquid and chewable versions of the medicines he told her to give the girl.

Opting for the liquids, she grabbed both, plus their dosage cups, and all but ran from the room. It smelled like him. And the large bed only gave her imagination fodder to build on the dreams that plagued her at night. She already woke up hot and bothered.

FIFTEEN

Fire tones rang through the station just as Wade finished his workout.

"Engine Three. Rescue Seven. Structure fire. Two-four-eight Michelson Street."

Cursing, he ran for the door. He was on Engine Three today. The gym was on the same level as the sleeping quarters, so he ran in to get his pants, where he left them on his bed. Toeing off his sneakers, he whisked his athletic shorts down his legs, then pulled on his pants, not bothering with his shoes since he'd just have to put his boots on.

Running from the room, he took the fire pole to the first floor and ran into the garage, donning his gear with the rest of his squad. He hopped onto the truck. His butt barely hit the seat before they rolled out of the garage bay, siren blaring.

The address was only two minutes away. Wade buttoned his coat and checked the straps on his helmet, so he'd be ready once they arrived. When the truck pulled to a halt, he and the others climbed out.

Smoke poured from the single-story house. Flames licked the gutters as they shot out from under the roofline. The interior through the windows looked dark. Wade was willing to bet the fire was in the attic.

"Kaczmarek, Oakley, get on the hose and go in. Do a search for victims. Durham, Smith, hook up two lines, and start spraying from out here."

Wade nodded at his lieutenant's orders and moved to the side of the truck to get a respirator. Checking the valves and oxygen supply, he put on the mask, then his helmet and gloves. "You ready?" He glanced at Will Oakley. The man nodded. Wade grabbed the end of the hose, now charged thanks to Durham and Smith. "Let's go."

Will grabbed the hose behind him and they walked toward the burning house. At the door, Wade opened it and stepped in. Thick smoke greeted him, obscuring his vision. He didn't see any flames, though.

Smoke alarms shrieked as they moved deeper into the house. The bedrooms and lone bathroom were clear. In the kitchen, flames roiled over the ceiling. He aimed the hose at the flames and opened the valve. It didn't take long for them to knock them down. Once they were out, he motioned to Oakley for them to go outside through the back door. The man nodded, and Wade led them outside.

Turning, he looked up. Flames rolled over the gutters, burning the roof tiles. They sprayed more water, choking out the flames. The force of the spray knocked off the charred roofing and allowed them to get water directly into the attic. Soon, white smoke billowed from the house, replacing the darker smoke from the fire.

With the visible flames out, Wade and his partner retrieved a ladder from the truck and made their way onto the roof. Durham and Smith joined them from the other side. They mopped up the few hot spots, making sure they had all the embers out.

Hot and sweaty, Wade descended the ladder and went

back to the truck to stow his respirator. He still needed to walk through the scene and determine the cause. But he needed a drink first.

Shutting the cubby door, He opened another and retrieved a bottle of water, guzzling it. Drops trickled down his throat, but he didn't care. The cool liquid felt good.

Water gone, he climbed into the truck and put it in the trash sack they carried around, then found his clipboard and a flashlight, as well as a mask to filter the air and the small digital camera he used to document his findings.

"Kaczmarek."

Wade turned at the sound of his name. His lieutenant, Nick Rutherford, stood at the front of the truck.

"You going in to determine cause?"

"Yes, sir."

Rutherford gave a short nod. "Holler if you need a hand."

"Will do." Wade tipped his head, then headed for the house. He rounded the side and went into the backyard. Most of the blaze was concentrated over the kitchen. He figured he'd probably find a short in its wiring somewhere in the attic.

Climbing the ladder, he stepped onto the roof and went through a hole they'd chopped in the shingles while checking for hot spots. With careful steps, he shined the flashlight on charred rafters and walls, looking for the telltale signs of ignition. Above the stove, he found the source. A set of wires for the hood vent.

Squatting, he took a closer look. Moving the wires to look at the charring around them, something about them caught his attention. He aimed his camera at them and snapped a picture, then pulled it up, zooming in.

"Damn." They'd been cut.

He looked up, glancing around. The cut alone didn't explain why they sparked a fire. The house was vacant. No one should have been attempting to use the hood vent. So, what made them spark?

Taking several more pictures, he climbed out of the attic, then went into the kitchen through the back door. He wanted to sift through the debris below the wires. Wade snapped several pictures, then squatted. Most of what fell down from the attic was insulation.

His hand hit something harder. And scratchy. He moved aside a piece of soggy, charred drywall to find a loosely crumpled ball of foil. Taking more pictures, he picked it up. Like everything else, it was charred, but it also had scorch marks.

Wade sighed. He wondered what the odds were that Tim Willard owned this house. Getting on his radio, he informed Rutherford they were looking at arson and asked him to have someone bring him an evidence bag and to call in a crime scene unit.

He stared at the ball of tinfoil. If this was the same person, what could his aim be? Did he believe they wouldn't think four fires were suspicious? Or that Wade wouldn't find evidence of arson? Was it more than just money he was looking to get out of it? Maybe he got a thrill now.

Regardless, Wade intended to look up the owner of this property as soon as he got back to his office. If it was Willard, it was time to pay the man a visit.

Sixteen

The ring of Alice's phone broke through the chirping birds on her walk with Henry and Elise. She stopped to dig it out of the diaper bag in the bottom of the double-stroller. Elise protested the lack of forward momentum and squealed.

"Hang on, sweetie." She found the device as it rang for the fourth time and saw Wade's name on the screen. Frowning, not sure what he could be calling about, she swiped her finger over the screen to answer. "Hello?"

"Hey, it's me. Are you able to stay late today? I have to go to Billings with Sheriff Lattimer for my arson case, and it's going to be probably seven or so before I'm back. If you can't, that's fine. My parents can take the kids. I hope."

"Oh, well, I guess that depends. I really need to work on some pottery. Do you mind if I take them up to the Stone Creek?"

"Can you keep an eye on them while you do that?"

"Yes. Jasper moved in with the sheriff and told me I could set up my pottery studio in his old house. I set everything up in the spare bedroom and can see the living room from it. I can bring some of their toys and Elise's highchair, so I can contain her for a bit if need be." Alice had been creating all her pottery at the house, then transporting it to a place in Billings to be fired until she had her house and could have an electrician install an outlet for her kiln. It drew too much power to just plug in anywhere.

"That sounds like a lot of effort. Maybe I'll just call my parents."

"Wade, I've been schlepping their double-stroller around any time we go out. The highchair is actually lighter."

He chuckled. "Are you sure? I'll come up there and get them, so you don't have to make another trip into town tonight."

"That works."

"Okay. Thank you, Alice. You've been a godsend. I don't know what I'd have done without you this past week."

Elise let out another shriek and banged her feet, cutting off Alice's reply.

"Everything okay there?"

Alice chuckled. "Yes. Your youngest is just protesting the fact that I stopped to answer the phone. We're headed to the park."

"Oh. Well, far be it from me to get in the way of park time. I'll see you this evening at the Stone Creek. Thank you, again."

"Not a problem. See you later."

They said goodbye and hung up.

"Was that Daddy?" Henry asked, twisting in his seat to look at her.

She nodded. "He's going to be late tonight, so you get to come to the Stone Creek with me."

"What's that?"

"It's a ranch. I'm living there while I wait for the sale on my house to go through." She hoped it would only be another couple of weeks. The owners were eager to sell and accepted her offer the same day she put it in. It just had to pass inspection and clear escrow and they could close on it.

"Are there horses?" His hazel eyes, so much like his dad's, lit up.

"Lots of them."

"Do I get to ride one?"

"Probably not. But I'm sure you can pet a few."

"Oh, boy! Wait until I tell Bronwyn."

His bright grin made Alice smile. "She'll be excited, I'm sure." She put her phone away, then started down the sidewalk again. "But right now, how about we go swing?"

He clapped and cheered. Alice picked up her pace.

It only took her a few more minutes to reach the park playground. She let Henry out of the stroller, and he ran off to climb on the equipment while she got Elise out. The girl refused to be held, so Alice set her on her feet, and she toddled off to a car on a large spring and climbed inside. Alice stood behind it and nudged it with her hand, making it rock.

They played for about forty-five minutes before it was time to head home for lunch. Neither child was ready to leave, but she pacified Henry with the promise of mac and cheese. Elise calmed down halfway to the house.

After lunch, she put the girl down for a nap and let Henry watch some television while she cleaned up the kitchen and checked her email. Her pottery had an online presence, so she got a few orders through her website every month. She checked every day to see if there were any she needed to fill. Today, she had an order for a set of four coffee mugs. She could throw those tonight, and decided to make some extras for the shop. Her original plan was to make bowls this evening, but if she was already working on mugs, she might as well keep it consistent.

With dishes and business out of the way, she tackled a few other chores, taking advantage of the quiet. By the time Elise woke up, she'd swept and mopped the floors on the first floor and cleaned all the bathrooms. Wade never asked her to do housework, but she didn't mind. It meant he could spend more time with his kids.

Putting Elise in the playroom with Henry, she packed a bag with extra clothes and snacks for the kids, then folded up the highchair and put it in her car. After wrestling Elise into her shoes, they headed out to pick up Bronwyn from school.

"I can't wait to see the horses. Do they have cows too? What about chickens? My grandpa sells food for amninals. I want a kitty, but Daddy says he's too busy for a pet. Do you have any pets?"

Alice smiled at his rapid-fire questions and mispronunciations, then shook her head. "Not at the moment, no. I'm like your dad and don't have time for a pet."

"If I had a job, I'd still get a kitty. It could go to work with me."

"You think?"

"Yep."

Alice chuckled. She turned into the school parking lot and pulled up behind the last car in line. She twisted in her seat to look at him. "I bet when you three get a little older and can help take care of a pet more, your dad will let you get a cat."

He gave her a solemn nod. "That's what he said."

Henry continued to talk while they waited. She needed to take the kids to the ranch more often. He was normally a quiet child, but the excitement of seeing farm animals in the flesh set his tongue loose. Even as his sister climbed into the car, he continued to talk, switching gears to tell her where they were going and why.

"The Stone Creek is where Olive lives. Will she be there?"

Alice nodded as she put the car in gear. "Most likely. I'm not sure if she'll be able to play, but we'll stop and ask, okay?"

"Goody!"

"We need to make a stop first, so I can pick up some groceries for dinner. How does homemade pizza sound?" She would borrow the ingredients for the crust from Daisy and get the rest from the store.

"Yummy!" Bronwyn threw her arms up in the air.

"I like pizza!" Henry clapped his hands.

"Perfect." She turned out of the neighborhood and headed for the grocery. A quick trip through the store and they were back on the road.

SEVENTEEN

Wade stepped out of the police cruiser at the Billings police station and glanced across the hood at the sheriff. Katy Lattimer was a tall woman who commanded attention. And not just because of her stature. She was beautiful. And young. But she was a good cop, and a balanced and fair leader. He liked working with her.

He held the door open for her, then they signed in at the front desk. The officer led them down the hall to a conference room where Tim Willard and his attorney waited for them. Wade was glad the man agreed to a meeting. He didn't have to, of which he was certain the man's lawyer would have informed him. Willard was either cocky as hell, curious to know what the police had and was hoping to get some information on that front, or he had no idea what was going on.

Katy thanked the officer, then entered the room and sat down across from Willard and his attorney. Wade sat next to her.

"Hello, Mr. Willard. Thank you for meeting with us. I'm Sheriff Katy Lattimer. This is my colleague, Fire Investigator Wade Kaczmarek."

Willard, a heavy-set man with thinning salt and pepper hair and muddy brown eyes, nodded a greeting. "I'm as eager as you all to find out why my properties keep going up in flames." He glanced at the younger man beside him. "This is my lawyer, Brad Purcell."

Wade offered him a tight-lipped but polite smile.

"Good." Katy shifted, opening the file folder with the fire incident reports and Wade's notes. "Let's not waste each other's time then, all right?" At their nod, she continued. "The first fire at one of your properties in Pine Ridge was six months ago, correct?"

Willard nodded. "That sounds about right. A vacant building."

"Yes. Then the second happened four months later outside a warehouse. It housed a mechanic's shop."

"Right." He glanced at Wade. "The fire investigator said it started in a trash bin outside the building. Oil rags that caught fire." A frown creased his eyebrows. "Something about homeless people in the area probably trying to keep warm."

"He speculated," Wade corrected. "He only noted that the rags caught fire, causing the blaze, but couldn't find any malicious intent."

"We all know this," Purcell cut in. "What's the point?"

Katy flipped a page. "Our point is that the next two fires are both definitely arson. Someone poured gasoline all over a house being renovated and put the electrician in the hospital with third-degree burns over twenty-five percent of his body. The latest fire was also at a vacant house owned by you, Mr. Willard. Mr. Kaczmarek found evidence that someone deliberately cut wires in the attic that go to the hood vent over the stove, then put aluminum foil under them. Our lab technicians found wax on the foil and iron oxide."

"What does that mean?" Willard's frown deepened.

"It means someone created a delayed aluminothermic reaction by burning a candle on top of aluminum foil coated with rust shavings." Wade sat forward. "When the candle flame reached the foil and shavings, it caused a small explosion that sent sparks flying, which ignited the insulation. They cut the wires when they set the candle, hoping the evidence would burn up in the fire and we'd chalk it up to a shoddy electrical job or a short in the wires."

Willard tipped his head, then shook it, his expression puzzled. "Why would someone light my buildings on fire? I just don't understand."

"Mr. Willard, where were you two days ago?" Katy asked.

The man sat straighter in his chair. He laid his hands on the table and leaned forward. The gold Rolex on his wrist flashed in the harsh lighting as his sleeves inched up. "Wait. You think I did this? That's just ludicrous. Why would I destroy my properties?"

Wade and Katy stayed silent. Willard huffed, sitting back, and looked at Purcell. The lawyer leaned in and whispered something in Willard's ear, who then nodded.

"I was here in Billings. I haven't left the city since my business trip to Denver a few weeks ago."

"Can you provide any evidence you were indeed here?" Katy picked up a pen and rolled it between her fingers.

"My secretary saw me. And I made several phone calls from my office. I also visited a couple of sites. I didn't do this, Sheriff."

She lifted a hand. "I have to ask. We'll check your whereabouts, of course, but it sounds like they should be easy to verify. Can you think of anyone who would want to harm you or your business?"

His mouth flattened. "Plenty of people. You don't get to be in my position and not step on some toes. What I don't understand is why it would happen in Pine Ridge, but not anywhere else."

"There haven't been fires at any of your other properties?" Wade asked. "Not even small ones that didn't do much damage?"

"I don't think so. I'll have to check, though. If they were minor, I might not have heard about them. My project managers would be the ones to deal with them. All the fires in Pine Ridge did more damage, so I got more information, quicker."

Katy uncapped her pen. "Who's your project manager in Pine Ridge?"

"There are two. Levi Rister and Edward Hughes."

Wade glanced at Katy. She met his gaze with barely banked surprise. Edward Hughes was Cynthia Hughes's son, and the brother of her chief deputy.

She wrote the names down. "Okay. We'll make sure to talk to them. Would either of them have a reason to want to burn down your buildings?"

"No. We have good working relationships."

"What about anyone else in town? Did you buy a building out from under somebody? Or outbid another contractor for a job?"

"Several times. But that's the nature of the business."

"If you could, I'd like to get copies of your records for your properties in Pine Ridge. The more information we have on them, the deeper we can dig into this."

Willard glanced at his attorney, who nodded.

"I'll have my secretary pull everything and make copies, then have a courier drop them at your office either late tomorrow or early the next morning." Willard sighed and ran a hand over his face. "I will cooperate in any way I can."

"I appreciate that." Katy gave him a quick nod, then looked at Wade. "Do you have any other questions?"

"Not at the moment, no." Willard's confusion and surprise when he described the method of ignition for the last fire told him the man either didn't do it or hired someone, but had no knowledge of how his employee set the fire. It was on Katy to figure that part out.

Katy gave another short nod, then pushed back her chair. They all stood. She held out a hand. "Thank you for your time, Mr. Willard. I'll keep an eye out for those files."

He shook her hand. "I'll call you when they're on their way."

"That would be great, thank you."

Wade shook Willard's hand and his attorney's, then followed Katy out of the room. They signed out at the front desk, then climbed into her cruiser.

"What's your take on him?" She glanced at him as she turned onto the main road.

"He seems genuine. It didn't feel like his surprise was fake. Or his frustration."

"I agree. I don't think he's our guy. We need to look into Hughes and Rister." She shook her head. "I can't see Ed doing this, though. He's a good guy. I don't know Rister. Do you?"

"No. I don't know Ed that well, either." He and his brother were several years Wade's senior. He only knew of them through their church.

"Ray's going to have a conniption when I bring his brother in for questioning."

"So will their mom. I do not envy you your job." He was glad Katy was lead. Dealing with the people element was never his thing.

She chuckled. "Thanks."

He grinned. "You're welcome."

"You feel like running through a drive-thru for some dinner? Or do you have plans with Alice?"

Wade looked at her, eyes widening a fraction. "Why would you think that?"

"Jasper said Asa told him she's been filling in for your

babysitter. I also heard from Daisy that sparks fly whenever the two of you are together." She shrugged. "I thought maybe you had plans to eat with her and your kids."

He drummed his fingers on his thigh and stared out the windshield. Daisy thought there were sparks between him and Alice? He'd admit he found Alice attractive, but he'd been so preoccupied with ignoring it, he hadn't stopped to consider how she might feel about him. Was she attracted to him too?

Did it matter? He still didn't want to get involved with anyone. Not even kind, sweet, beautiful Alice.

"No, no plans," he answered. "She was going to take the kids to the Stone Creek so she could get some work done. I have to go pick them up when we get back to town. I imagine she'll have fed them by then."

"Oh, yeah, probably. Okay. How do burgers sound, then?"

"Good." Honestly, he didn't care. He doubted he'd taste it anyway. His brain was so preoccupied with the revelation that his attraction might not be one-sided to register anything else. And it didn't matter that he held open the door to the vault where he'd kept that attraction. No matter how hard he tried, it didn't want to go back in now.

Grinding his teeth, he rested his elbow on the windowsill and ran a hand over his jaw. *Dammit.*

Eighteen

"Daddy's here!"

Alice heard Bronwyn's shout, then the sound of two sets of small feet running across the wooden floors toward the door.

"Don't answer it!" she yelled after them. Standing up, she grabbed a towel and wiped the clay and water from her hands as she hurried from the room. Both kids stood in front of the door. Bronwyn bounced up and down.

"Can I answer it now?"

Alice nodded, and the girl twisted the knob. Wade's gaze dropped to her, and he grinned.

"Hi, munchkin." He picked her up and dropped a kiss on her cheek, then did the same to Henry.

Elise ran over, holding up the wooden spoon Alice gave her to play with. "Dis!"

He scooped her up and gave her a soft toss. Her deep belly laugh filled the room. Tucking her close, he kissed her blonde hair, then looked at Alice.

She couldn't do more than blink at him. Even her feet

wouldn't respond to her commands to move. They'd grown roots to the floor as her ovaries took over. The sexiest thing about Wade was how he loved his children. And that was saying something, because he was the sexiest man she'd ever met before she knew he had kids.

"You look like you've been busy."

"Huh?" *Brilliant, Alice.* She blinked and swallowed, willing her hormones away. "Oh, yeah. I've been making coffee mugs."

"She plays with mud, Daddy," Henry said.

"She does?" He looked down at the boy.

"Yep. And she said when we had more time, she'd let us play with it too."

"Oh, boy." Wade turned an amused smile on her. "You don't shy away from a mess, do you?"

Alice smiled. "Not really, no. Art's meant to be messy. It's part of what makes it fun."

"I agree." He looked away to glance at the kids. "You guys ready to head home? You all need baths and to get to bed."

Henry and Bronwyn groaned.

"Your dad's right. It's time to head home. Help me get your stuff together."

They both grumbled again, but went to pick up the few toys she'd brought with them.

Wade put Elise down and went to help the kids. Alice retreated to the kitchen to wash her hands. Once she had the clay off, she repacked the diaper bag and folded up the highchair.

"I'll take that out if you want to help Elise into her shoes."

Alice grinned. "You just don't want to wrestle her."

He laughed. "Guilty."

"Chicken." She laughed and turned away to get the toddler's shoes. Her smile turned down when she discovered they weren't where she left them. When they arrived, she'd put them by the door with Henry and Bronwyn's, the girl's socks tucked inside, but now they weren't there. Hands on her hips, she walked over and stood in front of Elise. "All right, Missy. What did you do with your shoes?"

Elise held up her spoon. "Dis!"

Alice rolled her eyes and smiled, sighing. She got down on her hands and knees. "If I were an eighteen-month-old who hated shoes, where would I hide them?"

"Alse, hi." Elise patted her head.

"Hi, sweetie. Where are your shoes? It's time for you to go home."

She banged the spoon on the coffee table and bopped to her music.

Alice huffed a laugh and looked at her siblings. "Did you see what your sister did with her shoes?"

They both shook their heads.

"Great." She glanced at Elise. "You might be going home barefoot, kid." Like she'd care, though. The toddler was happiest with nothing on her feet. Not even socks.

Alice bent down and lifted the couch skirting to look underneath, shining the flashlight on her phone into the darkness.

"What are you doing?"

She let out a soft shriek, startled, and pushed up on her hands, glancing over her shoulder. "I didn't hear you come in. I'm trying to find Elise's shoes. They were by the door, but she did something with them."

He didn't respond. Just stared at her, his eyes a bit unfocused.

"Wade?"

He blinked, and his gaze cleared. "Sorry. What were you saying?"

She frowned, wondering what that was about. Maybe his

long day was catching up to him. That thought sent her to her feet. "Elise's shoes. She hid them somewhere."

"Oh. Right. She does that. Check baskets or boxes. I usually find them in a toy basket or the urn by the front door, where I keep the umbrella."

With a nod, Alice bit her lip and glanced around the living room. Her gaze landed on the trashcan. She pointed to it and walked over. Two pink and white toddler shoes sat on top of the crumpled tissues and papers. "Found them." She reached in and fished them out. The socks were still in them.

Elise saw them and held out a pudgy hand. "Leese shoes!"

Alice lifted her off the floor and sat down on the couch, putting her in her lap. "Yes. These are your shoes. Why did you put them in the trash? They still fit you, silly." She kept up a steady stream of conversation, trying to hold the girl's attention while she slipped the socks and shoes on her feet.

"Damn. You made that look easy. Half the time, I end up tucking her foot under my arm to get them on." Wade picked up the diaper bag and the bag of toys the kids cleaned up.

Grinning, Alice stood, holding Elise. "Some people are just talented."

He laughed. "Who knew putting shoes on a toddler was a talent?" He reached for the girl, who went to him willingly. "And it's one Daddy doesn't have, right?"

"Dada." Elise patted his face.

"I'm sure you have other talents." The words registered and her brain descended into the gutter. Cheeks heating, her gaze shot to his.

A wicked smile lit his face. "Many."

Blushing harder, she turned away. "Henry. Bronwyn. Are you ready?"

They nodded, moving toward the door. She opened it, holding it open so they could file out. Their feet thudded on the steps as they ran toward the car.

"Thank you again for keeping them late." Wade stopped in the doorway.

Alice's heart rate kicked up at his nearness. She could smell his cologne. Or aftershave. Or whatever it was that made him smell so good. He needed to walk down her porch stairs and get in his car. Sexy dad was rapidly eroding her willpower.

She offered him a smile. "No problem."

He perused her face, his hazel eyes a soft gray green in the evening light. His lips parted like he wanted to say something, but he pressed his lips together and nodded. "I'll see you tomorrow."

"Yep." Through her brain fog caused by his—everything—she remembered what day tomorrow was. "Oh, and if you don't mind, I was planning to make dinner tomorrow, then follow you to the school."

His eyebrows dipped. "Why?"

"Bronwyn's play?"

He groaned. "I forgot all about that. I don't know what she's going to wear. They're supposed to come as a woodland animal. She asked me about it last week, and I said we'd come up with something. I'm amazed she hasn't reminded me."

Alice laid a hand on his arm. Her fingertips sizzled, and she lifted it away. "Don't worry about it. We've been working on her costume."

"You have?" He blew out a breath. "I don't know why I'm surprised. You seem to have a better handle on this parenting thing than I do right now."

She couldn't resist touching him again. This time, she didn't pull away when she made contact. Her hand curved over his shoulder. "Don't be so hard on yourself. You have to work to support them. And they know you love them. It's obvious. Both that you do and that they feel loved."

"I know. It's just hard. Doing it all alone."

"You're not alone. It takes a village even when there are two parents in the house."

His smile was soft. "Thank you for being a part of that village."

An answering smile lifted her mouth. She reached out to smooth Elise's hair out of her face, her smile growing as she made eye contact with the little girl. "I'm glad to be part of it." She made the mistake of looking at him again. The heat in his eyes was enough to turn her knees watery. She tried to lock them, but she swayed closer instead.

He angled closer.

"Daddy! Can we go?"

Bronwyn's shout jerked them apart. Alice stepped back and crossed her arms.

Wade cleared his throat. "I better go. See you in the morning."

She nodded, and he hurried down the steps after one last look. Blowing out a breath, she watched him cross the grass to his car. He opened the door and put Elise into her car seat, then rounded the front to get to Henry and buckle him in. Once all the kids were secure, he climbed into the driver's seat. Alice's heart raced faster than any of her brother's horses the entire time. She had a feeling it wouldn't slow down until he was out of sight.

The SUV's engine roared to life. She lifted a hand as he rolled out of the driveway. When he tooted the horn in farewell, she backed into the house and shut the door.

Her head thunked against the wood. "Oh, man." She had no idea what she was supposed to do about this crazy attraction that wasn't as one-sided as she thought. It was easy—well, easier—to ignore it when she didn't think he felt the same way. But there was no mistaking what just passed between them. Should she act on it?

She let out a huff and pushed away from the door. That

was an answer she doubted she'd figure out tonight. Getting involved with Wade could do a lot of damage to her heart if things went sour. She'd fallen for his kids. It would devastate her if she couldn't see them anymore.

Groaning, she headed for her pottery wheel. She needed to lose herself in her art and not think about the sexy firefighter and his adorable children any more tonight.

NINETEEN

The murmur of voices surrounded Wade as he stepped into the auditorium at the high school carrying Henry, so he didn't get lost in the throng. They'd dropped Bronwyn off in the cafeteria with her teacher, then headed in to find seats. He glanced back, making sure Alice was still behind him with Elise. She was, so he continued down the sloped aisle.

A waving older woman caught his attention about two-thirds of the way down. It was his mom. He smiled and headed toward her.

"Hi." She reached up and gave him a hug and kissed Henry's cheek. "We saved you some seats."

"Great."

Elise let out a yell and strained toward her grandmother, trying to launch herself from Alice's arms.

Wade took the girl from her and passed her to his mom. "Mom, Dad, you remember Alice Duvall?"

"Of course." Peg smiled at her. "It's nice to see you." She slid down the row to make room for them. "How have things been going with these little rascals?"

"Oh, fine. They're good kids."

The older woman smiled. "They are. And we miss them. Any chance we can take them off your hands soon? We're feeling much better." Peg had caught what her husband had, but now they were both healthy again.

"Sure. You just tell me when."

"Maybe early next week? I'll get your number from Wade or at church on Sunday."

"That sounds good."

"Perfect." She turned her brown eyes on her son. "I'm still taking them Saturday, though. You get them back after supper."

"That's fine. I have plenty of things I can get done around the house without them there." Like mow the grass and do some other outside things he'd been putting off. And enjoy the quiet. He might even take a nap if he had time. Elise was still working on her molars, so she'd been up and down several times a night.

"What are your plans for the weekend, Alice?" Peg asked. Elise giggled as she bounced her on her knee.

Alice smiled at the toddler. "Work on some pottery. I need to take a load into Billings and pick up another. Throw some pieces to take next week. Paint some. I won't lack for things to do."

"I'd love to see your work sometime. I love handmade pottery."

"There will be plenty of it once Sofie and I open our store. But you're welcome to come out to the ranch and look at what I have anytime you want."

"I might have to take you up on that. My sister's birthday is in a couple of weeks, and I still don't have anything for her."

"When do you move into your house, do you know?" Wade asked.

"Closing's been set for ten days from now. It passed

inspection, so I'm just waiting on all the paperwork to be finalized."

"Where are you moving to?" Bill asked, leaning forward to see around Peg and Elise.

"Next door to Wade, actually. The tan Victorian."

"That's a nice place. And a lot of house."

"I know. Most of the upstairs rooms are going to sit empty for now. I couldn't pass it up, though. The price was right, and it's just gorgeous."

Wade was happy she found a place she loved. He wasn't sure he liked that it was so close to him, though. Temptation would be right next door for potentially the rest of his life.

He glanced away, rolling his eyes at himself, unsure when he became so dramatic. Probably the moment Alice walked into his life and set his emotions into a tailspin. They were getting harder and harder to shove back into their box every day. Coming home to her in his house was starting to feel more like coming home to *her* instead of just coming home. There were days when it surprised him when she announced she was leaving. It felt like she belonged in his home.

That scared him a bit, and he didn't really know what to make of it. So he ignored it the best he could.

They chit-chatted for several more minutes before the lights dimmed. Henry climbed onto Wade's lap so he could see. Elise crawled across the empty seat to sit with Alice.

One of the teachers got on stage to welcome them all to the program, then the curtain opened, revealing all the local preschoolers dressed like creatures from the woods. He found Bronwyn quickly. Alice did an amazing job of crafting an owl costume from an oversize hooded sweatshirt and some fabric. When she lifted her arms, she had wings.

The program was cute. They danced around the stage, and a few of them, including Bronwyn, sang short solos. It was over in twenty minutes, for which he was grateful. Elise was restless, climbing down from Alice's lap, then up again. A couple of times, she tried to get in his lap, but couldn't because of her brother. She wandered down to her grandparents, too, then back again. He was glad she refrained from screeching.

When the curtain closed on the kids, they got up, merging into the line of people exiting the auditorium. Someone bumped into Alice, knocking her back. Wade reached out and took her hand, hauling her through the throng and into the hallway.

"Hi, guys."

Wade glanced to his left at the feminine voice and saw Sofie and Knox coming their way from the other door.

"Hi." He smiled. Alice echoed his greeting.

"Did you enjoy the show?" Sofie asked as the pair came up alongside them. They continued toward the cafeteria.

"It was great. Alice did an amazing job with Bronwyn's costume. Olive looked great too." Their daughter was dressed as a fox. She'd come complete with face paint and pointy ears.

"Thanks. I can't take all the credit, though. Alice helped me come up with some ideas and put it together. I can create all kinds of things with metal, but fabric escapes me."

He glanced at Alice. "When do you find time to do all this?" She not only took great care of his kids, but he'd noticed his house was a lot cleaner since she showed up.

She smiled and shrugged. "Children are portable. I just take them with me. We had a sewing session at Sofie's earlier this week."

It struck him then how much Alice needed to be a mom. She was hands on, caring, and fun. But strict when she had to be. Any child would be lucky to have her as their mother.

His eyes strayed to the toddler in her arms. She was the kind of mom his children deserved.

He frowned. Was he doing his kids a disservice by closing

himself off to relationships? Was he, by protecting his heart, keeping them from having a wonderful mother? One who would love them as her own and never abandon them? Could Alice be that woman?

She squeezed his hand. "Wade? Are you okay?"

He blinked. "What?" Her question registered. "Oh. Yes, I'm fine. Sorry. I zoned out."

She gave him a curious frown, but didn't say anything.

"Daddy!"

Bronwyn ran up, Olive on her heels, saving him from closer scrutiny. He didn't want to explain why he zoned out.

"Did you see me? Did I do good?" She came to a stop in front of him, an enormous smile on her face.

"I did." He let go of Alice's hand and smoothed it over Bronwyn's head. "And you did great." He glanced at Olive. "You all did. And you know what else I think?" He looked down at his daughter.

"What?"

"That your performance deserves a milkshake from Sarafina's."

Her eyes lit up. "Oh, boy!"

Wade grinned and looked at Sofie and Knox. "Would you all like to join us?" He turned to Alice. "You too."

"Of course." She smiled at him, then Bronwyn.

"We'd love to," Knox said, eyes on Wade.

There was a glint to them that told Wade the other man hadn't missed him holding his sister's hand.

"Oh, goody." Bronwyn walked past them all. "Come on. I want to get there before she runs out of chocolate."

Alice laughed. "I doubt she will. That's her most popular flavor, I think." But they followed her, anyway.

The crowd had thinned, so they had an easier time navigating the halls to get outside. In the parking lot, Wade glanced at Alice as he unlocked the car. "Do you want to ride with us? Save a parking space at the diner?" The words were out before he thought them through.

"Oh. Um, sure." She opened the back passenger door to put Elise in her car seat.

Wade put Henry in his, then made sure Bronwyn buckled herself properly before getting in the driver's seat. He closed the door as he settled in, immediately regretting the invitation. Her scent, something soft, like vanilla, permeated the air in the car. And she was close enough their arms would brush on the console.

Steeling himself for the ride to Sarafina's, he buckled up and started the engine, pulling out of the parking space.

Bronwyn and Henry chattered from the back seat, and Elise babbled softly to herself. He focused on the road, trying to ignore the thrum of awareness flowing through his body. The thoughts he had in the cafeteria refused to be buried. Now, all he could think about was Alice as his wife, being a mother to his kids. To *their* kids. One particular image—that of her round with his baby—played loudest in his mind. She'd be stunning. She was stunning now.

The diner came into view, and he'd never been happier to reach a destination in his life. He desperately needed the distraction. Pulling into the parking lot behind Knox's truck, he parked and cut the engine. He got out and opened Henry's door, unbuckling him. Alice had the other door open and was busy working on Elise's buckles. Bronwyn unbuckled herself and followed her brother out through his door. The group traipsed inside, Olive and Bronwyn skipping ahead.

Sara looked up as they entered, smiling when she recognized them. "Hi." A curious frown softened her smile as she took in the girls' outfits. "Why are you all dressed up?"

"School play," Knox said.

"Ah. Let me guess. It's treat time, now?"

The girls nodded.

"We're having milkshakes!" Bronwyn bounced on her feet.

"Well, you came to the right place. Why don't you go sit in the big booth in the corner, and I'll be right over to take your orders, okay?" She smiled at the girls, then glanced at the adults.

"Okay!" They took off, the adults following at a slower pace.

Wade detoured to get a highchair from the stack near the restrooms, setting it at the end of the table. Alice put Elise in it and strapped her in, scooting her forward, then handed her a toy phone from the diaper bag. She slid into the booth next to Henry.

That left the end for him. Everyone else was seated.

He said a silent prayer for strength and sat down. Heat radiated from her body, warming his arm and making the hairs on the right side of his body stand on end. Gritting his teeth, he shifted, sitting as close to the end of the bench as he could.

Sara appeared with children's place mats and crayons. She laid them in front of the older kids, then took her order pad from her apron pocket. "Okay. Milkshakes. What flavor does everyone want?"

"Chocolate!" Bronwyn thrust an arm in the air, making everyone chuckle.

"Got it." Sara smiled and wrote down the girl's order. "How about the rest of you?"

They went around the table and told her what they wanted.

"Perfect. Give me a few minutes and I'll be back."

Wade watched her leave, then kept his eyes anywhere but on the woman beside him. He couldn't get his thoughts from earlier out of his head. They bounced around his brain like a ping-pong ball, each ricochet sending ripples of awareness and what-ifs through him.

"So, Wade. Alice tells me you're a firefighter?"

Wade turned at the sound of Knox's voice. The older man's icy blue eyes pierced him from across the table, telling Wade he'd noticed their hand-holding earlier and how easy he and Alice were with each other. He sat a little straighter. "Yes. I'm both an inspector and an investigator, and I work an overnight shift at the fire station once a week."

"Busy man."

"I am, but it keeps me home at night with my kids."

Knox gave a short nod. "How long have you been a firefighter?"

"In Pine Ridge, just over a year. Before that, I lived in Tennessee and worked for the forestry service."

"Why did you move here?"

Wade felt Alice stiffen beside him. He reached a hand over and laid it on her knee, squeezing it gently to let her know it was okay, then lifted his hand. "My wife left. This is where I'm from, so the kids and I came home."

Knox's eyes darted to Bronwyn and Henry, who were busy coloring on the children's place mats and talking to each other, then at Elise, who played with her plastic phone. Wade could see in his eyes that he didn't want to upset the kids.

"His parents own the feed store," Sofie told him, changing the subject.

"Bill's your dad?"

Wade nodded.

"I guess I see the resemblance now. I didn't know his last name. Do you have any siblings?"

"Two brothers—one older, one younger—and an older sister. They've all moved away."

"No one's taking over the feed store when your parents retire?"

"I can see my older brother Andy coming back. He's a sales manager for a seed company." He shrugged. "It might end up being me. Who knows? We all worked for them at some point, so any of us could step in. But dad's not ready to retire. Mom says he'll work until he's dead." He smiled. His dad enjoyed what he did. It kept him involved in the community. The man was a social butterfly.

"What about your mom? What does she do?"

"She taught kindergarten until she retired a couple of years ago. Now she does the books for the store and bothers dad." He smiled.

The others chuckled.

"You know, I wonder if she'd do ours for our store?" Alice nodded to Sofie. "Math is not my thing."

"Mine either." Sofie wrinkled her nose.

"You can ask her," Wade said. "But I don't think she'd mind."

"I will. Maybe she can come over for lunch one day next week. I know she said they want to take the kids for a day, but I'm betting they'd love to have her visit too."

Wade was both happy and worried that Alice and his mother got along well enough to be willing to spend time alone together without him. Emily never wanted to. She and his mom just tolerated each other.

"Did you two decide on a name for the store?" Knox asked.

"We haven't talked about it too much." Sofie glanced at him.

They'd bandied about a few names, but hadn't settled on one yet. "We're circulating a few."

"Like what?" Wade asked.

"The big two are Pine Ridge Artisan Gift Shop and Homespun Arts," Alice answered.

Elise dropped her toy phone. The clatter of it hitting the floor echoed through the restaurant.

"I like the last one." Wade bent over to pick it up, handing it back to his daughter. She banged it on the table, then punched some buttons.

"I do too." Sofie smiled at him. "I think that's the one we're leaning toward."

Alice nodded. "I agree. We'll have to decide for sure soon. We need to order bags and business cards, not to mention the sign for out front."

Sofie nodded. "And get the social media going."

Alice groaned and wrinkled her nose. "You're going to do that, right? I hate that stuff."

Giggling, Sofie shook her head. "We have to share it. Or hire someone."

"I vote for that."

"Vote for what?" Sara stopped next to Knox with a tray of milkshakes.

"To hire someone to handle the social media for our new store." Alice took the chocolate shake Sara held out and gave it to Bronwyn.

"What about Jasper's sister, Megan?" Sara passed the rest of the milkshakes around. "She's only twenty, so that stuff is right up her alley. And she was going to work for me this summer, but since she buggered up her ankle in that accident she had, she can't wait tables. I bet she'd love to help."

"That's not a bad idea," Knox said, glancing at his wife.

Sofie nodded. "Okay. I'll talk to her, if that's okay with you, Alice?"

Alice shrugged and peeled the wrapper off of Henry's straw and put it in his drink. "It's fine by me. I'll happily pay someone so I don't have to create content and manage the feeds."

Wade dunked his straw into his vanilla shake and took a drink, listening to the exchange. He liked seeing his town grow. He'd never really wanted to move away, but did so for the sake of Emily's career. It was nice to see younger people wanting to stay and not just work, but open businesses.

The group chatted and laughed while they drank their shakes. By the time they finished, Henry and Elise were both wilting. He hoped Elise didn't descend into angry toddler mode when he tried to put her to bed. It was past her bedtime.

"Are you ready to go?" Wade asked Alice. "I need to get the kids home."

She glanced at Elise and smiled at the girl, whose hazel eyes stared back between slow blinks. "Yes."

Wade slid from the booth, smiling at Knox and Sofie. "We're going to head out. Elise is ready to face-plant on the table."

Sofie chuckled. "I noticed. We should get going too." She looked at Knox, who nodded.

They all exited the booth and headed for the door, stopping long enough to pay their bill. Outside, he and Alice said goodbye to the Duvalls, then fastened the kids into the car. In minutes, they were on their way back to the school to drop Alice off at her car.

Her sweet scent permeated the car again. Wade cracked a window, glad it was warm enough outside that he could. He glanced over. She was resting against the seat, looking at the scenery.

"Thanks for coming tonight." His quiet voice broke through the sound of the wind coming through the open window. "It was nice not having to wrangle them all on my own."

She looked at him and smiled. "Oh, you're welcome. I wouldn't have missed it. And I was happy to help with the kids." She gave him a pointed look. "Off the clock."

He chuckled. "You're determined to not let me pay you, aren't you?"

Alice flashed him another smile, but said nothing.

Wade shook his head. Stubborn woman. He was still writing her a check when her time with them ended. If she didn't take it, he'd give it to Knox and tell him to deposit it into his sister's bank account.

The drive to the school was a short one, and he soon pulled into the lot, parking next to her car. Alice unfastened her seat belt.

"I'll see you in the morning." She twisted in her seat to look at the kids. "You guys be good for your dad, okay? Go right to bed for him."

Bronwyn nodded. Henry's nod was much sleepier. Elise only mustered up a long blink.

She chuckled and glanced at Wade. "Hopefully, you won't have much trouble. Two of the three are already almost asleep."

"Yeah. It's a good thing I don't have very far to go."

"For sure. I've had to wake Elise up from a nap to go somewhere. It's not fun. She's awake and doesn't want to be, but slept just enough to not be tired anymore."

That's what he was afraid would happen if she fell asleep before they got home.

Alice pulled on the door handle. "I'll let you get out of here. Goodnight."

"Goodnight. Be careful driving back to the Stone Creek in the dark."

She nodded as she climbed out of the car. "I will." Shutting the door, she walked to her car.

Wade watched her get in, then followed her out of the parking lot. He honked his horn and turned into his neighborhood while she continued on the main road to get to the highway that would take her home.

His jaw worked as their paths diverged. He didn't want her to go.

TWENTY

The vacuum left trails in the living room rug as Wade ran it over the surface. Pounding on the door, loud enough to be heard over the sweeper, drew his attention. He flipped the switch on the handle, silencing the machine, and went to answer the door.

When he opened it, his eyes widened. "Alice. Hi. What are you doing here?"

"I think I left my sketchbook upstairs in the spare room. I know you're probably busy—I heard the vacuum—but do you mind if I go look quick?"

Wade stepped back and motioned her inside. "Of course not."

She smiled and stepped over the threshold. "Thanks. I'll be fast, I promise."

He waved a hand. "Take your time. It's not like I'm eager to get back to cleaning."

She chuckled as she walked toward the stairs, where she paused. "You realize I cleaned pretty much everything this week? Including the rugs."

He huffed. Was she serious? "For real?"

She nodded.

Wade groaned and looked at the ceiling. "I knew things didn't seem as dirty." He glanced back down to see her staring at him with wide eyes.

"Did you really spend the day cleaning the house?"

"Not all day, but the last hour or so, yeah. Before that, I fixed the piece of flashing coming off the chimney, planted some flowers, put mulch down, and mowed the grass."

A quick laugh slid past her lips. "Is that how you normally spend a kid-free Saturday?"

"Trust me, it's easier to do all that without them around." He shrugged. "But what else would I do? I don't have much interest in going to the movies by myself. Some days, I build something, though."

"Like what?" A curious frown pulled her eyebrows down.

He shrugged again. "Tables. Dog houses. Benches. Usually, they're gifts for family and friends."

"Wait. The patio furniture out back. Did you make all that?"

Wade nodded.

"Wow. It's really nice. I'm impressed."

"Thanks." Embarrassment made his cheeks color. He wasn't used to praise for his woodworking. It was just a hobby. Most of the pieces he made were received well, but for some reason, her praise felt different.

"You're welcome." She hooked a thumb toward the stairs. "I better go see if I left that sketchbook here."

"Do you want some help?"

"No. I think I remember where it is. I'll be right back." She turned and hurried up the stairs.

Wade spun away from the sight of her butt flexing beneath her navy-blue leggings as she moved. Shaking his head at himself and his wayward libido, he walked over to the vacuum and unplugged it, wrapping up the cord. No point in finishing if she just did it.

Alice's footsteps on the stairs made him turn. She came into view, holding a large spiral-bound book.

"You found it."

"Yeah. I was working on some drawings when I was here Tuesday night of some pots I want to make, and I put it on the floor when I went to sleep. I must have kicked it under the bed and forgot about it until I needed it. I thought I'd put it back in my bag, but I didn't. I had to rough sketch the designs for the art gallery owner who wanted to see them."

"Art gallery?"

She nodded. "The place I've been taking my unfinished pottery to in Billings showed them to her friend who owns the gallery. He asked if I would make some pieces for them to sell. I wanted to show him what I was thinking."

"Alice, that's great."

She smiled. "Yeah. It's a small place, but it's still exciting. I've never had anything in a gallery before."

"You should celebrate."

She laughed softly. "By myself?"

"Why not?" He grinned. "Or you could celebrate with your brother. I bet he's proud of you." *He* was proud of her. "Or," he held up a finger, "I have beer in the fridge. It's a nice evening. We could sit out back and toast your success."

A quick widening of her eyes gave away her surprise at his invitation. Wade did his best to hide his own. The words just popped out before he had a chance to process them. He didn't take them back, though. He wanted to spend time with her.

"Oh." Her gaze darted past him, then she met his eyes again and smiled. "You know, that sounds really nice."

"Yeah?"

She nodded. "Yeah."

"Okay, well, let's go get that beer."

Her pretty smile drew one from him. He motioned her to precede him from the living room. Wade followed her down the hall, stopping to put the vacuum in the closet. Walking over to the fridge, he took out two craft brews. Alice grabbed the bottle opener from the silverware drawer and handed it to him. He popped the tops off, passing the opener back to her. She put it away, then followed him outside.

Wade sank into a patio chair. Alice sat down beside him, and he handed her a beer bottle, then lifted his and took a drink.

"I love your yard."

He glanced over. "Yeah? Me too. It was one of the selling points of this house. It's perfect for the kids."

She nodded. "I need to look into a fence for my house."

"Everything still on track for closing?"

"Yes. I'm excited to get moved in."

"Is the fence the only change you want to make?"

"No. I need to update the heating and air system. It needs a new electrical box, too, and I want to paint the exterior." She took a drink of her beer.

He grinned. "Not a fan of the brown on brown?"

She scrunched her nose. "No. I want to paint it a slate color with white and trim and an olive-green door."

"That'll look nice."

She nodded. "I think so. Was this house already navy blue when you bought it?"

"Yes. All I painted was the front door. It was white, and I wanted something that stood out a little more, so I went with yellow."

"It looks great."

"Thanks." He took another sip of his beer and stared out over the yard. "The kids will be happy to have you close still once Shelby comes back."

"I'll be glad too. I'm going to miss not being with them all the time."

In truth, he wished she could be. Shelby was a great sitter, and the kids loved her, but she wasn't Alice. There was just something about the way she interacted with them that made her fit in with their family like she belonged. If she didn't already have a job, he'd strongly consider making a change to his babysitting arrangements.

But that would also mean she'd stay off-limits to him. He wasn't so sure he wanted it to be that way anymore.

"So, Henry mentioned his birthday is coming up."

"Yep." Wade cleared his throat as his brain shifted gears. "In a couple weeks. I need to get his party organized." He frowned. "I should probably have done that already."

"Oh, let me do it." She leaned forward, her expression eager.

He arched an eyebrow. "You sure? I was just going to get a cake and some dinosaur decorations. He wanted to invite a few of his friends."

"Totally sure. I already have some ideas. It'll be something that will keep them all busy now that Bronwyn's out of school."

"I still can't believe she'll be in kindergarten next year." He shook his head. "Time flies."

Alice smiled. "It does. But each stage offers something new to be appreciated."

He glanced at her. "How did you get so wise for someone without any children?"

Her smile grew. "Teaching. I see quite a range in my classroom every day. From kindergartners all the way through fifth grade. Each age offers something special to be appreciated."

Wade brought his bottle up to his mouth. "I suppose that's true." He took a drink. "So tell me more about this art gallery thing. Do you have any ideas for what you're going to contribute?"

Her mouth twisted. "Some. It's not really a place to show off tableware, which is generally what I do, but I've done more decorative stuff before. I make a lot of vases, so I think I'll do one of those. I'll probably make a decorative bowl as well. Something you can set on a table and put things in."

"Like a dish for keys?"

"No. More like something for a dining table you would put other decorations in to make a centerpiece."

"Oh." He nodded. "That makes sense for a gallery."

"That's what I thought. I just have to decide on colors, though."

"Blue is always good."

She smiled at him. "Is that your favorite color?"

He grinned back. "Yes."

Alice chuckled. "It's a good accent color for interiors. I was thinking that or some teals and browns. I don't think I can go wrong with either."

Wade held up his hands. "Don't look at me. My sister and mom helped me pick out decorations and paint colors for this place. I gave them a budget and a general idea of what I like, and they went wild."

"Well, they have nice taste."

"Agreed." Wade raised his bottle and took another drink. He liked his home and the furnishings his mom and sister picked out. It was comfortable and kid-friendly.

Alice took another sip of her drink and slouched some in her seat, looking out at the yard. Birds flitted from bush to bush, and a squirrel chattered in the tree. Wade closed his eyes for a brief moment, savoring the breeze. The warm weather was nice.

"You know, we probably should have celebrated with water or soda. I still have to drive back to the ranch."

He frowned. "Sorry. I didn't think about that when I offered." He'd wanted to celebrate her news, then he'd been too flummoxed by his offer to think about the fact she still had a half hour drive home.

"I didn't, either." She shrugged. "I guess I'm hanging out in town for a while. Maybe I'll walk downtown and get dinner at Sarafina's."

"How about you stay here? I was going to throw a steak on the grill, but I can just as easily throw on two." Why did these invitations keep coming out of his mouth? He might be thinking about dating in a new light, but that didn't mean he was ready to start something. His brain had other ideas, though, it seemed.

"Oh, um, yes?"

He arched an eyebrow, one side of his mouth lifting. "You don't sound too sure."

A rueful smile stretched across her face. "You took me by surprise. We don't really spend time together without the kids."

Wade nodded. "I think I'd like to change that."

Her eyes went wide, and Wade's heart beat a little faster. Man, his brain was really getting ahead of itself today.

But he didn't take it back. Regardless of whether he'd thought it through, it felt right. So he held her gaze and waited.

Twenty-One

Alice studied Wade across the table. Her mind whirled as she processed his statement. Did he mean what she thought he did? Judging by the way he stared back at her, it appeared he did. Her heart thudded in her chest. Did she want to change their relationship too? She was attracted to him—more than any other man she'd ever met. But what happened to her relationship with his kids if they started dating? And she'd be living next door. If things went sour, they'd still be stuck in close quarters. Could she handle seeing him every day, but not getting to be with him and the kids?

She gave herself a hard mental slap. Why was she acting like it wouldn't work out? Saying yes today could be the best decision she ever made and could set her up for a lifetime of happiness.

It was that thought that made the decision for her. She couldn't live with the what-ifs and regrets if she said no. Whatever happened after this point, happened. But she wanted it to happen. To see what could become of the what-ifs.

"I think I'd like that too."

He sucked in a breath, then offered her a bright smile. "Okay. Great. That's great."

Alice chuckled.

Wade chuckled. "I'm really rusty at dating." He held up a hand and shook his head, his smile turning rueful. "I promise I won't always be awkward."

She laughed. "It's okay. I'm not that practiced at it, either."

"Which I still don't get. The men in Colorado must be idiots."

She felt a blush creep over her cheeks. "It's more a lack of options. And I refuse to settle for just okay. Not when it comes to the rest of my life."

He pulled in a deep breath, holding her gaze. "I won't either. Especially not with my kids involved." He took another shaky breath. "I have to admit, Alice, I never intended to get involved with anyone again. I thought Emily was it for me. I fell in love with her, knowing how she was. I don't think either of us realized that having children would affect her the way it did. She loves them, but she lost some of her independence when the kids came along. We both did. To me, that wasn't a bad thing. It's just the way it is when you have children. It was worth it to me. I thought it was to her too." A small frown formed between his eyebrows.

Something he said pushed its way to the forefront of her mind. "Do you still love her?" Because that could be a deal-breaker for Alice. She wouldn't compete with a woman who clearly didn't want to be part of her family.

"In a way, I think I always will, but I'm not in love with her anymore, no. She's the mother of my children, and she was my first love. There will always be a part of me that cares about her because of that."

Alice could understand that. And it told her something about Wade. When he cared, he cared deeply. She needed to be prepared to be loved for the rest of her life—no matter the outcome of their relationship. It was a nice thought, actually, to know there would always be someone out there—besides her family—who would care about her and think of her from time to time.

He leaned over and took her hand. "I'm a one-woman man, Alice. If I still loved Emily, another woman wouldn't even be on my radar."

She swallowed around the lump in her throat that formed at the intensity in his eyes. "Good to know."

He squeezed her hand, then let go. "Enough of the heavy talk." He stood up. "How about we get those steaks going?"

Alice looked up at him with a sweet smile. "Sounds good." She stood, setting her half-finished bottle on the table, and followed him inside.

Conversation flowed easily between them as they made dinner together and ate it on the back patio. She learned he loved steak, but hated shrimp. That they both preferred beer to wine. And neither of them liked asparagus. She also learned he had a serious addiction to vanilla swirl ice cream. When he pulled it out from the depths of the freezer after dinner, she had to laugh.

"I didn't even know that was in there."

"I hide it, so Bronwyn and Henry don't find it when they get popsicles."

Alice laughed. "Wise man." She leaned back against the counter and braced her hands on either side of herself as she watched him get out two bowls and the ice cream scoop.

"Unfortunately, it was a lesson learned the hard way." He popped the top off the ice cream. "Wyn saw it once not long after we moved in and wouldn't stop pestering me about it. Henry heard and added his two cents and suddenly, I no longer had any ice cream." He grinned at her and scooped ice cream into the bowls.

"So, how do you get away with having it now?"

"Once that carton ran out, I told them I only bought it on occasion. It's a total lie." He waved the scoop, then set it in the sink. "I buy it all the time."

Laughing, Alice turned and took two spoons from the drawer. She held one up to him. "Well, here's to secret ice cream and the joy it brings."

He grinned and took the spoon, tapping it to hers. "Hear, hear." He handed her a bowl.

"Speaking of the kids, when will they be back?" She leaned against the counter again.

Wade glanced at the clock on the microwave. "Another hour or so. Mom usually brings them back in time for a bath before bed."

Alice dipped her spoon into her ice cream and looked at him through her lashes. "Do you mind if I stay and help?" Her voice was soft. She didn't want to overstep or push things faster than either of them was ready for, but she wanted to be there when they got home. Any relationship she had with Wade would include his children. And they'd already come to mean a lot to her. She genuinely liked spending time with them.

"I don't mind. Do you mind the third-degree you're going to get from my mom?"

Alice tipped her head and took another bite of her ice cream. "I think the bigger question is, are we?"

His eyes widened a fraction, but then he shrugged. "I'd rather get it out in the open that we're exploring whatever this is between us than sneak around like teenagers and hide it."

She grinned, scooping up more of her creamy treat. "I don't know. Could be fun. Secret rendezvouses behind the oak tree, stolen kisses in the coat closet." She shrugged and ate the bite on her spoon.

Wade's eyes took on a heat she hadn't seen before. He set

his bowl on the counter and stepped closer. "Stolen kisses, huh?"

Alice swallowed the ice cream in her mouth. The cold feel of it as it slid down her throat did little to dampen the fire flaring to life in her blood as she stared back at him.

He edged closer, his head lowering toward hers. "Do they have to be stolen?"

Her heart rate increasing, she floated on a cloud as she gazed into his hazel eyes. Mesmerized by the flecks of blue and gold in them, she failed to answer his question.

His arm went around her waist. Taking her bowl from her hands, he set it next to his. "So, do they?"

She laid her hands on his chest, curving her palms over the firm muscles. "No."

Those beautiful eyes turned a dusky slate green, and he dipped his head. She felt his warm breath fan over her lips a moment before they sealed over hers.

Millions of tiny explosions went off inside her body. A soft moan escaped her, and she ran her hands up his chest and over his shoulders to tangle in his hair, kissing him back. He tightened his arms around her waist, tucking her closer to his muscled frame. His large hands roved over her hips and back, leaving a trail of need in his wake. Alice wanted to feel them on her bare skin. She wanted to feel *his* bare skin.

The bang of the front door, then the sound of little feet running on the hardwood floors, broke through the lust fog in her brain. She and Wade jerked apart, staring at each other for a moment, chests heaving.

"Daddy?" Bronwyn's voice carried through the house from the living room.

Wade cleared his throat. "In the kitchen."

Alice swallowed, looking away as she composed herself. She ran a hand over her face and through her hair. When she glanced back at Wade, her eyes widened. His hair was a mess, thanks to her fingers. She stepped closer, reaching for it.

"What are you doing?" He took her hands in his.

"Fixing your hair." If someone had asked her before this evening if she thought it was long enough to muss, she'd have said no. She'd have been proven wrong, because it was sticking up in several directions.

He let go of her and lifted a hand to his head, smoothing down the strands just as the kids burst through the door. They skidded to a halt as they saw her.

"Alice!" Bronwyn's pause was momentary. She launched herself across the room to give Alice a hug.

A wave of love crashed over Alice as she hugged the girl back. "Hey, kiddo. Did you have fun at grandma and grandpas?"

"Yep." Bronwyn leaned back. "They took us to the park, and we made lasagna for dinner."

"Oh, that sounds yummy." She smiled at the girl, bending down to pick up Henry and give him a squeeze before setting him on the floor.

"Speaking of your grandparents, where are they?" Wade glanced around with a frown.

"Grandma came in with us. Grandpa was getting the car seats out of the car. Hey!" Bronwyn's gaze landed on the bowls of ice cream. "Did you have ice cream?"

Alice smothered a smile and looked at Wade.

"Um." He looked at her, pleading for help.

She covered her mouth and shook her head.

He glanced down at his daughter. "We did, yes. Alice brought it."

Alice narrowed her eyes at him over her hand. The rat. Throwing her under the bus. She stifled another smile. She honestly didn't mind. But she couldn't let that slide.

Grin growing wicked, she looked at Bronwyn. "I did. And there's plenty more in the freezer."

Bronwyn cheered, drowning out Wade's soft groan.

"What's all the excitement about?" Peg walked into the room, carrying Elise. "Oh. Alice, hello." She smiled. "What are you doing here?" Her gaze roamed around the room, taking in the dishes in the sink. "Did you two have dinner together?" Surprise colored her voice. She turned wide eyes on her son.

Wade nodded. "We were just having dessert when you arrived. Why are you so early?"

His question distracted her from the others that Alice could see she wanted to ask. She shifted the toddler in her arms, lifting her higher on her hip. "Elise seemed more tired than usual. And she's been crabby today. I think she's getting sick."

"What?" Wade frowned and walked over to take the girl from his mom. Elise burrowed her face into her father's shoulder and popped her thumb in her mouth. He looked up at Alice with concern in his hazel eyes.

Alice pushed away from the counter and walked to his side. "Does she feel warm?"

He kissed the girl's forehead. "No." He dipped his head to look into his daughter's face. "What's the matter, sweetie?"

She blinked up at him with her large hazel eyes and said nothing.

"Are your teeth bothering you again? Can Daddy feel?" He slid his index finger into her mouth.

"I checked her gums, but didn't feel anything," Peggy said.

"I don't, either." Wade withdrew his finger.

"I'll go get the thermometer and start her a bath. We can put her to bed. Maybe she just needs some extra sleep." Alice patted the girl's back, glancing at Wade.

He nodded. "Yeah."

Smiling softly, Alice hurried out of the room.

Twenty-Two

Wade leaned against the doorjamb to Elise's room and watched Alice rock the girl as she read a story. His daughter clutched a stuffed llama and sucked her thumb as she listened. Her eyelids drooped, but she resisted the pull of sleep.

His heart flip-flopped in his chest as he watched them. He wasn't sure how it happened, but in just a couple of short weeks, Alice Duvall had become an integral part of their lives. His children adored her, especially Elise. After they checked her temperature—which was normal—they took her upstairs for a bath, then put her into her pajamas. Wade sat down with her to read her a book, but she'd squirmed and squalled and reached for Alice. Once they traded places, Elise calmed down and was now almost asleep. After shaking his head, he'd left her to it and helped Wyn and Henry get ready for bed. They were downstairs now, watching a cartoon while he checked on Alice and Elise.

The toddler's eyes finally closed and stayed closed. Alice's voice trailed off, and she closed the book, setting it on the shelf. Elise sighed and snuggled deeper into Alice's arms, her thumb falling free of her mouth as she relaxed into sleep. Carefully, Alice stood and walked over to the small bed. Wade pushed away from the doorjamb to help. He pulled back the purple and white blanket to reveal the soft gray sheets.

"Sleep tight, sweet girl." Alice pressed a kiss to Elise's temple, then laid her on the bed.

Wade drew the covers over her and bent to give her a kiss. He took Alice's hand and led her from the room, closing the door behind them.

In the hall, Alice glanced at him with a soft smile. "That was easy."

He returned her smile and tucked a strand of blonde hair behind her ear. "Yeah. She likes you." It seemed he wasn't the only one taken in by Alice's charm and beauty.

"I'm glad."

His smiled widened, and he pulled her close. "Me too." Wade pressed a tender kiss to the top of her head as he tucked her under his arm and turned toward the stairs. "Want to help me wrangle the other two? Then we can dish up two more bowls of ice cream, since we didn't get to finish it earlier."

She chuckled, pulling back to take his hand as they walked down the stairs. "That sounds good." She glanced at him. "So, did your parents say anything when I left you alone to get the thermometer?"

Wade blew out a breath. "Sort of. Mom just smiled at me and told me it was about time I found someone worthy. Dad looked at her and asked what she was talking about."

Alice laughed. "Did either of you enlighten him?"

"Mom patted his arm and said she'd explain later."

They reached the bottom of the stairs and turned into the living room.

"Did they go home?" Alice glanced around the room.

He nodded. "Yeah. Dad hooked the car seats back up in my car, then they left." He turned to the kids seated on the couch watching television. Henry's eyes drooped. "Come on, you two. Time for bed."

"Can we watch the rest, Daddy?" Bronwyn turned her dark eyes on him. She didn't look the least bit tired.

He leaned over the back of the couch and picked up Henry. The boy sagged against him and yawned. Wade looked at Wyn. "Did you brush your teeth like I asked you to?"

She nodded.

"Let me see."

She bared her teeth. They looked clean.

"Okay. Alice and I will be right back."

She spun around, already engrossed in the show again. A corner of Wade's mouth tilted, and he shook his head before heading for the stairs with Henry.

Upstairs, he put the boy in his bed, tucking the covers around him. "You get some sleep, Hen."

He yawned again. "Okay, Daddy." He stretched his arms up for a hug.

Wade pressed a kiss to the boy's cheek. "Goodnight, bud."

"Night-night." He yawned again and looked at Alice, holding his arms up.

She leaned in and gave him a hug. "Goodnight, Henry. I'll see you at church, okay?"

He nodded. "M'kay."

Alice tucked the blanket around his shoulders and smoothed his hair back. "Sleep tight."

His eyes fluttered closed. Wade and Alice backed away, closing the door as they left.

"You ready for round three?" He smiled at her as they headed for the stairs.

She gave him a half smile. "No. She's going to be harder. I don't think she's sleepy."

"I think you're right."

At the bottom, they turned into the living room.

Bronwyn poked her head over the couch, a frown on her face. "Do I have to go to bed?"

Wade walked over to her and picked her up, giving her a soft toss into the air, making her giggle. "Tell you what—how about Alice and I tuck you in, then you can look at your books for a bit on your own?" He settled her on his hip, then wagged a finger at her. "But you have to stay in your room. Deal?"

The girl's head bobbed once. "Deal." She held up a pinkie.

Grinning, he hooked his pinkie through her hers and placed a smacking kiss on her cheek. She giggled again as the three of them headed for the stairs.

It didn't take long to get Bronwyn settled in her room. Alice drew back her bedcovers and made sure she had all her stuffed animals while Wade helped her find some books. They tucked her into her blankets with a pile of them on her nightstand.

"Are you all set?" Wade propped his fists on her mattress, bending close to her.

"Yep." She smiled up at him.

"Good." He kissed her temple, then straightened, snapping on the lamp next to her bed. "Don't stay up too long. Look at your books, then turn off the light and go to sleep, okay?"

She nodded.

Alice stepped forward to give the girl a goodnight kiss. "I'll see you at church tomorrow." She tapped Bronwyn's nose, and the girl smiled. "Goodnight, sweetie."

"Goodnight." She opened her book.

Wade headed for the door, Alice right behind him. "Remember, not too long."

"Okay, Daddy."

Smiling, he waited for Alice to leave the room, then turned off her overhead light and closed the door.

"That was easier than I thought it would be. Nice bargaining skills, Dad."

"I really want that ice cream."

Giggling, Alice turned toward the stairs. "Last one there has to scoop."

With a laugh, he hurried after her.

Twenty-Three

At the knock on his office door, Wade looked up. Katy Lattimer pushed the door wide and stepped inside.

"Hey, Sheriff. What brings you here?"

"I have an update for you on the arson case."

"Oh?" It had been just over a week since they talked to Willard in Billings. He sat forward and motioned to the chair in front of his desk, eager to hear what she had to say. "Have a seat."

She sat down, adjusting her gear belt. "So, I talked to both Rister and Hughes. Neither of them has an alibi for any of the fires."

Wade's eyes widened. "How can that be?"

She shrugged. "They both live alone. Levi's never been married and Ed got divorced just before the first fire. But I also can't place either of them at the scene."

"Did the lab reports come back yet?"

"Just on the fuel used. It was gasoline. They're still processing everything else."

His mouth flattened. That they were backlogged didn't

surprise him. The crime lab was as short-staffed as the sheriff's department. "Do you have any other suspects?"

She shook her head. "Not really. Willard gave me the names of a few business contacts who'd like to see him ruined, but none of them are local." With a huff, she sat back and crossed her arms.

Wade arched an eyebrow as he studied her. "That little bit of news warranted you coming down here? You could have passed it all on through an email or a phone call. What's wrong?"

A muscle in her jaw ticked, and she glanced away for a moment. When her eyes met his again, they glittered, hard, in the overhead lights.

"Something about this case bothers me. I need a sounding board, and I can't talk to Ray because his brother is one of my suspects, so here I am."

"Okay." He sat forward. "What about it bothers you?"

She dropped her arms and sat up. "All the fires have been at either vacant properties or in places where they wouldn't hurt anyone, except for the fire where the electrician was present."

"Right."

"That's the one that bugs me. How did the arsonist not know he was there? They poured gasoline all over the place. It's not like they doused the back door, lit it on fire, then left. They walked around and through the house."

She had a good point. "Have you looked into the electrician's background?"

Katy pointed a finger at him. "You're a sharp tack. I need you in my department as a detective. And yes. Vincent Perabo did five years in the Colorado State Penitentiary for involuntary manslaughter and has been out just over a year."

His eyes grew wide. "Whoa."

"Yeah."

"So maybe this isn't about Willard at all."

"That's what I'm wondering. I've got a request in to the Gunnison PD to get the case file for his arrest and another in with the Gunnison County prosecutor's office for the trial transcript. I'm hoping it'll give me a direction to go in. I visited Perabo in the hospital, but once I started asking questions about his past, he clammed up and asked me to leave. Said it was all behind him and that he didn't want to talk about it."

"Damn. That would be the quickest way to get a lead too."

She nodded. "Yep. But he's not talking."

Wade frowned, wondering if there was more to that story than just painful memories. "Okay, so say this is about Perabo. Why have all the buildings been Willard's?"

"Not sure. Maybe we have a smart arsonist who's trying to throw the blame elsewhere. Maybe he's got something against Willard, too, and wants to kill two birds with one stone. It could be pure coincidence, though I find that unlikely."

So did he. But the other two? Both of those were valid theories. "I agree." He drummed his fingers on the desk once. "Where does that leave us, though?"

She sighed. "With too many damn questions. And I was only partially kidding about needing you as a detective. I know you're under the purview of the fire department, but you're a sworn officer of the law, right?"

Wade nodded.

"Perfect. Do you mind expanding your duties for this case?"

"No. I'd like to be as involved as I can be. I want to catch this guy before someone else gets hurt."

She smiled. "I was hoping you'd say that. I could really use the help since Ray can't touch this case. Do you think you could do a search for other arson fires in the Gunnison area that are similar to the ones here? Go back to before Perabo went to prison. I looked at his rap sheet, and he doesn't have any record of arson, but that doesn't mean he wouldn't be listed as a witness in another case."

"Sure. How far back do you want me to search?"

"Two years before his arrest? Just do Gunnison County for now. Once I get more information on his manslaughter case and find out a little more about him, we can expand or shrink the scope as necessary."

His head bobbed once. "Sounds good."

"Wonderful, thank you." She stood, rounding her chair, then paused to look back when she reached the door. "Do you have a sidearm?"

Wade blinked once with surprise. "Yes, but I rarely wear it."

"You might want to start." She glanced away, that muscle ticking in her jaw again, then looked back. "I don't like this case, Wade. Something doesn't feel right. Just be careful."

A wrinkle formed between his eyes, but he nodded. "I will."

"Good. Once I know more about Perabo, I'll be back."

"Okay. Thanks, Sheriff."

She nodded, then left.

Wade sat back in his chair and steepled his hands, resting his chin atop his fingertips as he stared out the window. Katy's nerves made him nervous. One thing he'd learned about their new sheriff was that she didn't allow emotion to rule her decisions. She approached the job with calm and level-headed thinking. For her to have such reservations about this case gave him pause. He intended to heed her warning. The handgun he kept locked in the safe in his closet would start coming with him to work.

His children's faces flashed through his mind. He hoped for their sakes he didn't need it.

Shoving his disturbing thoughts aside, he sat up and logged into his computer. He opened the criminal database and searched for arson fires in Colorado, limiting his search to Gunnison and the surrounding area. Finding several, he read through the details, jotting down the names of the departments and the email contacts and phone numbers for each. He fired off emails to them, requesting information on the fires, then shut down his computer. His first inspection of the day was in twenty minutes.

Gathering file folders with information on the properties he was supposed to inspect this afternoon, he shoved them and his clipboard with his inspection checklist into his briefcase and left.

The rest of his day passed quickly. After his last inspection, he went back to his office and wrote up the reports. Only one property failed inspection, but the fixes weren't difficult. He'd go back next week.

Before he left, he checked his email again. Several of the departments he emailed had gotten back to him. He glanced through the information they sent, but none of the properties listed Willard as the owner or Perabo as a witness or victim.

Wade sighed and shut down the system. Of course it couldn't be that easy.

Grabbing his briefcase, he locked his office and headed home, doing his best to push thoughts of work behind him. Knowing Alice and the kids waited for him made that easier.

Their bright, cheery smiles flashed through his mind, making him grin as he climbed into his SUV. He wondered if he could talk Alice into staying for dinner. Most nights now, she stayed and ate with them. One day soon, he hoped he didn't have to watch her walk out the door in the evening to go home.

But he was getting ahead of himself. They were a long way

from moving in together. Especially since she just bought the house next door.

Pine Ridge was small, and he was home in just a few minutes. As he turned into the drive, he frowned as he saw his mom's car instead of Alice's parked in the driveway. Wade pulled into the garage, then gathered his things and went inside.

When he opened the front door, he heard the kids talking in the kitchen. Following the sound, he entered the room to see them seated at the island while his mom stood in front of the stove.

She glanced up when he entered. "Hi, honey."

"Hey, Mom. What are you doing here? Where's Alice?"

"She had to leave. Sofie wasn't feeling well and Knox wanted to take her to the hospital to get checked out. She went home to watch Olive."

"Oh." He frowned. "Is Sofie okay?"

"I'm sure she'll be fine. Alice said she's been getting sick with some stomach virus and couldn't keep anything down. With her pregnancy, they were worried about the baby." She waved a hand. "Anyway, Alice called and asked if I could come stay with the kids so you wouldn't have to drive all the way up to the Stone Creek to pick them up later. She actually just left about half an hour ago."

Wade nodded, then wandered over to give each kid a kiss on top of their heads in greeting. Elise waved a wooden spoon, banging it on her highchair, and Bronwyn gave him a quick grin, then went back to coloring. Henry, though, wrapped his arms around Wade's neck and started chattering.

"Guess what Miss Alice and I did, Daddy?"

"What did you do?"

"We got lots of dine-saur stuff."

"You did?"

"Yep! Plates and cups and napkins. And balloons! And she said she's making a pi-nada."

"A piñata, huh? Let me guess. It'll be a dinosaur?"

Henry nodded, his little head whipping up and down. "A ter-dactal."

Wade ruffled his son's hair and pressed a kiss to his head. "Good deal, bud." He disentangled himself from Henry's arms and straightened, looking at his mom. "So, what are you making?"

"Minestrone. The kids asked for soup for dinner, and Alice already had it started." A sly smile tilted one side of her face. "Bronwyn said she stays for supper every night."

"She does, yes."

Peg's smile widened. "I'm glad. She's a nice woman, and you deserve to be happy. I think she's done that for you. I see a light in your eyes that hasn't been there in a long time."

He returned her smile. "Yeah. She's really great." He gave a soft shake of his head, lowering his voice so the kids didn't overhear. "I fought it at first. After what I went through with Em, I didn't want to put myself or the kids in that position again. But there's something about her."

"She's selfless."

A quick wrinkle marred his forehead. "Yeah. That's part of it for sure." Having watched Alice with his children the last couple of weeks, she was more of a mother to them than their own mother had ever been. She wasn't actively trying to take on that role, but her demeanor and interaction with them was motherly. She was a natural with children.

But it was also her beauty—inside and out—that drew him to her. He'd never met anyone like her.

"I like that smile." Peg pointed her stirring spoon at him.

He smiled brighter. "Me too. And speaking of Alice, you and Dad still okay to take the kids tomorrow, so she and I can go on a date?"

"Of course." Her sly smile came back. "We can take them all night, if you want."

He chuckled. "One day, but not yet."

She nodded once. "Good. I'm not saying go slow, but be sure before you reach that point. I don't think she's the kind of woman who's looking for a hot temporary romance."

"I'm not looking for that, either." He glanced over at his kids. "They deserve more than a string of women who mean nothing." He'd never been one to casually date or to have casual sex. He'd always wanted the deeper connection. Now that he had children to think about, he was even less reluctant to have that sort of relationship. If he didn't think Alice could be someone he could spend the rest of his life with, he wouldn't even be entertaining thoughts of dating her.

"Yes, they do. And I hope things work out between you two. I like her."

"Me too," he said again. Giving his mom another cheery smile, he moved away to set the table for dinner. As he took bowls from the cabinet, it hit him that he was happy. Happier than he'd been in a long time. All thanks to a sweet, kind-hearted blonde bombshell who liked papier-mâché and kids.

Twenty-Four

Alice brought her horse to a halt and glanced back, waiting for Wade to catch up. "Come on, slowpoke. I thought you said you knew how to ride?"

One corner of his mouth quirked, and he rolled his eyes as he crested the hill to stop next to her. "I do. But that horse of yours practically floats. This one doesn't." He patted his horse's neck.

Running a hand through her horse, Torrey's, mane, Alice smiled. "Yeah. Sorry. I would have put you on one of her siblings, but they can all be a handful. You said you don't ride often, so..." Her voice trailed away, and she shrugged.

He waved a hand. "It's okay. I'd rather be on a slow horse than one that doesn't want to go where I want it to without a fight."

She chuckled. "Yeah, Sherman and Lincoln would both try to forge their own paths. Regardless, though, we're here." She gestured ahead of them with a quick nod.

Wade's gaze shifted. "Oh, wow."

"Right? The Stone Creek has some beautiful vistas. I've been exploring in my free time. This is my favorite." They'd crested a ridge that looked down over the river valley below. In the bright sunshine, the water sparkled and wound its way through the wavy, deep green prairie grass below. Pops of color from wildflowers stood out against the grass.

"I can see why."

Alice smiled. "So you like my idea for a date, huh?"

"Definitely." He smiled back. "What else do you have to show me?"

She laughed. "Lots. Come on." She turned Torrey and headed up the trail. Her plan was to just ride and enjoy the beautiful countryside and each other's company. Wade said he wanted to take her to town to dinner later, so she only packed water and some essentials in their saddlebags.

"So, Henry regaled me last night with all the plans you've made for his birthday party."

Alice chuckled. "There really aren't that many. I'm making decorations. Daisy offered to make his cake. We made invitations for him to give to his friends. It'll be nice, but not over the top."

"Well, to him, it's the best thing ever. He's very excited."

"Good. It's been fun, and I'm glad he's happy."

Wade reached over and took her hand as they rode. "Thank you."

"It's just a birthday party."

He squeezed her hand. "Not just for that. I meant for loving my kids."

Alice's heart lurched at the look in Wade's eyes. It made her sad that he seemed amazed she could love them. "They're easy to love. They're great kids. And I'll never speak ill of their mom in front of them, but she's an idiot." She couldn't fathom how a mother could leave her kids—leave those kids. They were amazing.

"I agree. But I look at it as her loss. Does it upset me that they don't have their mom? Of course. But I can't help but wonder how happy they'd be if she stayed. She was never home. When she was, she didn't spend much time with them. She did at the beginning. When Bronwyn was little, and even after Henry was born. But once she went back to work after his birth, that's when things really changed." He shrugged. "Some people just aren't built to be parents. I don't regret our life together, because I could never regret having my kids."

Her heart flip-flopped again, but this time with a rush of feeling for Wade. She'd thought, based off her first impression of him in the barn, that he'd be some gruff, standoffish man, but he wasn't. He was guarded, but as they'd spent more time together, he'd opened up. She quite liked who he was.

He blew out a breath. "Enough about my ex. How are the house repairs coming along?"

Alice wrangled the emotions flowing through her as he changed the subject. "Good. The HVAC guy comes Monday. The electrician's already been there. It's quite convenient that you live next door, you know."

He smiled. "I agree." His eyes heated, and she felt an answering fire ignite in her belly.

She bit her lip and stared back.

Wade cleared his throat. "You know, I wanted to take this slow and really get to know you before we go any further. But one, I feel like I already know you pretty well. And two, I'm not sure slow is possible."

He'd get no argument from her on that. Watching him interact with his children, being in his home nearly every day, she'd gotten an in-depth look at the man. At who he was and what made him tick. Alice didn't need to know more to know she could very easily love him for the rest of her days.

Tugging on her hand, he reined his horse in, then leaned toward her. She met him in the middle for a tender kiss.

Torrey shifted under her, pulling them apart. She smiled at

him. "Maybe on horseback isn't the best place for a make-out session."

He laughed. "No, probably not. Come on. Let's finish our ride. We'll get some dinner, then have a proper goodnight kiss."

That fire kindling in her belly burned a little brighter. "I like that plan." She nudged Torrey in the sides, setting the horse in motion.

They stopped at several other spots before heading back to the barn to dress the horses down. Once they were brushed and had fresh hay and water, Alice and Wade walked outside to his SUV.

"I'm glad your parents were able to take the kids." She looked up at him as they stopped beside his car. "It's nice to spend some time alone together."

Wade leaned into her, sandwiching her between his body and the car. Tingles raced along Alice's spine and awareness pricked her skin.

"I agree, Ms. Duvall." He flashed that sexy smile she loved and leaned down.

Alice framed his face with her hands and stood on her toes to meet his kiss. She'd quickly come to crave his touch. It had been hard this past week to keep her hands to herself around the kids. They hadn't formally said anything to them about the change in their relationship, so any time they could steal a few moments alone, she let her hands roam.

Right now, they were fascinated with his jaw and the rough texture of his beard stubble.

He tore his mouth away from hers and put an inch of space between them. "You're lethal. Come on. Let's go get some dinner before we get too carried away."

With a soft laugh, she pecked his lips once, then ducked under his arm to round the car and get in. A hum of desire flowed between them as they held hands all the way to town.

At Sarafina's, they took a seat along the window, ignoring Sara's knowing grin. Alice picked up a menu and opened it, hiding her flaming face. She didn't know why she was blushing. It wasn't like she was ashamed of her relationship with Wade.

She blew her bangs out of her face and rolled her eyes at herself. It was probably because she wasn't used to being in a relationship. She didn't know how to act. The last boyfriend she had was in college.

"Hey, you two."

Alice came out from behind her menu to look up at Sara, who'd stopped at their table, order pad and pencil in her hands.

"Hi, Sara." She smiled at the other woman, who smiled broadly.

"I'm glad to see you both got your heads out of your butts and recognized what the rest of us saw weeks ago."

A laugh bubbled from Alice. "I've only been here a few weeks."

"I know. That's how strong the chemistry was between you two. It was there from the start."

Wade chuckled. "Yes, well, we had to recognize it for ourselves, it seems."

"I'm just glad you did. So, what can I get you to eat?"

Gratitude that she changed the subject rushed through Alice. She lifted the menu again and scanned it. "I'll take an iced tea and the chicken pot pie with a side salad." She tilted the menu down and looked across the table at Wade.

He glanced up at Sara. "I'd like—" His phone ringing cut him off. "Sorry." He put the menu down and lifted his phone from the table, frowning as he looked at the screen. "It's dispatch." He glanced at Alice, then Sara. "I need to take this."

Alice frowned, hoping their evening wasn't coming to an

early end. She knew he was on call, but had been hoping things would stay quiet.

Answering the phone, he slid out of the booth with an apologetic smile. Sara stepped back so he could get out, then looked at Alice, her mouth twisting.

"I hope he can stay."

"Me too, but I doubt it." She sighed. "I guess I'll get a head start on painting my house." She was going to wait until after the new heating and air unit was in, so she could use the air conditioning while she worked. It wasn't that hot today, though. She'd just open some windows.

Someone called Sara's name. She gave Alice a sympathetic smile. "I'll be back."

Alice waved away her concern. "You're fine." She slumped in her seat as Sara walked away.

Wade returned a few minutes later. She could tell by the hard set to his face and the thin line of his mouth it wasn't good news.

She wrinkled her nose as she looked at him. "Our date's over, isn't it?"

He nodded. "Yeah, I'm sorry. It looks like our arsonist might have struck again."

A frown marred her face. "Oh no. Is anyone hurt?"

"I don't know yet. The guys on scene learned who the property owner was and called me. They're still trying to put the fire out. Are you able to find a ride back to the Stone Creek? If not, I can drop you off at my house, then take you home later."

"Actually, can you drop me off at my new house? I'll do some painting while I wait on you."

"Are you sure? I might be awhile."

Alice slid from the booth. "Yep."

"Okay." He motioned for her to precede him. "I didn't know you already bought paint."

She grinned as they headed for the door, waving at Sara. "I bought it right after closing the other day. I didn't intend to start until after they finished the heating and air conditioning upgrades, but it doesn't really matter."

He held the door open for her. "Are you sure this is what you want to do?"

"Yes." She turned, walking backward, smiling. "I still need my goodnight kiss."

Twenty-Five

Brown-black smoke billowed from the house on Plum Street when Wade pulled up to it ten minutes later. He'd called his mom and dad on the way to tell them what happened. They were going to take the kids home to put them to bed, then stay until he got back. With that off his mind, he switched into investigator mode.

Climbing from his car, he opened the back to get his high-visibility vest. He shrugged into it as he made his way to the incident commander, Todd Verne.

"Hey, Verne, fill me in."

The older man glanced over and frowned. "It's not good. The boys just found a body."

Wade bit back a groan. "Well, hell. Any idea who it is?"

Todd shook his head. "No. It's a man, but that's about all I can tell you. He's pretty badly burned. I had them put him out back out of view. Don't need people taking pictures of that."

Wrinkling his nose, Wade nodded, grateful for the lieutenant's forethought. People took pictures of everything anymore. Covered or not, he didn't want those images getting out. Not until they knew who the decedent was.

"Is the coroner on the way?"

Todd nodded. "He should be here any minute. I called him right after I called you."

"Okay, thanks. Is there anything else you can tell me?"

"We found a gas can next to the body. And the kitchen area where the crew found him has sustained the most damage so far. It's likely the point of origin."

Wade frowned again. Did their arsonist accidentally light himself on fire? "All right. I'm going to go around and take a look at the body and start processing him." At Todd's nod, he ran back to his SUV to get his camera and the evidence collection kit he carried everywhere. With his gear in hand, he headed for the backyard by way of the neighbor's, staying clear of his colleagues working to put out the fire. The smoke was getting lighter as they battled back the flames.

The bright yellow tarp covering the body underneath the tree at the rear of the yard was easy to spot. He crossed the soggy grass to lift the tarp. The view—and the smell of burned flesh—under it turned his stomach. He was glad he and Alice never got around to eating.

Swallowing the bile rising in his throat, he forced himself into detached investigator mode and studied the body. Charred black in places, the man was slightly curled in on himself from the high heat of the fire. What was left of his clothes hung from him in burnt tatters. The crew had pulled him out before the fire sucked all the moisture from him, and his body wept, leaving a red-tinged puddle beneath him on the tarp. Any hair he had was gone, and Wade could see his skull in places. What he didn't see were any obvious wounds, though there could be ones he couldn't see with the way he was positioned. The man was on the heavy side, which had helped from an investigative standpoint. He didn't burn up as fast as someone who was thinner would have.

"Poor bastard." Wade hoped he was unconscious or already dead when the flames engulfed him.

Lifting his camera, he snapped some pictures of the body. He wouldn't move him until the coroner came.

"Wade."

At the sheriff's voice, he glanced up. "Hi, Katy."

She wrinkled her nose as she stopped next to him and looked down at the man. "That's terrible."

"Yeah." It wasn't the first burned body Wade had ever seen, but it had been years since the last one. Time didn't lessen the shock, though. "There's still a lot of tissue left, so the medical examiner should be able to collect DNA. And dental. His skull is intact."

She frowned and glanced away, swallowing hard before she spoke again. "Any ID?"

"I haven't moved him to check. Once the coroner gets here, we can do that."

She nodded. "Sounds good. I have a couple of deputies canvassing the crowd out front. Maybe someone will know who was in the house."

The coroner, Dr. Alan Sanchez, arrived, taking charge of the body. Wade helped the doctor roll him, then took more pictures.

"I don't see any signs of trauma." Dr. Sanchez glanced at Wade. "Until he's autopsied, I can't tell you for sure how he died, but from his burns, it was probably the fire that killed him. Though he could have been unconscious from the smoke first."

Wade hoped that was the case. He couldn't imagine burning alive and being awake through it.

"Let's get his hands bagged." Sanchez glanced over at his

assistant. "I doubt we'll get anything usable, but I don't want to lose anything on the off-chance something's there."

Already rising from his crouch, Wade paused halfway up when Sanchez lifted the man's left arm, his eyes on the gold watch. He dropped down and pointed. "Is that a Rolex?"

Sanchez looked at him and frowned, then lifted the man's arm higher to take a better look. "I think so, yes. Why?" He looked at Wade again.

Wade swiped a hand over his face. "Because I think I know who this is. It's Tim Willard. He owns the property." Biting back a groan, Wade looked away, thinking. What did it mean that Willard was their victim? Was this the last fire? Was Willard supposed to die in it, or did he surprise the arsonist? How did Vincent Perabo fit into things? Or did he? Could he have been a test run for Willard? Was Willard the arsonist after all, and accidentally lit himself on fire? Did he intend to die?

One thing was certain. Wade had many more questions than answers. Katy needed to get that report back on Perabo. Until they learned more about him, he doubted they would find answers to any of their questions.

Standing, Wade backed up so Sanchez's team could finish their assessment and pack the body for transport. He went around to the front of the house and found Katy again to tell her of his suspicions.

"I don't like that face." Katy drew a circle in the air at the level of his head as he approached. "What is it?"

"I think our victim is Willard."

Her eyes widened. "What? Why?"

"His general build plus the Rolex on his wrist. Willard had the same one on when we interviewed him."

She muttered under her breath. "Okay. Until we get confirmation, we assume he's still alive. I'll call him and his attorney. See if I can get a hold of him or find out when someone last spoke to him."

Wade nodded. "I'll ask Sanchez to put a rush on the ID."

"Thank you." She took out her cell, and Wade walked away to find Sanchez.

After asking the man to rush the victim ID, Wade wandered around the site, gathering information from firefighters and from bystanders about what happened. Once the fire was out, he donned his protective gear and walked through the smoldering ruins. Verne was right. The fire started in the kitchen. Char patterns showed someone dumped fuel all over the floor and splashed it on the cabinets. The old wood burned quickly.

It was dark when he finished at the scene. Tired and dirty, he climbed into his car and headed for home. He pulled into his driveway, but instead of parking in the garage and going into his house, he went next door. Mounting the porch steps, he could hear music coming through the open windows. Some bouncy song he could imagine Alice dancing to. He smiled and knocked on the door.

Through the beveled window in the door, he saw her come from the rear of the house. When she opened the door, all he could do was stare. Her honey-blonde hair was up in a loose knot on top of her head. Fly-aways fluttered around her face. Her blue eyes sparkled as she smiled at him. But what threw him the most was the sight of her wearing one of his old flannels. Paint dotted the fabric and her forearms below the rolled-up sleeves.

"Hi." She glanced past him at the darkened sky. "Oh, wow. I didn't realize it was so late."

Her words snapped him out of his trance, and he smiled. "How much did you paint?"

She stepped back so he could come in. "Two rooms. I started with the kitchen. Figured I'd tackle the hardest room first. I was just finishing up the first coat in the dining room."

She turned, motioning him to follow her and giving him a wonderful view of her pert rear.

Wade blew out a breath and raised his gaze. His jeans could only hide so much.

Luckily, they reached the kitchen and the new paint color distracted him. She'd not only painted the walls a soft mint, but the cabinets were now an off-white instead of gray.

"Damn. How long was I gone? You said you painted the dining room too?"

She smiled. "Yeah. But to be fair, the walls were easy. The cutting in takes the most time, but then you just roll the walls and you're done. I'd already removed all the cabinet doors, so I rolled several, painted some walls or the cabinets, then moved the doors to make way for more and painted those."

"Still." He glanced around again. "I'm impressed. This would have taken me way more than a few hours." He looked at her and smiled. "But you are an artist, so this kind of thing is right up your alley."

Alice chuckled. "Definitely." Tipping her head toward the doorway to the dining room, she took two steps in that direction. "Let me close up the paint and rinse my brushes, then we can go."

He nodded, following her and admiring her handiwork. "I like this color." White wainscoting covered the bottom half of the walls. Above it, she'd painted over the gray walls with a deep navy.

"Isn't it gorgeous? I saw that chandelier and knew I needed to do something dramatic in here." She nodded to the ornate crystal chandelier hanging low over the middle of the room, then crouched in front of the paint pan and picked it up, tipping it over the can to pour the paint back in.

Wade found the rubber mallet and put the lid on the can while she took the pan and brush to the kitchen to rinse them.

Once they had everything cleaned up, she took off the paint shirt and laid it next to the can.

"All set?"

She nodded. "I just need my purse, but it's by the front door."

He led the way, pausing for her to get her bag. Outside, he reached for her hand. "Sorry it's so late. That scene—" He paused and shook his head. "We found a victim in the rubble."

She gasped. "Oh, Wade. I'm sorry. Do you know who it was?"

"I have my suspicions. If I'm right, it just complicates things further." He sighed.

A frown marred her forehead, and she pulled him to a stop at the edge of his driveway. Reaching up with one hand, she stroked his face. "You look tired." Her frown deepened. "How about I stay in your spare room tonight? It'll take you an hour to drive me home and back. You need sleep more than I need to go back to the ranch."

His fatigue fled at her words. Having her under his roof, but not in his bed, would be torture. But he did like the idea of knowing she was safe in his house, and of waking up to her in the morning and sharing breakfast with him and the kids before church. "We can't linger in the morning if you want to go to church. I'll need to get you home so you can change clothes."

She chuckled and looked down at herself. "You don't think I can go like this?"

Wade ran his gaze over her tight jeans, boots, and turquoise t-shirt. "I mean, I like it, but you might get a few looks. Especially from people who saw you today." He gave her a wicked smile and put his hands at her waist, tugging her closer. "They might get the wrong idea."

Her hands landed on his shoulders, curling over them to link behind his neck. "Probably."

"We wouldn't want people to get the wrong idea." He shuffled closer. "It's all completely innocent." He lowered his head.

She nodded, her eyes heating. "Completely."

Warm breath puffed against his face and sent a shiver down his spine. He closed the distance between them and kissed her. She let out a soft whimper, fueling his need. Wade tightened his arms, hauling her against his chest as he deepened their kiss. He let his hands roam over her back, feeling the firm, supple muscles. They gave way to the soft curve of her hips. He cupped them, holding her to him. It was his turn to moan as she pushed against him, her body trying to get closer.

Tearing his mouth away, he rested his forehead on hers as he caught his breath. When they finally let this attraction have free rein, it would likely destroy them both. "Come on. Let's go inside before we give the neighbors a bigger show."

She chuckled and stepped back to look at him. Merriment and something sensual danced in her eyes. Wade's body tightened again.

"I'm not shy, but that's definitely pushing it."

Need flooded him, and he made a mental note to one day take her some place where he could strip her naked and enjoy her beautiful body outside without anyone stumbling over them. It became number one on his bucket list. Until then, though, he needed to get it together. "You're going to be the death of me." Dropping a quick, hard kiss on her lips, he took her hand and led her into the house.

Twenty-Six

"Here, Henry. Do you think you can carry this one?" She handed the boy a small box with some toiletry items. The kids were helping her move some things into her house. The heating and cooling systems were finally done, so she'd decided to bring some things over. She'd fully move in this weekend, but for now, she wanted to have some extra clothes and sundries handy, just in case.

It hadn't bothered her to stay at Wade's house the other night. But having him drive an hour to take her home so early in the morning and disrupting the kids' pre-church routine had. She would have liked to have been able to pop over to her house and change, then go to church with them, only going home after the service.

Henry grunted as he took the box.

"You got it?" She held on, not wanting him to drop it.

His tongue poked out, and a deep frown of concentration furrowed his brow. "Yep."

"Are you sure?"

He nodded. "I won't drop it. I promise."

She smiled and let go. "Okay. Take it inside and put it with the others."

Still frowning with fierce concentration, he walked away. Alice watched to make sure he got up the steps all right. It was slow-going, but he made it. She grabbed a larger box with her shoes and followed him in.

Elise threw a doll over the play yard at her as she walked inside.

"Are you upset that you're stuck in there?" Alice set her box down and picked up the doll.

"She wants to play with us." Bronwyn took the doll and walked over to her sister, handing it back.

"Soon. There's just a few more things to unload." She had some dresses to bring in and a couple jackets, plus the stair gate she bought yesterday. "I'm going to go get the rest. You three stay here, okay?"

Bronwyn nodded, eyes still on Elise.

Alice hurried outside and hooked her fingers through the hangers, lifting them out of the back of her car, then went inside. Opening the coat closet, she hung everything in there. She'd put it where it belonged later. She made one more trip for the gate, then let Elise out of her pen.

"You guys can play in here while I put this gate up." She unhooked one set of hinges on the yard, opening it up, then stretched it across the doorway to the living room, keeping the toddler from escaping down the hallway. The little girl didn't seem to care that she was stuck in the living room with Alice on the other side. She was just happy to have more space.

Keeping one ear on the kids, she opened the box and took out the gate pieces. Using the tools she borrowed from Wade, she installed the gate at the base of the stairs. She'd get another one later to put at the top of the staircase, but for now, one would do. She didn't intend to take the kids upstairs anytime soon, and they weren't staying long today.

With the gate in place, Alice gathered up the box and tools, putting both by the front door. She'd take Wade's tools back and take the box to the ranch with her to dispose of.

"Okay." She turned to the kids. "Who's ready for lunch?"

Two hands shot up. Elise ignored her, babbling to her doll.

"Perfect. How about we take a picnic to the park today?"

"Yes!" Bronwyn bounced and clapped her hands.

"Can we have peanut butter?" Henry asked.

"If that's what you want, sure."

He nodded.

"Okay. Come on. Let's go back to your house and get everything ready. You two can ride your bikes over."

Scampering for the door, she had to hold a hand out to slow them down. "There's no rush. Each of you gather up some of the trash and take it to the car, please."

They changed direction and picked up the empty box and packaging, dragging it out the door. Alice lifted Elise over the play yard, then picked up the toolbox and her purse and followed the kids to the car. She helped them load the packaging into the car, then locked it. They walked across the yard to their house.

After setting Elise up with some toys, Alice packed a lunch with Bronwyn and Henry's help. She stowed it in the bottom of the stroller, then helped the kids find their bike helmets and use the restroom. Once they were ready to go, she popped Elise in the stroller. They retrieved the older children's bikes from the garage and set off down the sidewalk.

At the park, Alice corralled them at a picnic table and made them eat before they got on the equipment. Bronwyn and Henry demolished their food, then asked to play. When she smiled and said yes, they ran off at top speed.

Alice gathered their trash, throwing it away in the nearby bin, then sat down while Elise finished smashing her PB and J all over her face.

"Kiddo, you're a mess."

Elise grinned and squealed, bouncing in the stroller. She held up a peanut butter-covered hand to Alice.

"I don't want it, thank you."

The girls shoved her fingers in her mouth. Alice gave a quick laugh and shook her head. It was a good thing she had a fresh pack of wipes in the diaper bag.

When Elise was done, Alice cleaned her up, getting off as much stickiness as she could. She'd wash her up better when they got home. She was just going to get dirty playing, anyway.

"Do you want to swing?" She lifted the toddler from the stroller and walked toward the swings, putting her in the baby seat and fastening her in.

A little boy of around four ran up and plopped onto a swing. "Mommy! Come push me."

"Please?" A dark-haired woman walked up, smiling at the boy.

"Please?" The boy bounced on the seat, eager to swing.

She walked around behind him and gave him a push.

Alice smiled at the woman, then went back to pushing Elise.

"Your daughter's adorable."

"Oh." Alice glanced over, smiling again. "Thank you, but she's not mine. I'm the sitter."

"Really? I would never have guessed. She looks like you."

Alice nodded. "We do have similar coloring." Elise's hair was almost an exact match to Alice's. But the toddler had hazel eyes like her father. Alice's were an icy blue.

"I'm Liz."

"It's nice to meet you. I'm Alice. This is Elise. Her brother and sister are running around over there somewhere." She pointed to the play equipment, spotting both children running through the structure. "I think her brother, Henry, might be your son's age. He'll be four this weekend."

Liz smiled and glanced at her son. "Did you hear that, Liam? There's a boy on the playground who's your age."

Liam dragged his feet and looked up at his mom. "Can I go play with him?"

"Sure." Liz stopped the swing, and he jumped off.

"He's at the top of the slide." Alice pointed. "His name is Henry."

"Okay!" He ran off.

Liz chuckled. "I wish I had his energy."

Alice laughed. "We need it to keep up with them."

"For sure. So, how did you end up as a sitter? No offense, but you don't strike me as a professional nanny. Are they your nieces and nephew?"

"No. They're a friend's kids. He was in a bind when his normal sitter broke her leg."

"Oh, ouch!"

"Yeah. He's a single dad and was running himself ragged, trying to work and keep an eye on them when his parents couldn't watch them, so I offered to help out. I'm the new art teacher at the elementary, but I don't start until the new school year, so it worked out great. Keeps me busy and keeps him sane."

"Wait. Are you talking about Wade Kaczmarek?"

Surprise made Alice's eyes go round. "You know him?"

Liz nodded. "I thought the kids' names sounded familiar, then you mentioned single dad and it clicked." She gave Alice a sad smile. "I was friends with their mom in high school."

"Oh, wow. I guess I was bound to run into someone who knew her sooner or later. It's a small town, after all."

"Yeah." Liz sank onto the swing her son vacated. "She was always a free spirit. I can't believe he got her to settle down at all, actually."

"So, you're not surprised Emily left?"

"No."

Alice tried to keep the anger off her face, but knew she failed. Emily's attitude toward her kids burned Alice's gut.

Liz met her gaze and tipped her head. "Why do you look angry? Some marriages just aren't meant to last."

Alice's eyebrows shot up. She bit her tongue to keep back the foul words she wanted to say and formulated a more polite answer. "It's not about the marriage. I'm aware not all people are suited to being married or being married to a certain person. I'm angry because she didn't just leave Wade. She left her kids. She hasn't had any contact with them since she left. Did you know that? Wade's tried to contact her, giving her updates and pictures, but she never acknowledges them, never calls. They don't even get cards or gifts on their birthdays. He doesn't even know where she is."

Liz's eyes widened. "I didn't know that." She glanced away, then shook her head before she looked up again. "She's in Los Angeles."

Alice's heart stopped, then jolted, racing in her chest. "What? How do you know?"

"Her social media. We follow each other. She's in L.A., working as a backup singer." She blew out a breath. "She looks happy." Her voice was quiet and subdued.

The anger simmering in Alice's gut grew hotter. "Good for her. I'm glad forsaking her family made her happy. If you talk to her, tell her that her kids are doing great without her." Unable to stand there and talk any longer, she lifted Elise from the swing and hurried away. Her vision swam, and she blinked furiously. She refused to cry over that woman. Emily Kaczmarek didn't deserve an ounce of her time, let alone her tears.

Reaching the play structure, Alice put Elise on the toddler slide and let the girl climb around while she watched. Now that she and Wade were involved, she felt like she had a bigger stake in the kids' lives, and their mother's actions irked her more than ever.

But she was also sad for the woman. She was missing out on so much love. Her children were wonderful, and it made Alice's heart hurt to know that both children and mom would never share that love or the joy of growing up together.

Pushing her melancholic thoughts away, Alice forced herself to enjoy their outing and the warm sunshine. She refused to let Emily's actions put a damper on her life or theirs.

TWENTY-SEVEN

"Alice, this really is amazing." Wade walked onto the back patio, carrying a platter of vegetables. He glanced around. She'd transformed his yard into a dinosaur wilderness. Cutouts of the creatures stood arranged against the fence and poking out from bushes. A pterodactyl piñata hung from the branches of the big maple. Fake rocks and dinosaur nests dotted the grass, complete with eggs. On the patio, helium-filled balloons flanked a long table that held the most amazing cake he'd ever seen.

From the base, which looked like a plant, the head of a raptor peeked out. Its mouth open, it parted the leaves with its long black talons. Daisy had outdone herself.

"It all turned out pretty well." Alice glanced around.

"Pretty well? They're never going to be satisfied with a box cake and a few balloons ever again." He walked to another table and put the platter down.

She laughed. "Well, so long as I'm around, they won't have to. This was fun."

He wandered over and gave her a quick kiss. "I can see you've enjoyed yourself."

The back door opened again.

"Wow!" Peg stepped out, Wade's dad, Bill, right behind her.

"Wow is right." Bill looked around the yard. "Alice, this is incredible."

"Hey," Wade said. "How do you know I didn't do all this?" A grin tilted one side of his mouth.

Bill rolled his eyes. "Because I've seen your idea of a birthday party. This isn't it."

Peg patted his arms. "You're good at other things, dear. Don't fret."

"Thanks, Mom."

"You're welcome. So, where are the kids?"

"My brother and his wife picked them up this morning so we could set everything up." Alice glanced up at Wade. "We decided to surprise Henry with the finished product."

"Good plan," Bill said. "He's going to love it."

Wade agreed. Alice had done a wonderful job.

"So," Bill clapped his hands together. "What can we do?"

Before Wade could open his mouth, Alice fired off the list of things that still needed to be done. His parents jumped into action. It didn't take the four of them long to get the rest of the food outside. The front door opened, and he heard his kids come inside just as he came back in from plugging in the crock pot.

"Daddy!" Henry ran into the kitchen. "Can I look now?"

Wade picked up the boy. "You sure can. Alice did an awesome job. You're going to love it." He sent a wink at her, then carried Henry outside.

His gasp made Wade grin.

"Wow! This is neat!" He squirmed, so Wade set him down. He ran out into the yard to look at the decorations.

Alice stepped up beside him. "I think he likes it."

"Yeah." Wade wrapped an arm around her waist and

pressed a kiss to her cheek. "You did good. It's nice to see him so happy." His smile faded a bit. "I wasn't sure how he'd react to today." He looked at her. "Without even a call from his mom. But I don't think he'll miss her. He's going to have too much fun."

"Good." Her mouth parted, like she wanted to say something else, then she frowned and looked away.

"What?"

She glanced at him, searching his eyes. "I don't want to talk about it now, but there's something you should know. Later. After the party."

He frowned. "Is everything okay?"

She nodded. "It's fine. I promise."

Wade studied her for another moment, then nodded. "All right."

Perplexed at what could put that pained look in her eyes, he stared at her a moment longer, but didn't press. If it wasn't serious, whatever it was, could wait. Right now, it was all about Henry.

TWENTY-EIGHT

Fatigue clawed at the back of Wade's eyes as he sank onto the couch. The kids were in bed, the dishes were done, and he was ready to relax with Alice for a few minutes before she left.

She sank beside him, leaning into his side with a sigh. "I'm going to sleep so well tonight."

"Same. I'd forgotten how exhausting children's parties are." He let his head fall back against the cushions and closed his eyes.

Alice poked him in the side. "Hey. No falling asleep. If you fall asleep, I'll want to fall asleep, and I need to drive home yet."

He grumbled and lifted his head to look at her. "Why don't you stay the night again? I know you moved some of your clothes in next door. Bronwyn told me."

She scrunched her nose. "You might not want me here after what I have to tell you."

Some of the fatigue cleared at her words. He frowned. "Oh, yeah. You had something you wanted to tell me. I thought it wasn't bad."

With a shrug, she glanced away for a brief moment. "I guess it depends on how you look at it." She took a deep breath, then continued. "So, I ran into an old friend of your ex-wife's at the park the other day. Liz? She said they went to high school together."

Wade's brow furrowed as he thought. "Liz McMaster?"

Alice shrugged again. "She didn't tell me her last name."

"Okay. So, how did you get on the subject of Emily?"

"She complimented Elise by telling me my daughter was adorable. When I corrected her and told her I was filling in for a friend's sitter who broke her leg, she knew who the kids were, then." Alice glanced away again. "She said she wasn't surprised that Emily left you."

Wade's breath stalled in his lungs. While he was no longer angry his wife left him, it was still a punch to the gut to know that others had expected their marriage to fail.

"It wasn't because of you, though. She called Emily a free spirit. Her cavalier attitude to it all made me angry, and I asked her if she knew that Emily didn't just leave, but that she cut off all contact with the kids. She said she didn't, but then she told me Emily was living in Los Angeles and seemed happy."

The breath stuck in Wade's lungs came out on a whoosh. He stood up and walked to the fireplace, staring at the wall for a moment before turning back to her. "How does she know that?"

Alice stood and walked over. "Social media. They follow each other."

He scoffed and shook his head. "I sent her friend requests, and she ignored me." He pinched the bridge of his nose. "I just wish I could understand why she doesn't want to be a part of the kids' lives." That old anger rose in his throat like a bitter pill. He clenched his teeth and swallowed it down. It didn't do him any good to get upset over it.

"I'm sorry. I wouldn't have said anything, but I thought you should know where she is. She is still their mother."

He cupped the side of her face, something shifting inside him. This woman was amazing. To know she cared enough to get angry for his kids, for him, and to not keep something like this a secret, even though it had the potential to throw a wrench in their relationship, endeared her to him all the more. She just wanted what was best for his children. "I know. And thank you for telling me. I don't plan to do anything with the information, but it's nice to have something to tell the kids if they ever ask. Once they're adults, I'll tell them whatever they want to know. They can make their own decisions then about whether or not they want to track her down."

He leaned in and pressed a gentle kiss to her lips. Pulling back, he looked into her beautiful eyes. His heart cracked open and feelings he thought were dead and gone erupted through the hole. Bringing up his other hand, he framed her face, holding her gaze. Words he didn't have a chance to process tumbled from his mouth. "I don't regret my relationship with her, because it gave me my kids. But I wish I'd met you first and you were their mother. It would have saved us all a lot of heartache."

Twenty-Nine

Shock made Alice go still even as her eyes went wide. Words failed her, and all she could do was stare at him.

He huffed a quick chuckle, one corner of his mouth lifting. "Alice Duvall, speechless. Bet that doesn't happen often."

She swallowed. "No."

His smile grew. "I didn't mean to freak you out."

Blinking, she shook off the surprise. "You didn't."

He arched an eyebrow, and she smiled.

"Not that much. It's more surprise. I know I like you—a lot. And that I want what's between us to continue to grow, so that one day we possibly become a family. I guess I just didn't realize you were in the same place."

Shivers went down the side of her face as he tucked a lock of hair behind her ear. "We're very much on the same page. I wish we'd started dating before you bought your house. I don't want you to leave."

Her eyes went wide again. He wanted her to move in? "Boy, you don't move any too slow, do you?"

He chuckled. "Honestly? All of this is hitting me now. My mouth and brain aren't currently connected, because these thoughts hit me and they're out before I can think about what I'm saying. But I don't regret saying them. I've never met a woman like you, Alice. Not even in the height of my relationship with Emily did I ever feel like this."

Shock edged back in, but so did something else. Warmth bloomed in her chest, making her smile. She raised her arms to wrap them around his neck. "You're right. We are on the same page."

His muscles tensed beneath her hands, and his pupils dilated. He swayed closer. "So, where does that leave us?"

Alice felt his breath puff over her lips. Her desperate need to kiss him meant she missed what he said and had to run it back through her brain. Looking away from his delectable mouth, she focused on his hazel eyes. "Committed. It leaves us committed. To doing whatever we can to make this work." She tangled her fingers in his short hair, running them over his scalp. "I don't want this to be a flash in the pan."

"Me either."

His low, growly voice sent pings of delight through her belly and lower. "Are you going to kiss me goodnight, or are we going to keep talking?" She couldn't take much more.

"That depends. Are you staying?"

Oh, how she wanted to. But the kids still didn't know about them. They'd been a little less careful about not touching lately, but they hadn't sat Bronwyn and Henry down yet to talk to them about their relationship.

Wade leaned closer, his lips just millimeters from hers. She wedged a hand between them and laid it over his mouth. "I'll stay, but I'm sleeping in the spare room."

He groaned, but nodded. "Fine. Can I kiss you now?"

For an answer, she removed her hand and replaced it with her mouth. They both groaned at the contact. In moments, Alice was nothing but a ball of nerve-endings. She wanted nothing more than to feel his touch electrify her body—everywhere.

He wandered away from her mouth to trail hot kisses along her jaw and down her neck. At the collar of her jersey dress, he hooked a finger in the stretchy fabric and tugged, exposing her upper chest to his mouth. "Just because we can't take this party upstairs doesn't mean we can't have a preview down here, right?"

Before she could answer, those strong hands of his wrapped around her waist and lifted her, scooting her back and laying her out on the couch. He rose, putting a knee on either side of her hips, and leaned down to kiss her again. Needing to anchor herself, she curled her fingers over the waistband of his jeans and clutched his belt. She felt like she could float away if he moved.

Those glorious lips left hers once more and beelined for her neck. He palmed her breasts, making the already aching globes swell further. His idea of a preview was going to drive her insane. She moaned into his mouth and tugged at his polo shirt tucked into his jeans, wanting to touch the skin beneath.

He sat up and smiled at her when she pouted. "Nope. If you touch me, I'll explode. This is a preview for you. Not for me."

"What?" She propped herself up on her elbows as he slid off the couch to kneel beside her. His hand landed on her exposed thigh, and her eyes widened. "Are you—?"

He nodded, sliding his hand under her dress. "Only if you want me to."

She wasn't about to say no. Not with her body already on fire and ready to shoot off like a rocket. "Oh, hell yes."

His wicked grin made her panties wet. She flopped back on the cushions and let one leg fall off the side of the couch, giving him better access.

He didn't need further invitation. Those long fingers slid

the rest of the way up her thigh to find the edge of her underwear. He curled a finger around the band on the side of her hip and tugged. Alice lifted her hips and let him slide them down. He whisked them off over her feet and dropped them to the floor.

"Don't lose those," she managed to say as his hand returned to her leg. "We don't need one of the kids finding them."

He chuckled. "I won't." His smile faded, and an intensity dropped over his face. His hazel eyes turned a steely green with hunger as he lifted her dress, exposing her to his gaze. Alice swallowed hard.

"It was murder watching you walk around in this dress all day. I kept imagining what you had on underneath and how easy it would be to flip it up and see." His fingers skimmed her hipbones as he talked.

"Now you know." She bit her lip, holding back the whimper.

"And then some." His hand slid toward her center, brushing the well-trimmed thatch of blonde curls shielding her.

Alice's breath caught. Anticipation made her hold it. She thought she'd pass out as he hovered over her, teasing. "Wade." Her breath left her on a harsh whisper.

That wicked smile slashed his face again, and he cupped her mound. One finger dipped between her folds, testing her wetness. Alice arched her hips, sinking the digit deeper, and she moaned.

"Oh, this is a bad idea," he muttered. "You're going to wake the kids."

A laugh started in her throat, but escaped as another moan when he added a second finger. "You started this."

His low chuckle added to the shivers coursing through her. "True."

Despite his words, he didn't stop. Alice did her best to muffle the noises he elicited from her with his talented hands. She felt her climax grow as he teased and stroked her body until she saw the crest. Slapping her hands over her mouth, she prepared to let go.

Just as she was about to reach the top, he withdrew his hands. Her eyes popped open, and she glared at him. "Why did you quit? I was so close."

"I know." He flashed that sexy smile again and rose, climbing onto the couch between her legs. "But I'm not done yet, so you're not done yet."

Alice groaned. She didn't know how much more she could take without coming apart at the seams. *But oh, what a way to go.*

He lifted her leg and put it on the back of the couch, then bent the other one, propping it on his shoulder. His eyes met hers, and the desire there was enough to make her core pulse. He wanted her as much as she wanted him. She knew he'd said this was a preview for her, but he was enjoying it just as much.

"You have no idea how much I want to carry you upstairs right now." The hands on her legs tightened briefly before he skimmed them along her skin.

She moaned again. "I can guess." Her head fell back, and she closed her eyes once more.

They popped open when his head dipped, and he ran his tongue along her seam. She let out a sharp shout, then slapped her hands over her mouth again.

It only partially muffled the noise she made, but she couldn't help it. She no longer had control of her body. That belonged to Wade.

When her orgasm broke, she turned her face into the back of the couch to muffle the scream. Riding the wave of bliss, she slumped, breathing hard. "Holy crap." What would that feel like when she came with him inside her? Would she survive?

His low chuckle made her look at him. He looked damn pleased with himself.

"I'm going to need to add some sound-proofing to the bedroom."

Alice laughed. "Just make sure there are plenty of pillows on the bed."

Smiling, he leaned down to kiss her. Her laughter melted into need again. How that was possible after that orgasm, she didn't know.

He pulled away to look down at her. "We will have as many pillows as you want." Pecking another quick kiss on her lips, he sat up and offered her a hand.

She took it, and he helped her sit up. Straightening her dress, she glanced around for her panties. Wade picked them up from the floor and held them up with one finger. That smirk came back.

"Should I help you put them on?"

"Will they actually make it to where they're supposed to go?"

His smile widened. "Probably not."

She snatched them from his hand.

"Party-pooper."

Casting him a mock glare, she wiggled into her underwear. Before he could stand, though, she pushed him back and slid to the floor in front of him.

"Alice? What are you doing?"

"Saving you from having to wait until you shower." She gave him the same smile he'd given her. "Besides, this way is more fun." Her fingers found his belt buckle and slid the leather through it.

He sucked in a sharp breath when her fingers skimmed the warm skin of his stomach. "Alice." He covered her hand.

She batted it away. "Nope. I agreed to wait to touch you, but I never said how long." She unfastened and unzipped his pants, exposing his dark teal boxers and the hard ridge hiding underneath. Her mouth watered. "Lean back and enjoy." She gave his chest a gentle shove, then focused her attention on bringing him the same pleasure he'd brought her.

Unfastening the button on his shorts, the material parted, and he sprang free, swollen and erect. She ran a finger along the pulsing vein on the underside until she reached the tip, where a dot of moisture beaded. Alice smeared it over the end of his shaft, then wrapped her hand around him and squeezed. He let out a harsh groan and bucked in her hand. More moisture beaded, and she leaned in, licking it away.

A strangled groan emanated from his chest. Alice smiled, then sucked him into her mouth. His hands clutched her hair, holding her in place as she swirled her tongue around his shaft and pulled. Beneath her hands, she felt his muscles flex and tighten as his climax neared. She bit down gently, and he exploded.

He let out a loud grunt, then clamped his lips together, his breath coming in quick spurts as he tried to stay quiet. Alice milked every last drop from him, only sitting up when his body went limp. She swallowed, then gave him a seductive smile.

"I'm not moving. I think I'll just sleep here."

She chuckled and got up to sit next to him, snuggling into his side. "You'll wake up with a crick in your neck."

He wrapped an arm around her. "My legs don't work, so it's inevitable." A smile quirked his mouth. "It was worth it."

Laughing again, she kissed his cheek. "Good."

THIRTY

Whistling, Wade walked into his office Monday morning with an extra kick to his step. This past weekend had been one of the best of his life. His children were happy and enjoying life, and he had an amazing woman in his life whom he and his kids adored.

After church yesterday, they'd packed a lunch and took the kids up to the Stone Creek, eating it in the yard behind the little bungalow where she had her temporary pottery studio. There, they'd asked Bronwyn and Henry what they thought about having Alice around as more than just their sitter. Once they grasped that it meant Alice could one day be their mom, they'd been excited. Henry had launched himself at her, hugging her tight and telling her he never wanted her to go. That he wanted a mom like his friends.

Until then, Wade hadn't realized how much Emily's absence affected his kids. They'd adjusted so well to life without her, but there were deeper wounds he couldn't see. He was more determined than ever to build a strong relationship with Alice. He couldn't let them lose someone else they loved. He doubted it would be hard, though, to make things work. Smitten didn't begin to describe how he felt.

Sitting down at his desk, still whistling softly, he logged into his computer to check his email. The whistling tapered off as he scrolled through his messages. He'd heard back from most of the departments he emailed in Colorado about their suspicious fires.

Wade scrolled through his inbox, making sure there was nothing more pressing, then went back to the top and started in on the first email. He grabbed a notepad and a pen, jotting down notes as he read through each message. An hour later, he finished the last email, then reread his notes. Several of the properties were owned by companies, but none he recognized.

"Okay, so who owns the companies?" He clicked to a different screen and pulled up the Colorado Secretary of State website and typed in the first company name. It yielded him an address and phone number, but no one individual. He repeated the process, finding a few names.

For the ones without an owner listed, he googled their websites. On the second to last name on his list, he froze when the "About Us" page loaded. Tim Willard's picture stared back at him. But the man didn't have his name. This man was Will Timmerman.

Wade picked up his phone and dialed the sheriff.

"Lattimer."

"Hey, it's Kaczmarek. What have you dug up on Tim Willard?"

There was a brief pause as she processed his question. "Willard? Hang on. Let me find his file."

Wade heard papers shuffling, then a thunk and a muffled curse.

"Sorry. Dropped the phone. Okay. Let's see. I remember seeing he's been in business in Billings for fifteen years." More papers rustled. "Before that, he worked for a construction company in Idaho as a project manager. He's fifty-two and was born in Boise. Never married, no kids. Why?"

"Did you check out his work history?"

"The company in Idaho is out of business, and I couldn't find a current contact. Wade, why are you asking all this?"

He pinched the bridge of his nose. "So, I heard back from the inquiries I sent out about suspicious fires near Gunnison. One of the locations I got back from Saguache County is owned by a company called San Juan Development Corporation. I looked up their ownership. I'm staring at a picture of Willard right now, but it says his name is Will Timmerman."

"Oh, hell." She blew out a breath. "Are you sure it's Willard?"

"It sure looks like him."

She sighed. "Give me the contact info. I'll see if I can speak to him."

Wade read her the phone number on the website. "You know what I don't understand, though?"

"Why he would allow his picture to be plastered on a public website when he's living under an assumed name?"

"Bingo."

"Maybe he doesn't know. Or maybe he thinks since they're different names, no one will connect them. His Billings company is small potatoes. It's regional. I'm betting that other one is too. Let me call this number, and I'll call you back."

"Okay. Bye."

"Bye." She hung up.

Wade looked at the receiver and blew out a breath, setting it back in the cradle. After they'd talked to Willard, Wade hadn't suspected the man was hiding anything, especially something of this magnitude. But some people were gifted liars. It's what made them good con-artists. What kind of trouble had come to their sleepy little town?

While he waited for Katy to call back, he pulled up the

background database and typed in Will Timmerman's name. He got a Colorado driver's license and address in return. Returning to the secretary of state website, he typed Timmerman's name in and discovered that he owned the residence listed on his license as well as another one near Telluride. He clicked over to Google Maps and input the address, changing the view to satellite, and zoomed in. It was a cabin in the woods.

His phone rang. He lifted the receiver to his ear. "Kaczmarek."

"The receptionist I spoke to said that Mr. Timmerman is currently unavailable. When I asked when he'd be free to speak with me, she said he's on an extended business trip and unreachable."

Wade scoffed. "Unless you're in some third world country backpacking or the wilds of Alaska, no one is unreachable. And I can't see a man of Timmerman's stature doing anything except riding around in a hired car and staying within walking distance of some decent restaurants."

"Agreed. I've already made a note to call the lab in Billings and get an update on our fire victim's identity. They should be close if they were able to find dental records for Willard."

"Tell them to check under Timmerman if they didn't find any yet. Maybe we'll get lucky and he uses the name here too. What about DNA?"

"Billings PD did a welfare check at his house. When no one answered and they couldn't reach him through his administrative assistant or his attorney, they got a judge to sign off on an entry warrant for his home. No one was there. They found his toothbrush and sent it off to be tested, but the results are still pending."

Wade frowned. There were times he wished crime labs worked as fast as they did on TV.

"What does that report say about the fire at Timmerman's property you mentioned before?"

Wade flipped through his notes. "It was six years ago. A residence undergoing renovation. The investigator found evidence of an accelerant near the stove." He glanced up, looking out the window. "Probably trying to make it look like a gas leak."

"Anyone injured?"

"No."

"Okay. Can you dig further and find out if there were any other fires connected to Timmerman or his company in the past? I'll dig into Timmerman himself."

"Yes. What have you learned about Perabo?"

"The case notes indicate he worked for a construction company called Build-Rite as an electrician. The prosecution alleged that he intentionally cut corners wiring a house because of budget constraints, which led to a short, killing a woman. His boss, Jim Tunney, also went to jail for the same charge. He died in prison six months before Perabo was released."

The company's name triggered something in Wade's brain. "Build-Rite. I've seen that. Hang on." He flipped through his notes, but found nothing. "Where did I see that?" Frowning, he looked up and went back to San Juan Development's website. He scrolled, and a logo caught his eye. "Got it. Timmerman's company uses several contractors for their properties. They're all listed on their website. Build-Rite is one of them."

Wade opened another tab as a thought struck him. "What's the name of Willard's company again?"

"TW Developments."

He typed the name into the web browser and clicked on the company's website. It too listed contractors, but Build-Rite wasn't one of them. "None of the contractors match

Timmerman's. You might want to look at employee records, though. See if anyone has worked for both."

She grumbled. "I don't have the manpower for that kind of search. This case is nuts. I'm seriously considering calling in the feds now that it's crossed state lines. Allegedly crossed state lines. We have to confirm Willard is Timmerman. Then I can call the feds." She sighed.

"Who was the victim in Perabo's fire?"

"Let me look. It started with an A."

He heard papers shuffle.

"Amber Mercer. Twenty-eight." She hissed. "Oh, she was pregnant at the time. Fourteen weeks."

"Damn." His heart dropped to his stomach. He couldn't imagine losing his wife and child that way.

"Yeah."

"Is there any other information on her or her family?" A death like that would leave someone with a strong motive for revenge.

"Just a husband's name. Joshua Mercer. Oh. He was a cop."

"Okay, he should be easy enough to track down. I'll do some digging on them both. Find out where he is."

"Sounds good. Does the report indicate who owned the Mercer's house before they bought it?"

"No. But I'll find out." He had a feeling it would be Willard. Or Timmerman. Or some other alias for the same man.

"Good. This case isn't going to have a happy ending, I have a feeling."

Wade agreed. This sounded more and more like a case of revenge, not someone out to get their kicks by lighting fires. "Yeah."

She sighed again. "Call me if you find something."

"I will. You do the same."

"Yep."

They said goodbye and hung up.

Wade put his elbows on his desk and ran his hands over his face. When he agreed to take on the part-time investigator role, he never imagined he'd be dealing with murder or a serial arsonist. Not here. Whatever the outcome of this case, he hoped he could stop the perpetrator before anyone else died.

A knock on his door brought his head up. "Come in."

His partner, Jed Braun, opened the door. "Got a minute?"

"Sure, what's up?"

Jed stepped inside and sat down. "I've been hearing about this arson case and read the reports. Do you need any help?"

Wade blew out a breath. "Actually, that would be great. I need to run down a couple of names. Do you think you could do a search of property fires in the Gunnison, Colorado region and find out if any of them are connected to a man named Will Timmerman or company called San Juan Development Corporation? We think Timmerman and Willard are the same person."

Jed's eyes widened. "What?"

"Yeah, I know. This case is just as crazy as it sounds. And I would greatly appreciate you going through incident reports. We need to go back a lot of years."

"Okay. I can definitely do that."

Wade's phone rang.

Jed stood. "Email me the specifics."

With a nod, Wade answered the phone. Jed gave him a quick wave and left.

"Kaczmarek."

His boss's voice came over the line, asking for an update. Wade blew out another breath. It would be a long day.

Thirty-One

"Oh, boy! There they are! Bronwyn! Do you see?" Henry pointed toward the horse barn and the corral behind it as Alice set him on the ground after lifting him from the car. He looked up at Alice. "I can't wait to ride one!" His eager expression morphed into a frown. "Are you sure we're allowed?"

She smiled at him. "Yes, I'm sure."

"And I won't fall off?"

"Nope. Knox or I will be right next to you the whole time, okay?" They were at the Stone Creek for a riding lesson. Horses were a large part of her life, even though she'd been living in town before she came to Pine Ridge. She rode several times a week when they lived in Colorado. If Wade and his children were going to be part of her life, she wanted the kids to be comfortable with the animals. When she told him that, he wholeheartedly agreed. She was excited to teach them to ride.

"There's so many!" Bronwyn came around to stand with them.

"There are, yes. Before long, there won't be, though. Once

Knox and Sofie move to their new ranch, a lot of these horses will go with them." She ushered the kids around to the other side of the car so she could get Elise. Unbuckling the toddler, she settled the girl on her hip, then grabbed the diaper bag and shut the door. "Come on. Let's go find Knox."

Henry and Bronwyn skipped ahead toward the barn. They stopped at the fence to look at the herd while Alice followed at a slower pace. Elise babbled in her arms, pointing at the horses and other things she saw.

She called to the kids and motioned them toward the man-door on the side of the barn. Their little voices bounced off the rafters inside. Knox poked his head out from a stall about halfway down the corridor.

"Hey, guys." He grinned, then glanced down as Olive stepped out beside him.

"Hi!" The dark-haired girl ran down the aisle and gave Bronwyn a hug. "I'm excited to go riding with you. Daddy's the best teacher!"

Knox chuckled as he walked up. "From the mouth of babes. No pressure, right?"

Alice grinned. "I believe her, though."

He smiled, then looked at Bronwyn and Henry. "You guys ready?"

They both gave an emphatic yes, bouncing up and down.

"Okay, then. Come on. I already put your horses in the arena. I was just readying Olive's. We'll do some basic safety with hers first." He gestured for them to follow, stopping in front of the stall he'd exited.

"This is Snowy." Olive reached up and pet the nose of the cream-colored, blue-eyed horse that poked its head over the door. "Her real name is Shasta, but I think she looks like a Snowy, so Daddy told me I could call her that."

"She's pretty." Bronwyn reached up and touched the horse's nose. "And soft."

Henry stretched a hand up, but couldn't reach the tall animal. Knox picked him up so he could pet the horse. The boy giggled as Snowy nudged his hand.

"Okay, first rule." Knox paused, making sure they were listening. "You never go into a stall or the corral without an adult."

Bronwyn and Henry nodded.

"Second rule, never run up to a horse. Always walk. And don't approach directly from behind."

They nodded again.

"Last rule, when you're in the barn or anywhere on the ranch where there's nothing separating you from the animals, you need an adult with you unless you're told otherwise, and you have to listen to instructions without arguing. If Alice or I —or Daisy or Asa or whoever—tells you to stop or back up or whatever, you do it, okay? You can ask questions afterward. It's a safety thing, all right?"

"Okay," Henry said.

"Yep." Bronwyn nodded.

"Good." He put Henry down next to Bronwyn. "Now, Olive's going to lead Snowy to the arena and we're going to follow far enough back we can't get kicked." He unlatched the stall door. "Step back."

Alice put a hand around Henry's chest, pulling him toward her as she took several steps back. Bronwyn moved next to her. Knox handed the reins to Olive, and the little girl led the mare from her stall. Knox dropped back with Alice and the kids.

"Where's Sofie? I thought she was going to be out here. You said she agreed to sit with Elise so I could help you with the lessons."

"She's in the arena. She wanted to sit down."

Alice frowned. "Is she okay? I thought she was doing better."

"She is, but she still gets tired. That virus packed a wallop."

"I'm sure it didn't help that she's pregnant. I haven't talked to her lately. I've been so preoccupied with my house and these three, I've been a terrible sister-in-law, not to mention business partner." Their new store, Homespun Arts, was set to open at the end of August. Sofie had been overseeing the renovations to the shop as well as the display installation.

"You're all right. She knows how busy you've been. And honestly, it's been good for her to have something to focus on. Keeps her mind off of being sick."

"So long as she doesn't overdo it."

"I won't let her. And she knows her limits. She wouldn't do anything to jeopardize her pregnancy."

They reached the arena, and Knox hurried ahead to open the gate so Olive could lead Snowy inside. Alice spotted Sofie sitting in a chair on the perimeter and wandered over.

"Hey." She smiled at her sister-in-law.

"Hey, yourself." She returned Alice's smile and got up.

"How are you feeling?"

Sofie waved a hand. "I'm fine. Fatigue is my new normal and will be for a while. Comes with the territory." She looked at Elise. "Hi, baby."

Elise, having never met a stranger, gave Sofie a toothy smile and waved one chubby hand.

"She's just adorable. You and I are going to have fun while your siblings ride." She turned and picked up the cloth bag next to her chair. "I brought some toys and coloring stuff for you."

"I brought some things too." Alice set the girl down, then opened the diaper bag, pulling out her toy phone and a silicone fidget toy. "There are some snacks in there, too, and her sippy cup."

"Sounds good." Sofie sank into the chair. Elise toddled over to her. "We'll be fine. Go teach."

Smiling, Alice bent and placed a kiss on top of Elise's head, then walked back to the gate and let herself in. Knox was explaining the parts of the riding kit to the kids. They listened with rapt attention.

Once he was finished, he took Henry and Alice took Bronwyn. Olive mounted her horse and followed along behind.

Alice followed Knox's lead. When he gave instructions to both, she helped Bronwyn put them into practice. Both kids picked it up quickly, Bronwyn especially. Henry looked a little unsure sitting astride the large animal, but by the end of the lesson, he'd relaxed.

When they were done, Knox and Alice, along with Olive's help, showed the kids how to dress the horses down. After unsaddling them, they led them to the big doors at the back of the arena. Knox removed their bridle and let them out into the pasture to graze with the other horses.

"Who's ready for lunch?" Sofie smiled at the kids, Elise on her hip. She'd followed them to the back of the arena and stood on the other side of the fence.

"Me!" Olive's hand shot up. Bronwyn and Henry echoed her affirmation.

"Well, come on, then. I've got stuff for sandwiches at the house. And Daisy made cookies especially for you."

"Chocolate chip?" Henry asked.

Sofie nodded. "Is there any other kind?"

"Oh, boy!" He ran up to Alice. "Come on, Alice. I'm gonna eat all my lunch so I can have a cookie!"

Alice laughed. "Sounds good, Hen."

They walked back through the barn and outside.

"Should we walk home?" Knox looked at Sofie.

She nodded. "I'm feeling good. Not too fatigued."

"Okay, then. Let's go."

The group headed for the cluster of small homes beyond the main house and entered one with ceramic pots of flowers lining the porch. They traipsed into the kitchen, where Sofie, Alice, and Knox put together some sandwiches and chips.

"Can we eat outside, Mommy?"

Sofie glanced at her daughter, then at Alice. "Sure. If that's okay with Alice?"

"It's fine with me. The weather's gorgeous."

Knox herded the kids outside, where they all crammed onto the picnic table benches. Alice put Elise in her lap and did her best to keep the toddler's hands out of her chips and on her own plate.

When they were done eating and had cleaned up, she let the girl down with her siblings and Olive. They ran around the yard playing tag, then with a ball Olive brought outside.

Alice sat in a lawn chair next to Sofie and her brother and watched, chuckling at Henry's attempt to catch the big ball.

"You've certainly taken to those three."

Alice looked at her brother. "It was easy. They're great."

He nodded. "They are. Are you sure you're ready to take on the role of mom, though?"

She frowned at him. "Why wouldn't I be? I've worked with kids for years."

"I know. But it's different when you're living with them. And you're young. A lot of women your age are just now having their first baby. You're taking on three children under the age of six."

"So? And I'm not that young. I'll be thirty at the end of the year. It's not like I was a teenager when Bronwyn was born. Wade's not robbing the cradle."

He held up his hands. "I'm just playing devil's advocate. I want you to be sure about what you're doing. Taking on the task of raising someone else's children is a huge responsibility."

"I know. But when you love them, it's not hard to put

yourself in the right mindset. I just want what's best for them."

He studied her for a moment, then gave a short nod. "Good." He smiled. "Welcome to the parenthood club."

She smiled back. "I'm not sure I can call myself a full-fledged member yet. Wade and I aren't married. We haven't even really talked about it. I mean, we've talked about how we want this to last. Neither of us is interested in a fling. But beyond that, we haven't discussed it." But even though it was still early in their relationship, if he asked her to marry him, she'd say yes in a heartbeat. She was rapidly falling in love with the man. She'd already fallen for his children.

Knox smiled. "I suspect that's coming, though. I've seen you all together. You act like a family. I really am happy for you, Alice."

"Same here," Sofie said. "Plus, I'm excited for Olive and this new baby to have cousins." She rested a hand on her belly.

"Me too." Alice glanced at the kids running around. They'd given up on the ball and just chased each other. Even Elise tried to join in, but stopped, distracted by a patch of dandelions. Alice chuckled. The girl loved her yard weeds.

Contentment washed over her. She'd always dreamed of having a family of her own. Up until recently, she hadn't worried about when it would happen. Not until Knox met Sofie. That made her think about her own future. She never thought she'd find love so fast, though. Wade and his children were a blessing. One she intended to hold close and treasure.

Thirty-Two

"You really got that thing loaded with just three people?" Wade stared at the kiln blocking the back of the trailer, then glanced at Knox, who nodded.

"Brady's a beast. He's got a couple of inches on Asa and probably thirty pounds of muscle. The engine hoist helped too." He grinned.

Asa patted Wade's shoulder. "Don't worry. I won't let Brady best us. Can't give that man the bragging rights."

Wade arched an eyebrow. Yes, there were four of them, but they were using carry straps. "If you say so. Make sure the women follow along behind with their phones in hand so they can call for help when it squishes one of us."

"Nah. Have some faith, Wade." Asa grinned and handed him the carry strap.

Shaking his head, he took the strap. "Sure." He just hoped it wasn't him that got squished. He had the most medical training.

"Let's get this thing unloaded so we can start on the rest of it." Jasper Hendriks, Asa's ranch hand and the sheriff's boyfriend, stepped into the trailer. Knox recruited him to help, knowing they'd need more people to move Alice's kiln.

They crowded around the kiln, and Jasper and Asa leaned into it, tipping it up so Wade and Knox could slide the straps underneath. Once they were sticking out on all four sides, the men spread around it and donned the straps, adjusting them so the kiln was level.

"Are we ready?" Jasper asked.

Wade and the others nodded.

At the tallest, Asa stepped out of the trailer first, keeping the kiln more level. Knox and Jasper came out next, and Wade brought up the rear. The weight pulled on his shoulders, but the padded straps kept it from hurting. He wouldn't want to go far like this, but walking to the firebrick pad Alice set up in her garage was doable.

Moving at a steady clip, they walked up the driveway and into the garage to the far corner. This past week, he'd helped Alice install firebrick on the floor and the walls around where the kiln would sit. She'd had an electrician come out and install a dedicated outlet for it as well when she had the electrical box upgraded.

"This how you want it, Alice?" Wade glanced at her as they positioned the kiln over the pad.

She eyed it for a moment, then nodded. "That works."

"Okay. Down on three, guys." Wade counted down, and they set the kiln on the bricks.

Alice squealed and ran up. "You have no idea how excited I am to have this thing hooked up again. No more trips to Billings, praying nothing shifts and breaks on the way there and back, or taking hours out of my day to do it." She sighed. "I can really make some headway on projects now."

Wade unhooked the straps from his shoulders and helped pull them out from beneath the kiln while Jasper and Asa tipped it. He glanced at her with a smile. "You'll have to make some pieces with the kids. My parents would love to have something like that for their birthdays or Christmas."

She smiled. "It's already on my list." She turned to her brother and Sofie. "For Olive too. Noreen and Silas will love it. So will Dad."

"They will." Knox rolled up a set of straps, while Wade rolled the other.

Jasper clapped his hands together. "Let's get this party in gear. I've got a date tonight." He blew out a breath. "So long as she doesn't get stuck at the office."

"Didn't she hire more staff?" Knox asked as they all walked out of the garage.

"She did. But this arson case is taking up a lot of her time."

It was consuming Wade's as well. He'd done plenty of digging on the Mercers this week with little to show for it. A few months after Perabo and his boss were convicted, Joshua Mercer disappeared. He'd sold his house, cut off the utilities, closed his bank accounts, and stopped using his credit cards. On the plus side, Wade now had a viable suspect for all the arson fires.

He shoved thoughts of work away. They had a trailer to unpack, and he wanted to be present for Alice and his friends. Not lost in his head.

With the kiln out of the way, they made quick work of moving in the rest of Alice's belongings. The furniture came first. Wade couldn't help but notice that she didn't have nearly enough to fill up this big house. The den and sunroom downstairs were virtually empty. Upstairs, only two bedrooms had beds; hers and a guest room. There were two more completely empty.

After dropping off a box load of books to the living room, he went back to the trailer to see what was left. There wasn't much, he knew.

"Three or four more trips and we should be done." Asa loaded several boxes onto the dolly Wade pushed.

"Sounds good. I'm ready for lunch." He had a decent breakfast but had quickly worked it off.

"We all are." Asa put the last box on the stack. "That's all kitchen stuff."

"Got it." Wade spun around and wheeled the dolly into the house. Moving down the hallway, he entered the kitchen. Alice, Daisy, and Sofie each had a box open and were wiping things down and putting them away.

He put the new stack in the corner. "We're almost done unloading."

"Awesome." Sofie stretched to put a stack of plates away. "I'm starving. You don't want the pregnant lady to get hangry, so step it up."

Chuckling, he gave her a quick, two-fingered salute. "Yes, ma'am." With a smile for Alice, he hurried out of the kitchen.

A police cruiser pulled up to the curb as he stepped outside. Katy climbed out, still in uniform, and made her way up the drive.

Jasper spotted her as he stepped out of the trailer, carrying two boxes of books. "Hey, babe. What are you doing here?"

She smiled and walked up to him, giving him a quick kiss. "I thought I'd eat lunch with you guys, if that's all right? I need to talk to Wade, anyway."

"I see how it is." Jasper rolled his eyes, but grinned. He bent, still holding the boxes, and kissed her harder.

She laughed as she pulled away. "Wade's just an excuse. I needed a Jasper pick-me-up."

He waggled his eyebrows. "You'll get a better one later."

Asa groaned. "Can it, Jazz. Geez."

Wade chuckled and pushed the dolly up to the trailer. "Like you and Daisy are any better?"

"Shh. Don't worry about that." Asa grinned and put a box on the dolly.

Laughing, Wade stacked another box. It was nice to be back among friends. He hadn't realized how isolated he was living in Tennessee until he came home.

"I think we're all guilty of it." He loaded a third box. "It's hard not to be when we're in love."

All movement stopped. It took Wade a second to realize what he said. When he did, his eyes widened, and he glanced up. Knox was in his direct line of sight.

"Dude. You can't tell us that before you tell Alice." Knox frowned. "Have you told Alice?"

Wade swallowed and shook his head. "No. The words just popped out. I don't think I actually recognized how I felt about her until now." But it was true. He loved Alice.

"No one says a word." Katy pointed at the others.

Jasper held up his hands. "Not my business." He mimed zipping his lips.

"No worries here. Daisy would kill me if I spilled the beans."

Knox narrowed his eyes, staring at Wade. "Do you really love her?"

Wade nodded. "With everything I have. She's amazing."

Silvery eyes, so much like his sister's, studied Wade. Knox nodded once. "Okay. Be good to her."

Heart thumping, Wade nodded again. "I will."

Knox grinned. "Now you have to go back in there and face her." He gestured to the house.

A fourth box landed on the stack on the dolly. Asa laughed. "Good luck. Maybe we should all go get lunch separately and leave them alone."

"I like that idea." Jasper gave Katy a hot look.

Knox wrinkled his nose. "Thank you for that image."

Katy smacked Jasper's chest. "Behave. I still need to talk to Wade, remember?"

He pouted. "Oh, yeah."

Taking a deep breath, Wade tipped the dolly back. "Let's finish unloading. And thank you for not giving me crap for blurting out my feelings."

Asa stepped out of the trailer with another box. "No worries, man. We all know exactly how you feel right now. Poleaxed, but happy beyond words."

That described it perfectly. A lightness filled Wade's soul. He couldn't wait to get Alice alone later. They had some things to discuss.

But first, Knox was right. He needed to face her with his newfound knowledge. Sucking in a fortifying breath, he headed inside.

Sofie eyed him as he entered the kitchen. "What took you so long?"

Wade glanced at Alice. His heart flip-flopped. Clearing his throat, he turned back to Sofie. "Katy's here."

"Oh?"

"She's going to eat with us. She also said she needs to talk to me."

Three identical frowns marred their faces.

"There wasn't another fire, was there?" Daisy asked.

He shrugged. "I don't think so. I'm on call, so I'd have probably heard about it by now. She probably just has an update." He unloaded the top two boxes, then spun the dolly around. "We should be done in just a couple of minutes. Why don't you three finish up and meet us outside?"

They nodded, and he left. Relief hit him as he turned away. He'd made it through his first interaction with her after his life-altering revelation without her getting suspicious. It wasn't that he didn't want her to know. He just preferred to tell her without an audience.

"This is it." Knox walked in with an armload as Wade reached the door.

"Oh. Great. I'll put this in Asa's truck, then we can all go get lunch."

"Sounds good."

In a few minutes, they were all ready to go and piled into Katy's cruiser, Asa's truck, and Knox's truck, then headed downtown. Daisy had called ahead to let Sara know they were coming, so when they got there, they made their way to the far corner of the restaurant, where Sara had pushed two tables together for them. They placed their orders, then relaxed, enjoying each other's company.

The bell over the door sounded, and Wade glanced up. Levi Rister walked in. He watched the man walk up to the counter and noticed Katy's attention drawn to him as well. From the look on her face, she still couldn't eliminate him as a suspect in the fires.

Wade studied him more carefully. The man didn't look like an arsonist or a killer, but didn't they always say it was the ones you'd never suspect?

The waitress manning the counter smiled at him, then retrieved a to-go order. Rister paid her, then left, never spotting them.

Sharing a look with Katy, he turned back to the conversation at the table, putting thoughts of the man on the backburner. He could focus on him later. Right now, he wanted to enjoy his lunch.

Sara came with their orders a few minutes later. Wade dug into his burger, not realizing just how hungry he was until he took the first bite. It didn't take him long to polish it off.

When they finished eating and were on their way out of the restaurant, Katy pulled him aside.

"Can you come back to the station with me for a few minutes? I'll take you back to Alice's afterward."

He nodded. "Just let me tell her where I'm going." He stepped away, finding Alice. After telling her he needed to go with Katy, she nodded and told him to take his time, then gave him a quick kiss.

Jasper gave Katy a kiss goodbye, then Wade got in the cruiser with her.

"I take it you found something?"

She smoothed a hand down her ponytail. "Maybe. A lot of the reports have come back. I want to run stuff past you." She made a turn and drove the few blocks to the police station.

More curious now than before, Wade followed her in the back door once she parked. They went straight to her office.

She sat down behind the desk and opened the top folder on a stack in the center of the blotter. "The medical examiner finally ID'd the body. It's Willard. I took your advice and also asked him to look for dental records under Timmerman's name. He found some in Colorado. They're a match as well, minus some recent fillings. The bone structure and previous work are the same. Did you find out anything on the fires connected to Timmerman or his company?"

"I had my partner run the search. He found several minor ones, and one larger house fire. All were ruled accidental. I reviewed the reports. There's nothing to indicate they weren't."

"What about the Mercers and their house?" she asked, her tone distracted as she took notes.

"I can't find Joshua Mercer. After Perabo and his boss went to jail, he disappeared."

"What?" She looked up. "People don't just vanish."

"He did. He sold everything, stopped using his credit cards and closed his bank accounts. I can't find him. As for their house, Build-Rite actually owned it before the Mercer's bought it. I dug deeper into the company, and it's a shell corporation. I haven't been able to find the parent company, though."

She nodded. "I might have the answer to that. I looked into Timmerman's background. That's his real name. Willard is the alias. I traced his driver's license back to when he got it in Colorado. He switched from a Nevada license. He grew up in Las Vegas, started doing some construction and made enough to buy a house and flip it. His business grew from there. It looks like he was on the up and up until an incident a little over fifteen years ago. Part of a foundation collapsed on one of his houses. It brought down the second story, killing the elderly couple asleep upstairs."

Wade winced.

"Yeah. But investigators couldn't prove Timmerman's company or contractors were at fault. They used low-grade materials, but they were considered acceptable. The stink of it stuck with him, though, and his company struggled. Tim Willard showed up in Billings not long after that."

"But he never gave up on his original company?"

She shook her head. "No. I think he was just trying to escape the fallout from the house collapse. Maybe build up some cash to keep his Colorado company afloat."

That made sense. "I think I want to take a closer look at the first fire here. Jed ruled it accidental, but I'd like to review the photos from the scene. Maybe I'll spot something he missed now that we have more information. I'll talk to him, too, about helping chase down the parent company to Build-Rite."

Katy frowned. "I don't want to think he missed anything. Or that our housing inspector did. That could spell more trouble for more than just this case."

Wade agreed. But they had to be thorough, no matter the consequences. "Billings should do the same."

Her frown deepened. "I'll call them. And I'll email

Mercer's photo to them, too, so they can keep an eye out for him. I think he's who we're looking for. The fires started after Perabo's release from prison."

"Do you have a protective detail on Perabo?"

"Not yet, but that's the first thing I'm doing after we wrap up this meeting. I'm going to attempt to talk to him again too. Maybe he'll be more forthcoming now that Timmerman is dead."

Wade hoped so, but he wasn't sure it would do any good. Perabo wouldn't know where Mercer was. He'd want to stay as far away from the man as he could.

THIRTY-THREE

Alice waved goodbye as the last of her helpers walked down the porch steps. She waited until Knox and Sofie were ensconced in their vehicle before going inside and closing the door.

"That everyone?"

She turned, smiling at Wade as he emerged from the kitchen. "Yes." Her gaze landed on the two champagne flutes in his hands. "What's this?"

He stopped in front of her and held one out, a playful smile on his face. "I figured we should celebrate your first night in your new house."

Taking the flute, she looked at the pale amber liquid, then up at him through her lashes with a small smile. "When did you get this?"

"Earlier this week. I ran over and got it from my fridge while you were saying goodnight to Knox and Sofie."

"Oh?"

He nodded and lifted his glass. "To new adventures and old Victorians."

She grinned. A soft tink rang through the room as she tapped her glass to his. "To the future."

They each took a sip of the bubbly champagne. Alice's mouth tingled from it, but the wine was crisp and refreshing.

Wade's arm went around her waist. "We have something else to celebrate."

"Oh?"

"Mom left a note on the counter. She and Dad took the kids home for the night."

Heat flooded Alice's system, pooling low in her belly. "Really?" She wrapped her free hand around his shoulders. "What are you going to do all night? Alone."

He leaned closer, a smile tugging at his lips. Alice lifted her face, pulled to him like a magnet.

"Who says I'll be alone?" His low voice whispered over her senses, making her dizzy.

"Yeah?" she breathed.

"Oh, yeah." He closed the distance, sealing his mouth to hers.

Alice tasted the crisp champagne on his tongue. It mingled with something unique to Wade and sent a heady feeling through her. The world spun, and she gripped the hair at the back of his head.

He broke away to stare at her. "I don't want to be presumptuous. Would you like to go upstairs?"

Something inside Alice shifted. A crack appeared and emotions flooded out, making her heart ache with joy. She moved the hand on the back of his head around to cup his jaw, staring into his hazel eyes, which were currently a steely green. Amazement rose above the riot of feelings. That this kind, considerate, sexy man wanted her blew her mind. What she did to deserve him, she'd never know, but she would cherish him the rest of her life. She loved him.

A smile blossomed on her face. "Yes, please."

He swooped in, pressing another hot kiss to her mouth. Alice swayed, the dizziness getting worse with her arousal. She wouldn't know up from down by the time they were finished.

"Come on." Stepping back, Wade took her hand and led her to the stairs. They ascended them together, moving silently through the upper story to her new bedroom.

Crossing the threshold, Alice flipped on the light, then paused as she caught sight of the bed. A laugh bubbled free.

"What?"

"We need to make the bed first."

He turned to look at it, then chuckled. "Do you know where the sheets are?"

She gestured around the room. "In a box." Alice sighed. She should have labeled things better. All she wrote on each one was the room it went in.

Wade took her champagne flute and set it on the dresser along with his own. "You take one side, I'll take the other."

With a nod, she walked to the closest stack of boxes and started opening them. Most of the ones they'd brought into this room were filled with clothes. And all the boxes were the same size.

Six boxes in, she hit pay dirt. "Found them!" She lifted the light blue sheets free and held them up.

Wade took them, and she lifted the comforter from the bottom of the box.

"You keep looking for the pillows." He unfurled the fitted sheet over the bed. "I'll put these on."

Sexy and he made beds? Alice's heart fluttered. She turned back to the boxes and started opening more. It took her longer to find the pillows. Wade had both sheets on the bed by the time she found them on the other side of the room.

She stuffed them into their cases, then helped him spread the comforter over the sheets.

"There." He looked at her. "Do we have everything now?"

"I think so."

"Good." He jerked the covers down on the newly made bed, then grabbed her by the waist and tossed her onto the mattress.

Alice let out a little squeal as she bounced, then laughed. Chuckling, he joined her.

"Getting impatient?" She curled her hands in the front of his shirt.

"Very." He kissed her, his intent clear in the way he invaded her mouth and took charge.

A shiver ran through her. She remembered the other night on his couch and couldn't wait for the full show.

His mouth left hers to trail down her jaw and neck. She tilted her head to give him better access, loving the contrast between his soft lips and coarse beard stubble on her skin. She wanted to feel it everywhere. And she wanted him naked. She wanted them both naked. Now.

Alice pushed on his shoulders.

He lifted his head. "You okay?"

She nodded and pushed again, sitting up as he sat back. "I hope you don't want slow." She whipped her shirt over her head. "Because I can't go slow. Not tonight."

His pupils dilated as he took in her purple lace bra and the curves spilling over the cups. "No. Slow is overrated." He traced the edge of the lace.

Goosebumps erupted on Alice's skin and her nipples beaded beneath the fabric. Breath coming in short pants, she managed a growl of warning. "Wade."

A wicked grin slashed his face. "Then again, maybe it's not." His voice dropped. "Should we bet on if I can make you come without even taking off your clothes?"

She growled again and grabbed his face, kissing him. He grunted, returning her kiss for a moment before pulling away to take off his t-shirt.

Her gaze landed on his bare chest. She pressed her hands to the hard muscles, tracing their sculpted edges. He was perfect. Michaelangelo couldn't have done better.

He didn't give her much chance to explore. Tipping her back on the bed, he attacked the button and zipper on her pants. She helped him tug them and her underwear down her legs. He stopped to admire her, but she growled a third time and reached for his belt.

Laughing, he pushed her hands away and stood to divest himself of his remaining clothes. "I'm going to start calling you tiger."

She grinned. "What can I say? You bring out the animal in me." Her expression went slack as he shucked his pants, exposing him to her view. She'd seen him the other night, but standing and wearing nothing, he looked even more impressive.

Climbing back onto the bed, he crawled over her, his eyes locked on hers. Alice didn't feel much like that tiger. More like the antelope it wanted to eat.

She quaked as need rushed through her. She was okay with that.

He tucked her body tight into his, then lowered his head to her breasts, caressing the sensitive flesh with his mouth and teasing the tips to taut peaks. Pulses of need washed over her in time to her heartbeat. Alice moaned, lifting her knees to frame his hips. She ran a hand down his side and around his hip bone. Finding his hard shaft, she squeezed him once. She might be the prey, but that didn't mean she was willing to wait. She wanted all of him. Now. "Please, Wade."

With a moan, he lifted his head to stare at her. "We probably should have discussed birth control before we got naked. I don't have any condoms."

For once, Alice was happy she had heavy menstrual cycles.

She'd gone on the pill in college to help with them and still took it. "I'm on the pill."

He froze. "Are you sure? I've only ever had unprotected sex with Emily."

She nodded, bringing one hand up to run through the short hair on the side of his head. "I'm sure." She took a deep breath. "I love you, and I want this—us."

His pupils dilated, and all his muscles went taut. He held her gaze another long moment. Alice stared up at him, feeling as though time stood still. Until a bright, joyous smile spread over his face.

"I love you too."

Her breath stuck in her throat, and her eyes went wide. "You do?" she squeaked.

"I do." His voice was soft, almost a whisper. He lowered himself down onto her.

Alice moved her hand to clutch at his firm butt.

"Alice." He leaned in, nuzzling her ear with his nose and lips.

"Hmm?" Her eyes rolled back. He bumped her entrance with the head of his shaft, sending a shock wave through her.

"You're it for me. I'm never letting you go."

"Ditto." She squeezed his butt and lifted her hips. A whimper escaped her as her actions pressed him against her core.

He groaned, then reached between them to position himself. Dragging himself through her wetness, he found her entrance and pushed inside.

Alice's back arched, and her breath froze in her lungs. "Oh!" Her muscles clenched around him, giving her a preview of what was to come.

Wade groaned again, sliding in and out several times until he was fully seated within her walls. Holding onto her hips, he glanced at her. "You okay?"

"Yes." She squirmed, wanting the friction, but he stubbornly held still.

That wicked smile crossed his face again. "Hold on." He withdrew, then slammed into her.

Stars danced in front of her eyes, and her breath left her on a long moan. Grasping his biceps, she did as he suggested, anchoring herself as he drove her to the most intense orgasm she'd ever experienced. Howling, Alice dug her fingers into his arms as she came apart.

Before she could put herself back together or even come down, he flipped her over and raised her hips.

"Got another one in you?"

"What?" She turned her head to look back at him.

He stared at her, eyes glittering with heat.

Hers widened. "Wait. You didn't go?"

He shook his head and shuffled closer on his knees. He bumped her entrance from behind.

Alice's eyes rolled back again, only to fly open as he drove into her. "Oh! Oh, do that again." Pleasure raced through her, touching every millimeter of her body all the way down to the ends of her hair. She reached for the top of the headboard and held on as he pounded into her.

This time, they went over together. As Alice cried out and bucked against him, he stiffened, then let out a loud growl. His body curled around hers, and they collapsed onto the bed, still intertwined. He rolled them, and they separated, but he tucked her close.

Taking deep gulps of air, Alice tried to slow her racing heart. "That was intense."

"Yep." His chest heaved against her back.

She turned, putting her arms around his neck to give him a long, tender kiss.

Wade brushed her cheekbone with his thumb and pulled back. "I love you."

Smiling, she caressed his bottom lip. "I love you too." Something he said came back to her, making her chuckle.

"What's so funny?"

"You know how you said you weren't letting me go?"

"Yeah. I meant it."

"I know. But it just hit me. What are we going to do with two houses?"

A wrinkle formed on his forehead before his expression cleared, and he chuckled. "Maybe we should keep this one as a sex den. You were pretty loud."

Alice laughed. "Might not be a bad idea." She bit her lip, her blood firing again. "Wanna see how loud you can make me get?"

Fire leaped to life in his eyes. "Hell yeah."

THIRTY-FOUR

Darkness enveloped them as Alice and Wade shared a goodnight kiss in the yard between their houses. Just as things started to heat up, Wade pulled back and rested his forehead against hers. Alice let out a sigh. She was tired of goodnight kisses. She wanted good morning kisses. While they were still in bed.

"I'm going to get Mom and Dad to take the kids again this weekend. Maybe we can run off to Billings or Bozeman for a night. No distractions."

She leaned back to smile at him. "I like that idea. What about your arson case, though?"

He frowned. "It's stalled. Still no line on Joshua Mercer or the shell companies. And I reviewed the case files from all the fires connected to TW Developments. Nothing seems amiss that wasn't already noted. Katy interviewed Perabo again, but he still refuses to talk. With Timmerman dead, we might be looking at the end of it."

A deep line had formed on his forehead as he talked. Alice smoothed it away. "I'm sorry."

He pecked a kiss on her lips. "Thanks. It's just frustrating, you know. A weekend away with you is what I need, though. It won't help solve my case, but it'll mitigate some of the stress." He smiled, lowering his head to kiss her more deeply.

Alice gave a soft laugh and kissed him back. Their embrace ended all too soon, though.

"I need to get back."

She nodded. Elise had been a light sleeper the last few nights. Her molars were giving her hell again. "Okay. I'll see you in the morning."

With a nod, he gave her another quick kiss. Squeezing her hand, he backed away. "I love you."

"I love you too." She'd never get tired of hearing that. "Goodnight."

"Goodnight." He let go of her hand and turned, jogging back to his house.

Alice let out a long sigh and went into hers. One day, it wouldn't be like this. She still didn't know what they were going to do about having two houses. Maybe she could rent hers out.

Inside, she checked her email and jotted down a couple of pottery orders, then shut the lights off downstairs and headed up to take a shower. Once she was clean, she walked into the bedroom to dress. Her gaze went to the bed, and she pressed her lips together, remembering what happened there days earlier. Her body heated and she turned away.

Donning an oversize t-shirt and panties, she picked up the remote for the TV hanging on the wall and clicked it on. She'd watch something funny for a little while and distract herself.

She shut off the overhead light, but left the fan on, then climbed into bed and flipped through the channels until she found something that interested her. Settling against the pillows, she forced her brain to concentrate on the show and not remember how it felt to have Wade lying next to her.

After an hour, yawns started to overtake her, so she shut

the TV off and snuggled under the blankets. Silence engulfed her. Without the noise of the television to distract her, thoughts of Wade crept back in. Of his hard, perfect muscles, and his heavy erection doing things to her body that sent her soaring into the clouds.

Moaning, she rolled over and tried to think about pottery. She had a bunch of pieces to throw tomorrow and several others to paint. She was well behind on her orders, but was hopeful she'd catch up soon. The kids' regular sitter, Shelby, was supposed to come back to work. She'd miss them during the day, but it would be nice to get caught up again. And to help Sofie with the store. There were several displays that needed to be put together, and they'd received the first deliveries from local artists to stock the shelves.

Her mind drifted as sleep edged in. Thoughts of her art and the store gave way to Wade's handsome face, then to his naked body, moving over hers. Her blood heated and sleep vanished.

"Oh, come on." Blowing out a breath, she puffed her hair out of her face and glanced at the clock. She really needed to go to sleep. But her body was on fire.

Alice stared up at the ceiling fan, then rolled over again, kicking the covers away. She doubted it would help, though. She wasn't hot from the room temperature. It had been five days since she'd screamed the roof off in this very room. They needed to figure something out soon. Now that she knew what sex with Wade was like, she craved more. Every day it didn't happen, the more she craved it. It would drive her mad before long.

With a huff, she sat up. She'd go down and drink a cup of chamomile tea. If that didn't help, she'd start on her pottery backlog. She figured if she was going to be awake anyway, she might as well be productive.

Leaving the room, she tread down the stairs, her bare feet

barely making a sound. She rounded the banister and went down the hall to the kitchen, where she filled a mug with water and put it in the microwave.

While it heated, she leaned on her hands on the counter and stared out at her darkened yard. After a moment, though, her brain cleared long enough for her to realize something didn't look right. It was brighter than usual.

Was there a full moon tonight?

She quickly shook off the thought. The color wasn't right for moonlight.

Curious now, she went to the back door and stepped outside. As she cleared the door frame, a brighter light drew her attention, and she looked to her left toward Wade's.

"Oh my God!" Flames engulfed the second and third stories.

Alice didn't think. She just ran. Hurrying through her yard, she opened the fence gate on his property and ran to the back door. Her fists landed on the tempered glass, and she pounded on it. "Wade!" Smoke alarms shrieked inside. She cupped her hands on the door and peered in. The kitchen was dark and silent.

"Oh please, no." She backed away, glancing around the yard. The light from the fire illuminated it well even through the smoky haze filling the air. There was no one out here with her.

She spun toward the gate and ran around the side of the house, hoping they'd gone out the front. Rounding the corner, heart in her throat, it sank like a rock when she didn't see him and the kids anywhere.

Desperate now, she ran up the porch steps and banged on the door and punched the doorbell. She could hear it sound inside. "Wade!" She tried the door, but it was locked and her key was at her house.

Moving to the window, she looked through, slapping the

pane with the flat of her hand as she yelled his name again. The front of the house had a lot more smoke than the back. She couldn't see anything.

Call for help.

Alice's conscience broke through her panic. It was right. She dashed off the porch and through the yard again, flying into her house and upstairs to get her phone. Out of breath, she dialed 911.

"Campbell County emergency dispatch. Can I have your name, please?"

"Alice Duvall. My neighbor's house is on fire."

"Okay. What's the address?"

Alice rattled it off. "Please hurry. I think he and his children are still inside. I can't find them, and I know they're home."

"I'm sending help now."

"Okay, thank you." She didn't wait for the woman to say goodbye or ask more questions. She hung up and dashed into her closet, yanking on the first pair of pants she saw. After stuffing her feet into some tennis shoes without socks, she snatched her phone off the bed, then ran downstairs and outside, grabbing her keys as she fled through the door.

Wade and the kids were still nowhere to be seen.

The bottom floor was still untouched. Alice ran up the porch steps and banged on the door again. Something hit the window from inside. She hurried over and saw the tips of Wade's fingers.

"No." The word ripped from her throat on a harsh whisper. She couldn't let them die.

Alice glanced around, looking for something to break the glass. Her gaze landed on the planter by the steps. Stuffing her phone and keys into her pockets, she ran to it and tipped it over, dumping out the dirt so she could lift it. It was still heavy, but she barely noticed the weight with all the adrenaline flooding her system.

She carried it to the window, then hurled it at the glass, praying it was enough. It hit, shattering the outer pane and breaking the pot into several pieces. She picked up one of the larger chunks and threw it at the inner pane like a baseball. The glass broke and smoke billowed from the opening.

Coughing, she grabbed another piece of the pot and used it to clear the broken glass from the frame. "Wade! Honey, it's me. Are you there?"

Elise appeared in front of the opening, hanging from her father's hands. The girl cried silent tears and coughed violently. Alice grabbed her. "I've got you sweetie." She pressed a kiss to the girl's head, then turned back to the window. Wade's hacking cough sounded over the roar of the flames. Sirens split the night, but they were still minutes away.

Henry's head appeared. Alice put Elise down and helped him through the window. "Sit with your sister." She pointed to the toddler, who laid on her side, coughing. Henry nodded and sank down beside her, coughing so hard he folded in on himself.

Alice looked at the window again, expecting to see Bronwyn. "Wade!" Her gaze searched the smoke, but she saw nothing. "Wade, where are you? Where's Bronwyn?" *Please, please, please.*

Relief made her knees weak when Bronwyn's soot-streaked face appeared. Alice hurried forward to help her through the window. The girl fell to the porch, barely conscious.

Alice dropped down beside her and made sure she was breathing. Bronwyn opened her eyes and looked at Alice, then tried to sit up. A violent coughing fit wracked her little body. Alice helped her sit, then hurried back to the window, pulling her shirt up over her face as she leaned through to look for

Wade. She searched the smoky darkness until her hand bumped his body. *Oh, thank God!* She curled her fingers into the fabric of his shirt and tugged. "Wade, get up! I can't lift you." He shifted but stayed down.

Tears streamed down her face from the smoke and from fear. "Please! You have to get up. Your kids need you. I need you. Don't die on me!"

He shifted again, rising onto his hands and knees. Alice wrapped more fabric around her hand and pulled, hoping to give him the incentive to keep coming. He lifted a hand to the windowsill. She grabbed it and pulled. He coughed, the sound harsh.

"Come on. We need to get off the porch." She tugged on his clothing again.

He fell over the sill, his legs still inside.

Alice grabbed the waistband of his shorts and pulled. He was virtually a dead weight, but her efforts gave him the impetus to raise his legs over the sill and tumble onto the porch.

The sirens grew louder. Red and blue lights flashed in the night sky as they neared, competing with the fire.

Alice picked up Elise and Henry, dashing down the porch steps to her front yard. She set them in the grass by the sidewalk. "Stay put."

Henry wrapped an arm around his sister. Alice ran back to get Bronwyn. Wade was on his hands and knees as she mounted the steps, crawling toward his daughter.

"I've got her." She scooped the girl off the porch. Her barking coughs shook her entire body. "Can you walk?" Alice laid a hand on Wade's shoulder.

"Yes." He coughed again and struggled to his feet.

Alice wrapped his arm over her shoulders and helped him down the stairs. They stumbled across the grass as the first firetruck turned down their road.

Wade fell to his knees next to Henry and Elise. Alice put Bronwyn down beside him, then ran to the firetruck as it pulled to a stop.

The doors opened, and four firefighters poured out. One of them turned to her. Even in the dark, she could see the worry on his face. He knew who lived here.

"Where are they?"

"In my yard." She pointed behind her. "They've all inhaled a lot of smoke."

The man nodded, then looked back. "Smith! Burgess! Get the oxygen!"

Two firefighters opened compartments on the side of the truck and withdrew oxygen tanks. Alice led them to her yard and helped them put oxygen on Wade and the kids. From the corner of her eye, she saw the other firefighters, plus those from a second truck that just arrived, attach lines to the fire hydrant, and attack the flames.

Wade sat up, the oxygen reviving him. He glanced at the kids. Alice did too. Bronwyn struggled, coughing harder than anyone. She'd perked up some with the oxygen but couldn't control her coughing.

"Wyn?" Wade crawled closer.

"Does she have asthma?"

Alice looked at the firefighter who'd spoken. The name "Smith" was emblazoned on his helmet.

A hard cough wracked Wade's body, so Alice answered for him. "No. None of them do."

The man's mouth flattened. "We've got medical on the way. She'll be priority."

A tear leaked from Wade's eye. Alice grabbed his free hand, sniffing back her own. They were out of the fire, but they weren't safe yet.

THIRTY-FIVE

Wade's chest ached. And his eyes and throat burned like the devil. He ignored it, his attention on his kids. Elise and Henry, while both coughing, were in much better shape than Bronwyn. His oldest had been closest to the fire. Her room was filled with smoke, and flames roiled over the ceiling by the time he found her. She'd been on the floor, nowhere near her door, disoriented from the inability to see where she was going.

It was a miracle they'd made it downstairs at all. He hadn't been able to see. He'd crawled down the upstairs hallway with Elise tucked into his chest and the older kids holding onto his t-shirt. They'd slid down the stairs on their butts. He'd relied on muscle memory to get them to the front door.

What he found there had ignited a fire in his blood as hot as the one burning down his house. Someone had screwed it shut.

Anger still simmered in his gut. He'd spooked the arsonist with his digging. But instead of skipping town, the bastard thought it was a good idea to take him out. But he'd tried to kill Wade's children. There wasn't a force on Earth that would stop him from hunting the asshole down now.

Gratefulness that he was still alive to do that—that they all were—washed over him. He looked at Alice. She'd saved their lives. He pulled down his mask. "Thank you."

Tears filled her eyes. She looked down at Elise, who sat in her lap, and brushed the toddler's hair back. "I wasn't about to let you die." She glanced up. "I can't live without you. Any of you."

He wiped away a tear that slid down her cheek. "I love you, woman."

"I love you too." She touched the hand holding his mask. "Now put that back on."

He tried to laugh, but it came out as another hacking cough. That was going to stick around for a while.

Paramedics arrived and started to assess them. Bronwyn still struggled. The first crew loaded her onto a gurney to take her to the waiting ambulance. Wade glanced between her and his other kids, torn about where to go.

Alice laid a hand on his arm. "Go with her. I'll stay with Henry and Elise."

"Are you sure?" The mask muffled his voice.

She nodded. "We'll see you at the hospital."

"Okay." He pulled his mask down again long enough to give Henry and Elise each a kiss. "I have to go with your sister. She's very sick. Alice is going to stay with you, all right?"

Henry nodded. Elise, scared and confused, clutched Alice's shirt with one hand and batted at her mask with the other.

Wade kissed the girl again. "It's okay, baby. You're going to be fine." Tears wet his scratchy eyes. He sniffed and got to his feet. He looked at Alice. "Take care of them."

"Always. Go."

Heart hurting at having to leave them, but knowing

Bronwyn needed him more, he followed the paramedics loading his daughter into the ambulance.

Inside, the older woman glanced at him as he sat down. He knew all the EMTs and paramedics and was glad Carrie Bledsoe was the one treating Bronwyn. She knew her stuff and had a gentleness about her that made her great with kids.

"Hi, Wade. Have a seat there." She nodded to a seat built into the wall.

He sat.

"Let me get an IV started on her and then we'll do you."

"I'll be fine. Take care of her."

She nodded once, then looked at her male colleague, Drew Kurtz. "Let's do this."

Wade sat forward, putting a hand over Bronwyn's leg as he explained to her what was happening. Her frightful gaze broke his heart, but he kept it together through her cries while they started an IV in her hand.

Carrie turned to him. "Your turn."

He waved her off. "They can do whatever to me at the hospital. It's not far. I've got oxygen. I'm fine."

She stared at him for several long moments, then seemed to decide not to waste time arguing with him. Instead, she glanced at her colleague. "Let's go."

Drew nodded, then climbed into the front. In moments, they pulled away from the curb, speeding toward the hospital. Leaning his head back, Wade closed his eyes and prayed everything would turn out all right.

The ride was a short one. In minutes, they pulled into the ambulance bay. Drew climbed out and came around to open the rear doors. Wade got out first, then stood to the side to let them unload the gurney. A nurse met them as they entered the emergency room and directed them to a trauma bay.

"Sir, why don't you come with me and let us check you

out?" Another nurse touched his arm and gestured down the hall.

"No. I'm fine." His hacking cough belied his words. He got it under control and continued. "You can assess me when you're done with her. And my other children. They're in another ambulance with my girlfriend." He coughed again.

She frowned but didn't argue. "Well, at least sit down. We need to switch out your oxygen, anyway." She grabbed a rolling desk chair and positioned him out of the way before fetching the supplies to hook him to the hospital's oxygen system.

Once he was situated, she and another nurse moved the patient from the bay next door to make room for Henry and Elise. They had the area cleaned just as the ambulance carrying them arrived. The paramedics walked in, pushing a gurney with both kids and Alice on it. She held them in her lap.

Relief that his family was together and alive flooded him. Tonight could have been so much worse. Sagging in his seat, he watched the medical team work on Bronwyn. One of the nurses came up and started an IV on him, hanging fluids and injecting medications to counteract the toxic substances he'd inhaled.

He moved the curtain separating Bronwyn's bay from the one next door to check on Henry and Elise. Both kids still sat on Alice's lap while the staff attempted to start their IV drips.

His baby girl was having none of it, though. She screamed and tried to squirm away. Alice spoke softly to her, trying to calm her down, but the toddler was beyond frightened by the night's events.

Wade glanced at Bronwyn. She was calm, and the staff had her condition well in hand. He caught the nurse's attention, then pointed to the next bay as he rolled that way. She nodded, and he stood, pulling his IV pole with him.

"Alice."

She glanced up, as did the medical team.

"You're dad?" one of the doctors asked.

Wade nodded.

The man's eyes did a quick assessment of Wade's body. "Why don't you trade places with this lady and hold your little girl? We can check you both over at the same time." He looked at Alice. "We'll have you sit in a chair with Henry."

"That sounds like a good plan." Alice shifted to swing her legs down.

A nurse helped Henry off the bed as Alice got up, holding Elise. Wade took her place, and she settled the inconsolable toddler in his arms.

He cradled her to his chest. "Hey, sweet girl. It's okay. We're safe. These people want to help us, okay?"

She pushed against his chest, wanting down.

"Honey, stop. Look at Daddy. Look, I'm wearing a mask just like yours."

Her eyes flicked to his face.

He touched his mask. "See. I need it too. And Henry has one. So does Bronwyn in the next bay."

She began to calm the more he talked to her. He glanced at the doctor. "See if you can get the IV in now."

The nurses jumped into action, bringing over the supplies to start the line. Wade held tight to Elise's arm and body. With his help, they had the IV in with one stick.

Controlled chaos reigned in the trauma room for the next thirty minutes as the medical staff assessed each of them and started the appropriate medicines to keep swelling and edema at bay. Fatigue weighed on Wade's shoulders as he laid there, both from what he'd inhaled and from the adrenaline crash. Sleep was the furthest thing from his mind, though. He had a million questions he wanted to ask the fire lieutenant from the scene. And he wanted to talk to Jed. He also needed to call his parents.

Once they were stable and had chest x-rays, they were sent upstairs to patient rooms. It about killed him to be separated from his kids, but they were better off with pediatric doctors who regularly treated children. It helped to know that Alice was with them. This hospital had double rooms, so they put Henry and Bronwyn together. The nurse told him Elise would be across the hall. They would be okay with Alice watching over them.

His bed bumped as the orderly wheeled him off the elevator and down the hallway. They turned through the doorway to his room, and he came to a halt next to the bed already in place there. A peppy nurse walked in, smiling.

"Hello. I'm Tillie, and I'll be your nurse. Are you able to get into the other bed, or do you need us to help you?"

In answer, Wade swung his legs over the side of the gurney.

"Oh, here, hang on." She hurried forward to lower the rail on the other bed.

"Thanks." He stood, took a step, then turned and sat, scooting himself up.

The orderly wheeled the gurney out of the room and closed the door.

"I just need to get a set of vitals on you, then I'll leave you alone." Tillie picked up the blood pressure cuff hanging from the hook at the base of the monitor on the wall.

He nodded, leaning his head back, fighting exhaustion.

She wrapped the cuff around his arm and pushed a button on the monitor. While it inflated, she clipped a pulse oximeter onto a finger on his other hand, then ran a thermometer over his forehead. The machine beeped. She took off the cuff, but left the pulse-ox clip on his finger.

"Okay, Mr. Kaczmarek, you're all set. Can I get you anything?"

"A phone? I need to make some calls."

She pointed to his nightstand. "Dial nine to get out, then the number."

"Thank you."

She gave him a bright smile. "Of course. Here's your call button and television remote." She lifted the remote over the top of the bed and laid it next to his hand. "Call us if you need anything. Otherwise, I'll be back in a couple of hours."

"I will, thanks."

"You're welcome." Spinning on her heel, she left.

Wade picked up the phone and called his parents. The phone rang four times before his dad's groggy voice came over the line. "Hello?"

"Dad?" A cough wracked him.

"Wade? What's wrong?"

Getting himself under control, he tried again. "Someone burned my house down with me and the kids in it. We're at the hospital."

"What!"

He heard his mom ask what happened. Bill's voice grew muffled as he told her.

"We're fine," Wade continued. "Some smoke inhalation. We've all been admitted." He coughed again, wincing as pain lanced his chest.

"Christ almighty, son. Okay. We're on our way."

Wade heard his mom's voice in the background, urging Bill to get out of bed.

"Dad, don't. We're fine, and it's late. Wait until morning."

"Son, if you think your mother and I will go back to sleep now, you're crazy. We'll be there soon. What room are you in?"

He sighed and told him his room number. "I'm not too sure about the kids, though. They're in the pediatric ward. Alice is with them." His breath caught. "She saved our lives. I couldn't get the door open. It was screwed shut. She broke the window and got us out."

A short pause came over the line, then Bill cleared his throat. "Thank God she was there."

Wade coughed. "Yeah."

"Hang tight. We'll see you soon."

"Okay. Bye."

"Bye." Bill hung up.

Pushing the button to get a dial tone again, Wade searched his cloudy memory for Jed's phone number. When it came to him, he dialed, then waited for his partner to answer.

"Braun."

"Jed, it's me. Are you at my house?"

"Jesus, Wade! Are you all right? Are the kids?"

"We're fine. Smoke inhalation. Tell me what you know."

"Um, not much yet. It's still smoldering. How about you tell me what you remember?"

Wade closed his eyes, thinking back. He relayed what he remembered from the time the smoke detector went off to the time he crawled through the front window.

"Damn. If she hadn't been there, you'd have all died."

"I know." Emotion made his voice thick. But it hardened on his next words. "I want this bastard, Jed. He tried to kill my children."

"I know. And we'll find him. I swear. But for now, you get some rest, okay? I'll come see you tomorrow afternoon and tell you what all I found here."

"Yeah. Okay, that works. Thanks."

"No problem. Get better."

They said their goodbyes and hung up. Another hacking cough rattled his body. Once it passed, he glanced at the clock. He had another call to make, but he needed someone's phone for that. He couldn't call long-distance from the hospital.

Setting the phone down, he closed his eyes. That call could wait.

Thirty-Six

Alice jerked awake as Elise's door opened. She sat up in her chair and glanced at the door. Peg and Bill walked in.

"Oh! My little angel." Peg walked up to the crib to look down at a now sleeping Elise. "Is she doing okay?"

"Yes." Alice stood. "She just fell asleep."

"This is just awful." Peg stepped away from the bed to give Alice a fierce hug. "Thank you, my dear."

"For what?" Alice pulled back to look at her.

"For what?" Confusion lit Bill's voice. "You saved them."

"Oh, that. I didn't, really. I just broke a window."

"Don't be so modest," Peg said. "We just left Wade's room. He was losing strength and would never have found something to break the window before he passed out."

A soft blush stole over Alice's cheeks. She just did what she had to. It never occurred to her that he might not have found a way out. She thought she'd just helped speed up the process. "Oh."

Peg hugged her again. Wiping away tears, she pulled back. "Do you need anything?" She looked at Alice's clothes. "You should probably run home and change. And get something to drink. Probably to eat too."

Alice made a face. She wasn't sure she could go back there yet and see the ruins of Wade's house. It was still too fresh in her mind. Plus, there was the matter of not having a way home.

"I don't have my car. I rode in the ambulance with the kids. I don't have my wallet, either. Just my phone."

Bill took out his wallet and gave her a ten-dollar bill.

"Oh, you don't need to do that. I can probably get some crackers and applesauce from the nurses."

He rolled his eyes and held the money out again. "Take it. Get something substantive."

His expression—so very much like one she'd seen on his son—told her he wouldn't be dissuaded. Rather than argue, she took the money. "Thank you."

"It's the least we can do. And we can give you a ride home too. Whenever you want it."

"Okay. Maybe in a few hours. I'm not ready to leave yet."

"Have you called your brother?" Peg asked.

Alice glanced at her. "No. It's still too early." It was just after four o'clock. "I'll call him in a couple of hours." Her stomach rumbled. The adrenaline dump left her ravenous. "But I do think I'll go find that snack now." And peek in on Wade.

"We'll sit with Elise." Peg plopped down in Alice's chair and smiled. "You go get cleaned up and eat. Take your time. We aren't going anywhere."

Giving them a grateful smile, she left the room. After a quick peek in on Bronwyn and Henry, who were both sleeping, she meandered down the hall until she found a restroom. Wetting some paper towels, she cleaned her face. She felt gritty from the smoke. What she really needed was a shower. She'd go home in a few hours and clean up. After she had a chance to better process things.

Her face clean, she found the vending machine and fed it the money Bill gave her and bought a Snickers bar and a bag of pretzels. It wasn't the best thing in the world, but it had protein. She also bought a bottle of water.

Snacks in hand, she took the elevator down to Wade's floor. She didn't know what room he was in, though. They'd only mentioned what floor he'd be on when she left the ER with the kids.

A nurse looked up as she approached. "May I help you? Visiting hours don't start until eight."

"I know. I'm Alice Duvall. My boyfriend is Wade Kaczmarek. He and his children were brought in from a house fire. I rode with the kids in the ambulance. I just want to check on him and give him an update on the kids."

"Oh. Goodness! Yes, okay. He's right through there." She pointed to her right.

"Thank you." Alice turned and went in the door she indicated. Wade opened bloodshot eyes as she came in.

"Hey." His voice was muffled by the oxygen mask over his face.

She smiled and walked to his bedside, sitting in the chair there. "Hey yourself." She took his hand. "I didn't mean to wake you."

"You didn't. How are the kids?"

"They're doing all right. Responding to treatment. Elise was sleeping when I left her with your parents. Bronwyn and Henry were too."

"Good." He coughed.

"How are you doing?"

"I'm fine." He coughed again.

Alice arched an eyebrow. "Sure."

He smiled. "I am, I swear. It'll be a few days, though,

before they'll discharge any of us. Smoke inhalation injury can appear up to forty-eight hours after the event if not treated properly. They need to give us certain medications on a set schedule to keep that from happening." He grimaced. "That's probably not a bad thing. It gives me a chance to figure out where we're going to go."

"My house." He was daft if he thought she'd let them go anywhere else.

"I guess this solves our problem of what we were going to do with two houses."

She smacked his arm. "That's not funny. You almost died." Tears welled in her eyes, and she dipped her head, letting her hair hide her face.

"Hey." He let go of her hand to lift her chin. "Baby, we're fine. A few days, some medicines, and we should be on the mend. Because of you. You saved us all."

She sniffed. "That's what your parents said. I didn't realize you were so weak when I broke the window."

He nodded. "It took me a while to gather all the kids and find the stairs. I spent precious time trying to get the door open before I felt the screws going through into the doorjamb."

Alice shuddered. "Why would someone do that?"

"I'm getting too close. Though, I don't know what they hoped to accomplish by taking me out. Jed would take my place and be doubly determined to find the culprit. So would Katy."

She scooted closer, propping an elbow by his shoulder so she could run her fingers through his hair. With her other hand, she toyed with the hem of the hospital gown at his neck. "So, what happens now?"

"We see what evidence my house offers. Hopefully, it'll lead us to whoever's behind this." He turned his head, pulling his mask down for a moment to place a kiss on her fingers.

"Right now, though, I just want to sleep. It's all catching up to me."

"Okay." She pulled her hands back, sitting up, but he snagged one.

"Stay. Until I fall asleep, at least?"

Alice sagged back onto the chair. "Of course."

His eyes closed. "Thank you for being here."

She rose up and kissed his cheek. "Nowhere else I'd be. I love you."

"I love you too."

Alice sat down and started running her fingers through his short hair again. His breathing evened out—interspersed by coughs—and he dropped off. She sat there for a while, watching him, and thanking God for saving him and the children tonight. For putting her in the right place to get them out. She couldn't imagine life without them.

Thirty-Seven

Wade stared at the ruins of his house. The charred shell held none of the structure's former glory. Now, it looked like a bunch of burnt toothpicks sticking out of a sad pile of rubble. He rubbed his chest, feeling the ache in his ribs from coughing the last few days. He'd take it. It meant he was alive. And so were his kids. Nothing else mattered.

He glanced at Alice's house. Bronwyn and Henry had only gotten a glimpse of it when they pulled into her driveway a little while ago. Now, they were making cookies with Alice. She'd come up with the plan to keep them busy when he mentioned he wanted to go poke through the debris.

Blowing out a breath, he stepped into his yard and walked up the steps to the porch, testing each board before he continued. He went up to the window they came out of and looked inside. More charred wreckage greeted him. Emotion clogged his throat as he looked at the remnants of the life he'd built here over the last year.

Wade forced his mind to compartmentalize so he could look at the scene objectively. Jed had given him the report on what they found so far. Gasoline and doors that were screwed shut.

But something about that didn't sit right with him. Wade didn't smell gas before they went to bed. And he didn't hear anyone moving around, either. The floors in the house creaked like mad. No one could walk around on the second or third story without being heard.

Lifting a foot through the window, he went inside. The right side of the house, where the fire originated, collapsed. He saw Bronwyn's bed frame poking through a section of wall lying on the floor. She'd come so close to dying.

Wade swallowed around the lump in his throat and kept looking. He didn't know what he was hoping to find. Just something to answer the nagging feeling in his gut.

He pulled a flashlight from his pocket and swept it over the rubble. To the left of the stairs, he saw part of his bedroom furniture, charred and broken, peeking through the remnants of the walls. Most of the second story had come through to the first.

His light bounced off something that wasn't charred wood. Wade squinted and realized it was the small lock box he kept in his closet. It held important papers and his service weapon. Finding his way carefully over the debris, he picked up the box, then continued his exploration of the rest of the house.

In his office at the rear, he found charring that indicated an accelerant was poured and lit on fire. Bending low, he peered through the doorway at the collapsed room. Jed said the fire started in this corner of the house.

Staying low, he stepped in and went to the wall to look at the wiring. It was obvious someone poured fuel on the house, but he wanted to know if they used the house's wiring as an ignition source. He shined the light on the wires, following them from the outlet and up as far as he could see. They disappeared into the ruins. He'd need special equipment to get into the areas above. It wasn't stable enough to climb.

Disappointed, he made his way out. The chirp of his cellphone broke the eerie silence around him and he jerked. Cursing, he took the phone from his pocket. Alice had ordered it for him the other day online and it arrived this morning. It still had the default ringtone, which was rather loud.

A glance at the screen revealed an area code he didn't recognize. He slid his thumb across the screen and lifted it to his ear. "Kaczmarek."

"What is so blasted important that my attorney left me eight messages? One for every time you called and demanded I call you back?"

Wade froze. The charred walls and floor around him faded as a voice he hadn't heard in over a year filled his ear. "Emily."

"Yes. Now, what do you want?"

Anger surged at her tone. "What do I want? Not a damn thing. But I thought you should know that your children were in a house fire and nearly died. They're going to be fine, though." Once he got some sleep that first night, he'd used his dad's phone to contact Emily's attorney to get a message to her to call him back. And she was right. He'd left eight.

A beat of silence passed.

"Oh."

He waited, expecting her to say more. When she didn't, his anger flared more. He had to force his teeth to unclench so he could speak. "Is that all you're going to say? You don't want to know their condition? Or let them know you love them?"

She uttered a long sigh. "Wade—"

He cut her off. "Tell me why, Em. Why don't you call or send cards? I understand why you left us, but why did you cut all ties with them?"

"Because it's better this way."

"For you, maybe. Children need a mom. They need you."

"No. You're right that they need a mom, but not me. They deserve someone who's going to be around and can go to the parent-teacher conferences and the ball games. Who bakes cookies and can help with homework. I can't do that. And being in their lives part-time would only hurt them more in the long run. I don't want to keep disappointing them. I love them enough to let them go."

He scoffed. "No. If you did, you would make an effort not to disappoint them. Divorced parents have good relationships with their children all the time. But you are right about one thing. They deserve a mom who will be there for them, and I think I've found her. So don't worry. They'll be well taken care of. I won't bother you again." He took the phone away from his ear and smashed "End Call."

Anger still vibrated his body, but a strange calm descended over him. Alice's smiling face floated through his mind. With it, the anger faded, leaving behind a feeling of acceptance. Emily would never be the mother his kids needed and deserved. But Alice would. And Wade didn't care that they'd only known each other a little over a month. He intended to marry her as soon as he could. He didn't need any more time to know he'd never find another woman like her.

Moving back through the house, he went through the window and back to Alice's. She looked up with a smile as he entered the kitchen.

"Hey. You're back sooner than I thought you'd be."

"I can't get to much. The back corner, where the fire started, collapsed. I saw the fuel burns Jed told me about. It definitely started in my office." He left out about the part about speaking to Emily. That was a conversation they could have without the kids around.

Alice frowned. "Your office? No. That's not right."

It was his turn to frown. "What do you mean?"

"I came out my back door. I couldn't sleep that night, so I got up and came downstairs to make some tea. While I waited on the water to heat, I looked out the window and realized the light didn't look right, so I stepped outside. The flames were coming out the second and third stories. There was no fire on the first, and I don't remember seeing a glow in your office window."

"That can't be right. There's clear evidence of accelerant use in the far corner of my office."

She shrugged. "I don't know what to tell you. It wasn't on fire when I came out."

Wade's mind digested that bit of information. How was it possible there was evidence of an origin point that didn't burn first? Was Alice wrong?

He quickly discounted the idea. No, the moment was likely burned into her brain as clear as a photograph. If she said there was no fire on the first floor when she went outside, there was no fire on the first floor.

So, why were there accelerant burn patterns, and why did Jed say that's where the fire started?

Elise's squeal and subsequent banging of a wooden spoon on a plastic pot brought him out of his thoughts. He didn't have answers for that yet, but he would.

"What's in the box?" Alice nodded to the firebox in his hands.

"I found it in the house. It was in my closet. It's got important papers and my service weapon." He set it on the counter and dialed in the combination, then thumbed open the latches. Lifting the lid, he saw that the box functioned as it was intended. Everything looked fine.

He removed his weapon and the box of ammunition with it.

"Fire investigators carry guns?"

Wade glanced at Alice, then nodded. "I'm a sworn law enforcement officer. I don't usually carry my gun, though. Only when I need to make an arrest."

"I didn't know that."

"Yep. I used to carry one all the time when I worked for the forestry service in Tennessee." He checked the weapon and the ammo, finding that all was well. Unfastening his belt, he slid it free of a couple of loops, then slid the holster on and refastened the belt.

"What are you doing?"

"I'm going to talk to Jed and Katy. See what else they might have turned up. And considering someone tried to kill me, I'm not leaving the house unarmed." He picked up his badge from the box and clipped it onto his belt, then shut it.

She frowned, but nodded. "Makes sense. Just be careful."

He walked over to her where she moved cookies off of a tray and onto cooling racks. "I will." Giving her a quick kiss, he waved at the kids and headed for the door. "You three behave, okay?"

"We will." Bronwyn waved back.

"Yeah. Because we've got cookies!" Henry held one up before he took a big bite.

Chuckling, he left the house and went out to the garage to get in his SUV. He'd been lucky. The fire didn't spread to his detached garage, so his car was fine. Knox and Asa moved it off his property yesterday, once Jed gave the all-clear to go in. Somehow, his keys also survived the blaze. Probably because they were by the front door, where the fire never reached.

He started the engine and backed out of the driveway, pointing the car toward the police station. He wanted to run his thoughts past Katy and see what she had to say first.

At the station, he parked at the rear of the building and used his key fob to get in the back door. It was a short walk to

Katy's office. Her door was ajar, so he knocked, then pushed it open. "Hey. Got a minute?"

"Hey." She glanced up with a smile. "Sure. How are you feeling? How are the kids?"

Stepping into the room, he sat down in the chair in front of her desk. "I'm doing much better. So are they. Bronwyn's still more fatigued than the rest of us, but she's home. Alice has her parked at the kitchen island making cookies right now."

"If that's Daisy's recipe, bring me some."

He gave a short laugh. "You're welcome to stop by anytime."

She smiled. "So, what brings you in? You should be home baking cookies too."

Wade's smile faded. "I went into my house a little while ago. I know Jed's already been all through it, but I wanted to see the damage for myself. I'm glad I did. Something's not adding up. I don't know if he missed something or if he just hasn't completely finished his inspection, but the point of origin is wrong."

"Oh?" Her forehead creased with a slight frown. "How so?"

"He told me it started in my office. And he's right that there's a burn pattern from an accelerant—gasoline, according to the readings he took. But I mentioned it to Alice, and she said when she went outside, the first floor wasn't on fire. Only the top floors."

Katy shifted in her seat. "Your office is at the back of the house. She might not have seen it."

"That's the thing, though. She went out the back door. She'd have looked right at that part of the house as she came across the backyard. From the way she described things, I think the fire started on the third floor and spread down."

"Okay. How do we prove that?"

"We need a cherry picker and a backhoe with a claw to move things in small sections. I want to examine the wiring. I'd bet my badge the guy used the foil, rust shavings, and candle method again. It's effective, and he would be long gone before it ignited."

"Then why the gasoline?"

"I don't know. And I doubt we'll figure that out until we catch the guy. Do you have any leads at all?"

Her face scrunched, and she shook her head. "No. Joshua Mercer's still in the wind. Ed's got an alibi for your house fire. He slept on his brother's couch after having a few too many beers. Levi Rister doesn't, though. He was home alone. And boy was he pissed when I showed up at his house asking questions. I won't get another crack at him without a lawyer present."

"He's our best suspect, then. Can we put all this up on a board somewhere? I need to see it all and how it's connected."

"Sure." She picked up a stack of folders from the desk behind her, then turned and held them out to him. "This is everything I've got on all the fires connected to Timmerman under both names. There's a whiteboard in the conference room. If you want to go in there and get started, I'll print off pictures of all the players and meet you there."

"Sounds good." Wade took the folders and stood. He wandered down the hall to the conference room. The white board was shoved into the corner. Setting the folders on the long table, he pulled it further into the room, then started writing things on it.

"You haven't talked to Jed about your suspicions yet, right?"

He glanced back at her, marker raised. "Not yet, no. I wanted to run through the case first. Get all my facts straight."

She walked toward him with the color photos she'd run off

in her hands. "Okay. I called him and asked him to join us. Might as well get all the information at once."

"Works for me." He took the tape dispenser she held out and tore off strips of tape, handing them to her so she could hang the pictures. Once they were all up, he started writing more information under each.

The board was full by the time Jed arrived.

"What's all this?"

Wade glanced back from staring at it to see his partner standing in the doorway, eyes on the board.

"I needed to see it all out. There's something here, nagging at me. It's probably so obvious, but it's just not coming to me." He crossed his arms, eyes roving over the information once again.

"Maybe we should go over it. Talk it out," Katy said.

Wade sighed. "Sure. Couldn't hurt."

Katy tilted her head, then started talking, going over what they knew and how each person was connected. Wade stared at their only viable suspects, Joshua Mercer and Levi Rister. He wished they could get a lead on Mercer. He was the only one who truly had motive.

When Katy got to the inconsistencies in the fire's origin at his house, she paused, looking at him to continue. Wade looked away from the photographs and turned to Jed.

Something clicked in his brain. He stared at his partner, then glanced back at the board. He caught Katy's eye.

She frowned at him. "What?"

Wade swallowed and looked at Jed again.

Something imperceptible flickered in the man's eyes. He frowned at Wade and echoed Katy's question. "What is it?"

Backing up, Wade took Joshua Mercer's picture off the board and looked at it. He tried to imagine the man without the beard and with brown eyes instead of blue.

"Jed?" Wade looked up, turning the picture around. "Or should I call you Joshua?"

Jed's dark eyes went wide for just a moment before he schooled his face. "What the hell are you talking about?"

"This is you, isn't it?"

"What?" Katy snatched the picture from his hand and looked at it. Her gaze flicked between it and the man standing a few feet away.

Jed rolled his eyes. "I think the smoke addled you more than you thought. Why don't you go home and get some rest?"

Wade shook his head. No, he was right about this. Without the beard Joshua sported in his picture, Jed's facial structure was the same. And he was the right age. "I'm not addled." Anger ignited in his gut. "You're Joshua Mercer. What I want to know is why you torched my house. You nearly killed my children! Your own unborn child died in a house fire. Why would you try to kill my kids?" He balled his fists at his side to keep from lunging at the man and strangling him where he stood.

A hard glint entered Jed's eyes. He was done pretending Wade didn't know what he was talking about. "You were too close to finding the truth. I needed you to stop digging. I've built a good life here. Everything was fine until Perabo showed up." He shook his head. "I couldn't believe it when I saw him in town." Twin pops of red bloomed on his cheeks. "I'd put Joshua Mercer behind me. He was dead. As dead as Amber and the baby. But the sight of that man brought him back to life like that." He snapped his fingers.

"I knew I had to do something. Lisa doesn't know who I am. We met after I changed my name—my identity. I couldn't let her find out."

"Why not?" Katy asked. "You didn't kill your wife."

"Because I didn't save her!" Red-faced now, tears streamed

down his face. "I was in our home gym with my headphones on, working out, when the fire started. I didn't know she was home. She'd gone out to get ice cream—pregnancy craving. I thought she was still gone. It wasn't until the firefighters radioed in that they found a body in the kitchen that—" His voice broke on a sob. Sucking in a breath and composing himself, he continued. "It's my fault she's dead. I should have looked for her." He sniffed.

"I couldn't handle the stares. People looking at me with pity. Others with blame. So I left. I had a contact through the police department. He put me in touch with a man who created a new identity for me. One that could stand up to deep background checks." He held his arms wide. "And I became Jed Braun. Became a firefighter so I could save others and make up for not saving Amber."

He shook his head again. "After I saw Perabo and had calmed down enough to think, I dug into his life. He was working for Timmerman."

Wade's eyes widened a fraction. "Wait. Did you know who he was?"

Jed shook his head. "Not at first. But once I dug into Perabo's background, I saw the blurb about his old company, Build-Rite, on San Juan Developments' website. That led me to the picture of Timmerman. When I looked into property developers around here, I saw Willard's picture and put two and two together."

"And that's when you hatched your plan." Katy rested her hands on her hips.

"Yeah. Multiple fires to keep you two clueless while I took out the two responsible for Amber's death." His mouth twisted. "Perabo should have died. I don't know how he made it out. Timmerman, I made sure he couldn't flee." His jaw worked. "That greedy bastard got what he deserved."

"You still haven't explained why you tried to kill my kids. I get that you wanted me dead, but my children too?"

"There was no other way to make it look like an accident. You had to die. I needed to take over the investigation and keep the heat off myself."

Wade took a step forward as fury overrode his rational mind. Katy's hand on his back stopped him.

"Jed, I need you to turn around. You're under arrest for the murder of William Timmerman, the attempted murder of Vincent Perabo, Wade Kaczmarek, Bronwyn Kacz—"

"No!" Jed drew his sidearm and pointed it at Wade. "I did not rebuild my life, only to have it all taken away. I'm not going to jail."

"Jed." Wade raised his hands, his heart thumping. "Put the gun down. You don't want to shoot me. If you do, Katy will shoot you." The sheriff had her gun trained on Jed. Wade's was still holstered. "Plus, you're in the middle of the police station. Where are you going to go?"

"Not to jail. And I don't want to shoot you, but I will. You ruined it all. Why couldn't you just leave it alone? It was perfect! No trail. Nothing to point to anyone in particular. Just a bunch of loose ends that went nowhere." His words ended on a growl. He flicked the safety off his weapon. "Now, I'm going to walk out of here." He backed toward the door, rounding the table.

Wade put a hand on the butt of his gun, stepping to the side so Katy could lead.

Jed made it to the door and reached back for the doorknob.

Katy edged closer. "Jed, I can't let you go out there."

The man's gaze flicked between them, then his eyes turned hard.

"Don't do it, Jed." Wade flicked open the clasp on his holster.

Jed yanked open the door and dove out, firing blindly.

A bullet slammed into the wall behind Wade. He drew his weapon and followed Katy to the door. Shouts filled the hallway and the bullpen beyond.

"Do you see him?"

She shook her head. "I need to get to the other side of the door."

He raised his gun and nodded. "Go."

In one long stride, she was on the other side. Another bullet slammed into the door frame. Katy backed up, then returned fire. Another set of shots sounded from deeper in the building.

"I think he's pinned between us and the deputies who were in the bullpen." She edged closer to the door and peered out again. No shots rang out this time. "Come on." On light feet, she stepped into the hall.

Together, they advanced to the next office. She cleared it, and they kept moving. As they reached the end of the hall, another shot rang out. Wade heard a deputy shout moments before Jed came around the corner, fleeing. He skidded to a stop and raised his gun, pointing it at them.

Wade fired. Katy shot at the same time. Both bullets hit him center-mass, and he fell backwards, landing hard on the tile floor. He didn't move.

They ran forward, guns still trained on him. Katy kicked his gun away while Wade dropped to check his pulse. Jed's eyes fluttered, and he gasped. Blood welled through the two wounds on his chest.

"Call for help." Wade holstered his gun, then put his hands over Jed's wounds and pushed, trying to stem the bleeding. The man's head lolled to the side, and the gasping breaths turned to shallow draws. He heard Katy radio for help. As the dispatcher replied that an ambulance was on its way, Jed quit breathing.

Blood filled the hallway and covered Wade's hands. He sat back and stared at the man who used to be his friend. "Dammit." Standing, he paced a few steps away. A deep sadness filled him. So many lives lost—so many ruined—because of greed.

He looked at Katy. She was pale, but still in control as commotion erupted around them. Deputies flooded the hallway. She gave a sharp whistle, reining them in, then started tasking them. Wade leaned against the wall, sad for the way things ended, but glad it was all finally over.

Thirty-Eight

Two months later...

"I'll get it!" Henry ran for the door at the sound of the doorbell.

"Henry, no. You let me." Alice ran after him, balancing a half-dressed Elise on her hip. She'd been in the midst of a diaper change when someone rang the bell.

She blew her bangs out of her face, glancing down at him as she caught up. "Step back, please."

He moved to her side, and she opened the door. It was the mailman.

"Hi, Ms. Duvall. Sorry to bother you. I need a signature for this." He held up a manila envelope with Wade's name on it.

She frowned. "Does it need to be Wade's? He's at work."

He shook his head. "No, yours will do." He produced a tablet and stylus.

Alice scrawled her name over the screen, then took the envelope. "Thank you."

"Yep. Have a nice day." He smiled, then waved at Henry and Elise before turning and walking down the porch steps.

"What is it?"

"I don't know." Alice closed the door and looked at the envelope. It was addressed to Wade at the house next door and from an attorney's office. She frowned. What in the world would someone send him from an attorney's office via certified mail?

"Can I see?"

She blew out a breath and glanced at the boy. "Not right now. It's addressed to Daddy. He can open it when he gets home tonight."

"Then can I see?"

"Maybe. Depends on what's inside." She turned him around. "Go find your shoes so we can get going. Tell your sister." They were getting ready to go to her new store to meet Sofie. They had a few last-minute things to hash out before their grand opening next week. She was beyond excited. They were expecting a decent turnout for the event. The gallery in Billings, where she took some of her pottery, contacted the local news outlets about the store. They'd already given several interviews.

"Let's get you dressed, huh?" She gave Elise's cheek a few smacking kisses, then went back to the living room to get the toddler's pants. At least she got the diaper on before the mailman knocked.

The door opened again, and her head shot up. "Henry!" She blew out a breath. He better not have gone outside. The kid loved to sit on the porch and sometimes he forgot to tell her when he wanted to go out.

She stuffed Elise's legs into her pants and pulled them up, standing in the same motion.

"Hey, hon." Wade appeared in the doorway.

"Hi. What are you doing home?"

"I forgot my lunch and didn't want to eat at the diner."

"Oh." She walked up to him and raised her face for a kiss. Alice felt him smile against her mouth when Elise reached up and patted his cheek.

"Dada."

He pulled back. "Hi, munchkin."

The girl fell toward him, and he took her from Alice's arms.

"We were just getting ready to leave. Sofie and I have a few things to go over for next week."

"Don't let me hold you up." He lifted Elise in the air and gave her a gentle toss. The girl squealed and laughed. "I can't stay long, either. I have an appointment in an hour."

Alice smiled at father and daughter. "We can stick around for a little bit. Oh! You got something in the mail." She turned around and picked up the letter from the coffee table, holding it out to him. "I had to sign for it."

A curious frown creased his forehead as he took it and looked at the return address. Some of the color left his face, and his frown deepened.

"What is it?" Alice's frown mimicked his.

"It's from Emily's attorney."

Her eyebrows shot up. "What? Why would she send you something from her attorney's office?" Worry churned her gut. Had the woman decided she wanted to be a mom after all and was suing for custody? Alice narrowed her eyes. She'd fight that tooth and nail. The kids were happy. They didn't need the upheaval her presence would bring, even if she was their mother.

"I don't know." Wade handed Elise back to her, then tore open the flap, taking out a sheaf of papers. He scanned them, his eyebrows going up over ever-widening eyes as he read.

"What? What does it say?"

He looked up at her, incredulity on his face. "She's signing over her legal rights to the kids."

Alice continued to frown. "What does that mean?"

"It means that she'll no longer have any right to them whatsoever. I've had full custody since she left, but she could always stick her nose into things and get a say in stuff, like their medical care or their school. But this means she can't do that anymore." He paused, holding her gaze. "It also means they can be adopted."

Confusion quirked her brow before his meaning sank in. Then her eyes went wide as saucers.

He grinned and reached for her hand. "Come here."

Unsure what was happening, Alice let him lead her to the room he'd taken over as an office. He and the children had moved in after the fire and never looked back. The rubble from their house was gone, and the lot stood empty. He still owned it, but they were trying to decide what to do with it. They'd talked about just fencing it and adding to their yard space.

Wade pulled her behind the desk, then opened the bottom drawer, reaching inside. Her hand flew up to cover her mouth when she saw what he held. Tears swam in her vision, obscuring his face and the ring box in his hand.

"You know, I think it's fitting that you're holding my daughter while I do this. The kids are what brought us together. And it was the love and care you showered on them that made me fall in love with you." A grin tilted his mouth. "That and your kind spirit and your ability to knock me for a loop with just a kiss." He dropped to one knee. "I love you, Alice. Will you make us a family and marry me?"

Alice heard a gasp from the doorway. She glanced back, and through her tears saw Bronwyn and Henry standing there.

"You're gonna be our mommy?"

"She hasn't said yes yet," Wade told her.

"Only because I didn't get the chance." She looked at Wade, smiling as tears ran down her face. "I love you, Wade." She glanced at the kids. "All of you. Yes, I will marry you."

Bronwyn ran to her side and wrapped both arms around Alice's waist. Henry wasn't far behind. Wade leaned in to kiss her.

A joy that lit her up from the inside filled her and warmed her heart. Alice kissed him back with all the love straining every fiber of her being. When they broke apart, her smile on her felt like it could split her face in two.

"Can I call you Mommy?"

Alice looked down at Bronwyn. She smoothed a hand over the girl's blonde hair. "If you want to, I'd love that."

"I want to. I already think of you that way."

More tears spilled over Alice's eyelids. She needed to remember to thank her brother for falling in love. It had changed her life too.

～

THE END

Thank you for reading *Homespun*, book 5 in the *Pine Ridge* series. I hope you enjoyed it and will leave a rating or review. There is a bonus scene available for this book that is exclusive to newsletter subscribers. Visit: https://ashleyaquinn.com/bonuscontent to sign up, if you haven't already joined. If you have, follow the link to download your bonus content!

For a sneak peek at *Smoky Mountain Murder*, book 1 in my next series, *Foggy Mountain Intrigue*, keep reading.

Prefer to dive right in? Follow the link below!
https://geni.us/SagV

CHAPTER 1

Trowel in hand, Gemma Mabley sat back and surveyed her handiwork. Pops of color shone brightly in the now filled flower beds surrounding the house she shared with her brother, Tristan, just outside of Foggy Mountain, North Carolina. The late-May sun beat down on her, making her sweat. She swiped at the beads of perspiration trickling down the side of her face, leaving behind a trail of dirt. Her shoulders and arms ached from all the planting, but the satisfaction from the result dulled the pain. Hot out or not, she was happy to feel the warm sun on her skin and see the brilliant shades of red, yellow, pink, and purple lining the front of her house. The winter had been brutal, and she'd done a happy dance the first day the temperatures rose above freezing and stayed there. She'd waited no longer than necessary to usher away the last dregs of the cooler weather by planting a plethora of flowers.

She had other reasons, though, for deciding today was the day to plant flowers. Her brother knew no boundaries. Three hours ago, in an attempt to use mindless action to calm herself, she returned from the local garden center with a trunk load of flowers. After donning her gardening clothes, she attacked the flowerbeds with a vengeance befitting Genghis Khan, imagining her brother's face with every stab to the dirt.

Gemma loved the man dearly, but she'd had it with his overprotectiveness. At twenty-eight years old, she did *not* need her older brother continually butting into her love life. In the past year, he'd sabotaged four different relationships. Every time she got remotely close to a man, Tristan stepped in and intimidated the guy to the point he would rather cut and run than be subjected to the "I'm a badass" stare her brother perfected over the years in the military and as a cop.

And, if the stare wasn't enough, the questions certainly were. One of her dates compared his questioning tactics to the German Gestapo.

Tristan claimed it wasn't him who was the problem. It was the men she dated. He insisted that when she found the man worthy of her, he wouldn't scare away. Gemma kept insisting that if he didn't even give anyone a chance to try to get to know her first, none would ever bother to try. She couldn't fathom there was a man on the planet who would willingly subject himself to that kind of treatment for a woman he didn't even know. Every time a new relationship crashed and burned before it ever left the ground, she and Tristan had the same argument. It had grown beyond tiresome.

Gemma sighed as she started on the final row of flowers. Last night's fiasco was the last straw and the reason she was out here imagining her brother's face in the dirt. She'd kept her relationship with David Masterson a secret for two months before she finally let him pressure her into telling her brother about them and arranging a meeting.

She'd had such high hopes for David. Gemma had gotten to know him better than any other man since college, and he'd been fully briefed on how difficult Tristan could be. David reassured her repeatedly he could handle whatever Tristan dished out. She foolishly thought their relationship had a footing strong enough to withstand Tristan's probing.

Gemma scoffed as she scooped more dirt and plunked a small flower plant in the hole she created. One look at Tristan's scowling face, his six-foot-two-inch frame packed with muscle, and the gun and badge attached to his belt, and David started to quake in his fancy Armani loafers. He stood strong through most of Tristan's interrogation—he was an attorney, after all —but Tristan could scare the paint off a barn.

And Tristan was smart. And ruthless when it came to his baby sister. She saw the gleam enter his eyes when he noticed David shrink back from the sheer weight of his presence. The blasted man pressed his advantage until David's normally warm skin tone was pasty white. He all but fled from the house once Gemma convinced Tristan he should save some of the questions for another time—she wouldn't want him to come up short, should he get a second chance to peel away the flesh from her date.

Her evening with David was a slide downhill to disaster after that. They ate a very stoic dinner that settled like lead in her stomach. David's normally engaging and friendly demeanor turned polite and reserved, and she once again felt like a piece of spun glass that was to be admired only from afar. After dinner, David drove her home and deposited her on her doorstep with a pat on the shoulder.

Dirt flew as she dug the final hole, muttering to herself. She still couldn't believe he'd patted her like a child. On their last date, he had his hand up her blouse, for crap's sake!

The front door slammed. Gemma looked up to see the object of her ire hurry outside, gun and badge clipped to his belt, truck keys in his hand.

Alarmed, she stood up. Today was Saturday and Tristan's day off. If he'd been called in, something terrible must have happened.

"Gotta go, Sis." Tristan cleared all the porch steps in a single leap and flew past her to the large gray truck parked beside her SUV in the driveway.

"What's going on?" she called after him.

"Dead body in Pisgah National Forest. Up near Hot Springs," he said over his shoulder. "I'll call you later."

Gemma felt her anger at him die as he roared out of the drive. She could never stay angry with him when he was going off and putting himself in the line of fire. She learned that early on after he joined the Army and headed off to Afghanistan. He might drive her nuts, but she knew it was because he cared, and she would be lost without her big brother around.

She sighed the tired sigh of long-suffering little sisters everywhere and bent down to tuck the last bit of soil around the last plant. Giving the dirt one last pat, she gathered up her tools, praying all the while that Tristan would be safe.

～

The warm sun beat down on Special Agent Ben Davidson's back even through the tree canopy as he stood near the trailhead, talking to the local sheriff, John Raymond. Parked next to them, the medical examiner, Dr. Cullen Tate, rummaged around in the back of his van, gathering supplies to assess the body in the field.

A headache brewed between Ben's eyes as he thought about what awaited him in the woods. If this was the work of the serial killer he'd been tracking, it promised to be gruesome. He just hoped this woman's body yielded more clues than the last four. This killer was rather adept at leaving a clean crime scene. As a result, Ben had very little to go on after over a year of investigating and four murders.

Getting a bit impatient, he resisted the urge to tap his foot as they waited for Raymond's detective to arrive. On the off-chance this wasn't his case, Ben had agreed to wait to have a local detective join them. Even if it was the work of the killer he was after, he would still work closely with local law enforcement until he exhausted all leads or the killer was caught. He didn't want to burn any bridges or step on anyone's toes by charging full steam ahead, leaving people out of the loop. His life was much easier if the locals cooperated.

"Major Davidson?"

Startled at the title he hadn't heard in years, he turned to see a chestnut-haired man looking at him in surprise. Sunglasses covered his eyes, but Ben knew that if he took them off, they would be a brilliant blue. "Captain Mabley?"

"It's Detective Mabley, now." Tristan extended his hand, smiling, as the two men took stock of each other.

A lifetime ago, Ben had been the commanding officer of their Ranger unit. Tristan Mabley was his second-in-command. The younger man left the service before Ben's last deployment, and they lost contact. The back of beyond in North Carolina was the last place he ever expected to see him again.

"Sir, it's good to see you. I heard you retired after your last tour went sideways. How's the leg?"

Lifting his left foot, Ben's mouth tilted slightly. "It works, but not as well as it used to." He'd taken shrapnel to his leg, shattering the bones and tearing up the soft tissue. It was a testament to the dedication and talent of the Army doctors that he still had a leg to walk on, let alone one that functioned as well as it did.

"So, what brings you out to my neck of the woods?" Tristan gestured around them. "Literally."

Ben held up his badge. "You aren't the only one with a new title. Seems my case may have landed on your doorstep."

"FBI, huh?" Tristan frowned. "The DB in the woods is yours?"

Ben nodded. "I think so. I've been tracking a serial killer in the region for a little over a year now. We've got a flag in the system to alert us to bodies found in wooded areas. As soon as the location of this one hit the airwaves, I got a call. I was on my way back north to Richmond when it came in, so I detoured here. From the cursory description we've gotten from the people who found her, it sounds like she may be related to my other victims."

"Great. A serial killer is just what we need roaming the hills. There are so many places to hide in the Smokies."

Ben agreed. It made tracking someone difficult.

"How many victims have you attributed to the guy?"

"This one, if she is in fact connected, will make five we know of. This case landed in my lap when he crossed state lines from Tennessee to Virginia. He's left two in Virginia, two in Tennessee, and now this one."

Sheriff Raymond, who'd been silently listening to the exchange, motioned toward the trees. "Well, let's get on with it before we're finding victim number two around here."

Dr. Tate stepped down from the van just then, a large bag slung across his chest. His assistant, a young man in his twenties, stepped out of the van as well, a camera around his neck and a hard case in his hand.

Silently, the men filed into the woods behind the park ranger, who answered the initial call from the hikers who stumbled across the body.

The stench of death assaulted Ben's nose about the same time the yellow police tape came into view. It didn't matter where or when a murder occurred, Ben could always count on the smell to point him to the body. Even the recently deceased had a smell. It hung in the air like smog on a hot day, and it was unavoidable.

He bent beneath the crime scene tape and got his first glimpse of the body as he passed through the trees. Taking in the grim scene with a detached eye, he assessed it for similarities to his other victims. The woman swayed in the slight breeze, where she hung by her neck beneath the branches of a large oak. Completely naked, evidence of torture was apparent on her bloodied body. Deep gashes marred the skin of her torso. Purple bruises colored her legs, and her fingers looked like gnarled willow branches. Where blood had once flowed freely, it was now dried on her fingertips. Ben felt a sinking sensation in his gut. At just a quick glance, she was identical to the other four victims. He suspected when the M.E. did the autopsy, he would find she'd been raped, that both her legs were broken in several places—crushed by a hammer or pipe—and that she died from a broken neck or asphyxiation from hanging.

"Jesus."

He spared a glance at the sheriff, who stopped beside him. The man's face was devoid of all color, and Ben could see him fight to keep the contents of his stomach where they belonged. Ben was far past being affected by grisly sights. He'd been cured of that after his first tour in Afghanistan. Now, nearly two decades later, he examined scenes like this one with a calculated eye, looking for clues to help him bring down the monster responsible. He sincerely hoped this woman yielded more answers than the previous four victims.

The M.E. stepped forward to look at the body as his assistant snapped pictures in quick succession.

"She hasn't been here long," Dr. Tate remarked. "There's not much decomp yet, and she's still in full rigor." He glanced back at Ben and the other investigators. "Once we get her down, and I get a liver temp on her, I can give you a more accurate time of death. But just based on looking at her, I'd say she died sometime late last night or very early this morning."

Ben felt a surge of hope. None of the other four victims were found so soon after death. In every other case, nature had a chance to wash away vital evidence. It hadn't rained last night, so they might very well find clues on or around her.

Tristan seemed to be on the same wavelength. The doctor's proclamation galvanized the man into action. Ben watched as he made a beeline for where the rope was tied, eyes trained on the ground.

"There are fresh prints here. Definitely male, probably a size ten or eleven." Tate's assistant came over and started snapping pictures of the indentations. "We might get a weight on the depth of the tracks," Tristan remarked, reminding Ben how astute the younger man was. He was damn glad to have the man working this case with him.

The team worked diligently for several hours, processing the scene. Even with the freshness of it, there wasn't much forensic evidence. They found tire tracks to an ATV in addition to the boot prints, but little else. The rope was a generic nylon sold in many sporting goods and hardware stores. Unless the killer slipped up this time, there wouldn't be any DNA evidence on the body. With the lack of clothing and other belongings, they likely wouldn't find any fingerprint or fiber evidence, either.

Frustration gnawed at Ben. He just wanted a break in this case. It haunted him on dark nights that he couldn't figure it out. He hated unfinished business.

"So, what's the plan?" Sheriff Raymond asked as they gathered in the parking lot after Dr. Tate drove away with their victim.

Ben glanced around at the crime scene techs packing up their equipment and at the spectators the police presence had drawn. "All my files on this case are in Richmond. I'll call my office and have someone drive down with them tomorrow. In the meantime, make sure we get statements from the hikers who found her and interview the park rangers who work this area. Find out if any of them have noticed anything unusual."

He looked down at the older man. "Sheriff, this is your territory and the people know you, so why don't you handle crowd and media control? I'd like to take Detective Mabley and head to the station to run down the woman's identity."

Sheriff Raymond gave a short nod and walked off to delegate interviews and handle the inevitable press that came with a case like this.

Ben turned to Tristan and swirled his finger in the universal "saddle up" gesture. "You lead, Mabley."

I hope you enjoyed this sneak peek of *Smoky Mountain Murder*. If you would like to read the book, please visit the link below to get your copy. Thanks again for reading!

Get *Smoky Mountain Murder*: https://geni.us/SagV

Wagner Brigade

Ford's Fight

Dean's Dilemma

Jordan's Journey

Sam's Salvation

Asher's Assignment

Max's Mission

Parker's Landing

Midnight Secrets

Midnight Witness

About the Author

After spending most of her adulthood moving around the U.S. and Europe, romantic suspense author Ashley A. Quinn has settled in South Dakota with her husband, two kids, and a menagerie of pets. Her first novel, *Smoky Mountain Murder*, came out in 2016, and she has since published more than two dozen books. When not writing, you can find her with her nose stuck in a romantic thriller or binge-watching British TV dramas and reality shows. She is an avid baseball fan and also enjoys growing all the things in her garden and bookbinding. To find out more about her and her books visit https://ashleyaquinn.com.

goodreads.com/ashleyaquinn

amazon.com/Ashley-A-Quinn/e/B07HCT4QST

facebook.com/ashleyaquinn.writer

instagram.com/ashleyaquinn.writer

tiktok.com/@ashleyaquinn.writer